ANGELA M. SANDERS

Dior or Die

WIDOW'S KISS

Copyright © 2014 by Angela M. Sanders

Printed in the United States of America

First Printing, 2014

ISBN 978-0-9904133-2-5 (pbk.)
ISBN 978-0-9904133-3-2 (e-book)

Widow's Kiss
P.O. Box 82488
Portland, OR 97282

www.WidowsKiss.com

Book design: Eric Lancaster

To my grandmother,
Marjorie Alta Miller Sanders,
who taught me to see the beauty
in everything from lipstick to
pickles to wild blackberry bushes.

ALSO BY ANGELA M. SANDERS:

The Lanvin Murders

Dior
or Die

Chapter 1

Joanna Hayworth fidgeted with her pearl ring, twisting it around and around her finger. The lot she wanted was up next. With any luck, everyone would be bidding on the sterling flatware or oriental rugs and not care about the three trunks of vintage haute couture.

Once again she scanned the warehouse floor, lined with bidders in folding chairs. No, no other vintage clothing dealers she knew. Still, the lot was important enough to draw bidders from Seattle or even San Francisco to the Portland auction house, and she wouldn't recognize their faces. Plus, proxy bidders stood next to the phones at the counter.

Her gaze rested on a tall woman with short, egret-white hair. Something about this woman — the graceful way she'd taken her seat, her removed but clear interest in the auction — put Joanna on alert. The elderly woman was dressed simply, all in gray, without the alligator handbag or Bakelite bangles that were the usual trappings of a vintage clothing hound, but that didn't necessarily mean anything. The woman's eyes, intensely blue, met hers. Joanna looked away and twisted her ring again.

"Attention, please." Poppy, the auctioneer, banged her gavel on the podium.

Joanna's heartbeat quickened. Here it comes. Two men wheeled a trunk onto the stage and set it upright. One of the men unclipped its door, revealing dress skirts of stiff satin and organza. Another two trunks were wheeled onto the stage and opened. Poppy stood close to her podium, surrounded by tufts of chiffon and smooth gabardine suits. Joanna held her breath.

"Now we have lot two-thirteen, containing vintage couture clothing. Condition ranges from good to very good," Poppy said. "Do I have twenty-five hundred dollars?"

Joanna's hand shot up. The recorder made a note. A proxy bidder nodded, and the recorder once more bent over her pad. Joanna searched the room again to gauge her competition. The white-haired woman sat calmly, her hands in her lap.

When Poppy, a good friend, had asked her to come down to the auction house a month earlier to see if the clothes were worth having appraised, Joanna had never expected to find crisp Mainbocher suits, Jacques Fath evening dresses, and even a wasp-waisted Dior Bar suit from his New Look collection. Ah, the Dior. Yards and yards of wool had gone into the skirt alone, an incredible extravagance in post-war Paris. Joanna had let its jet-black jersey pour over her gloved hands as she searched for frays on the hem or loose threads along its hand-basted seams. The clothes were from the collection of Vivienne North, a Parisian model who married a G.I. from Oregon.

"What do you think," Poppy had asked in her New Jersey accent. With her tiny frame and delicate features, she looked like a Southern belle. But she talked like a mobster. "They look valuable to me, but I have no idea where to start the bidding."

Joanna had still been in a daze. "I've never seen such an amazing wardrobe. In real life, at least. If you advertised, you'd have museums calling about it."

The second she left the auction house, she'd called the bank to have her credit line extended. She had to buy this collection.

The bidding was now up to five thousand dollars. Joanna bit her lip. Her credit line was twenty thousand dollars. If she cleaned out her savings she might be able to pull together twenty-three. Still, the wardrobe would be a bargain at that price, and with careful marketing she could make back the money many times over. In fact, she'd have to, and fast, since the bills at her vintage clothing boutique, Tallulah's Closet, were stacked high. Sales had been slow, and a pipe had burst the week before. Besides the plumber's steep bill, she'd had to shell out for a new carpet. Plus, her plans to upgrade the store would have to be put on hold—unless she won this lot.

Still, every one of these dresses would be hard to let go.

The door creaked, letting in a gust of wet spring air. Eve Lancer burst into the room in a blur of gold hair and clattering heels. "Ten thousand dollars," she shouted as she grabbed a bidder number.

No, not her. Joanna groaned. She waved her bidder number when Poppy asked for twelve thousand dollars. Eve didn't need these clothes. She didn't even care about them, she was just going through a phase of playing the vintage clothing dealer.

"Thirteen thousand," Poppy said. Eve nodded. Eve spotted Joanna and smiled confidently, making a production of laying her Burberry trench coat over a folding chair.

"Do I hear fifteen?" All bidding had dropped away except Joanna and Eve. The proxies had moved from the phones.

Joanna lifted her card.

Eve smiled again, revealing Hollywood-perfect teeth. She raised a hand, a diamond ring sparkling even in the dim light. "Twenty-five thousand dollars." She leaned back in her chair without even looking up.

Poppy turned to Joanna, giving her a moment longer than she would another bidder. Joanna's heart sank. There's no way she could come up with that much money. Besides, Eve would run the bidding as high as she needed to get these clothes. Thanks to her daddy, twenty-five thousand dollars was small change. With regret, Joanna shook her head at Poppy and glanced at Eve, whose fingers flew over her phone's keyboard, seemingly already having forgotten the auction. So strange that a face angelic enough to rival Gene Tierney's could hide such a foul interior.

"Sold to bidder number three-eight-seven for twenty-five thousand dollars." Poppy banged her gavel. The assistants closed the trunks and wheeled them off the stage to clear the floor for the next lot.

Joanna watched them roll away. Goodbye, lilac organza Fath. So long, Dior Arsène Lupin theatre dress. The afterglow of Vivienne's post-war afternoons at the Café de Flore and evenings dancing at the Hôtel Meurice disappeared with them. Damn. She gave her ring one more twist, this time in frustration, then dropped her hands to her side.

When Joanna turned to get her coat, Eve was standing at the counter next to the coat check. She was tempted to leave her coat at the auction house and return for it another day, but decided she wasn't going to be humiliated—or at least let it show.

"So sorry you didn't win the clothes." Eve examined her fingernails. "I'm sure Tallulah's Closet could have used them."

"Congratulations." Joanna forced a smile. Where the hell was the coat check person? In the background, Poppy's voice started again, calling the next lot.

At last, a lanky man in horn-rimmed glasses came to the counter holding a sheet of paper. Ben, Poppy's house manager. "I'm sorry," he said to Eve, "The credit card you used for your bid number was declined. Do you have another one?"

White-faced, Eve dug through her purse. She pulled out a thin Hermès envelope with her driver's license and nothing more in it. "No, my main wallet is at home. I forgot and brought that card with me on vacation — just got back from Aspen — and haven't paid the bill yet." She leaned forward and smiled. "But I can bring a credit card later, right? Maybe with a little more money — say, a hundred dollars — for your trouble?"

Joanna's gaze shot to the clerk.

He shook his head, unfazed by Eve's pleading smile. "You'll need to pay now, or we'll put the lot back out to bid."

"I'm good for the money," Eve said, her voice taking a shrill edge. "Who's your boss? Let me talk to him."

"Poppy's the boss." Ben nodded toward the podium. "She's busy right now."

"Is there a problem here?" asked a voice with a slight French accent. Joanna turned to find the white-haired woman she'd seen earlier standing behind her. Up close Joanna saw that her jacket, while plain, was expertly tailored to mold to the woman's thin frame. A gold crucifix pendant caught the light as she turned.

"Oh, Ms. North, there's nothing to worry about. The winning bidder's credit card was declined, so we'll put the clothes up again after this lot. It happens from time to time, not a big deal."

Joanna's eyes widened. This was Vivienne North, the estate's owner.

"Do you work here?" Eve raised her voice. "I won those clothes fair and square. All I'm asking is for an hour to get my other credit card. I don't need some minimum-wage flunky telling me — "

"She was the next highest bidder, for fifteen thousand dollars.

Correct?" Vivienne turned her head toward Joanna. Their eyes met again. Ben nodded. Vivienne's glance passed over Joanna's 1940s suit, stopping for a moment at the peacock-shaped brooch on her lapel. The glimmer of a smile played on Vivienne's lips. "Then give her the clothes." Without waiting for a response she returned into the main auction room, a wisp of tuberose perfume in her wake.

Joanna realized she was holding her breath when it escaped with a whoosh. She had secured her bid with a certified check. She thought of the Diors, the Balenciagas, the Mainbocher suits, and a surge of happiness shot through her, reminding her of one of the paintings that had sold earlier, the one with parted heavens and putti swimming in sunlight.

Eve turned for the front door. It slammed behind her. The auctioneer's voice steadily rattled bids in the background.

"Here's my bidder number," Joanna said, her coat forgotten. She almost laughed.

Chapter 2

Dot's Café was a cave, especially compared to the warm light and frothy fabric at Tallulah's Closet next door. Joanna and Apple, her best friend and part-time sales assistant, found seats between a pool table and a painting of a toreador on black velvet.

The bartender wiped her hands on a dishtowel. "Martini?" she asked Joanna. "And a tall mint tea for you, Apple?"

"Champagne," Joanna said. "We're celebrating. You have champagne, right?" Dot's was known more for beer and burgers than fine wine.

The bartender dusted off a bottle of Veuve Cliquot before finding an empty margarine tub to use as an ice bucket. She carried them to the table. "I knew we'd sell this thing eventually. Always have a bottle of champagne around, I told the manager. No coupes, though. I'll grab wine glasses."

"When are you going to pick up the clothes?" Apple asked. Her style couldn't be more different than Joanna's. Today she wore a 1970s Indian caftan, and sometimes she'd even work the store barefoot. Despite her Haight-Ashbury look, Apple could knock out a fully accessorized 1950s cocktail ensemble that would make a customer seem to have stepped from a George Cukor movie.

"Tonight, after the auction house closes," Joanna said. "Poppy arranged for her trucking company to help. I can't wait."

"Tell me about the celebration," the bartender said. The hollow pop of the champagne cork drew the attention of the two skinny men drinking at the end of the bar.

"I just bought some vintage couture. I'm talking the real thing, too — clothes the owner had to buy in Paris or New York."

"Anything in a womanly size?" She put a hand on her ample hip.

"Small. Fours and sixes, mostly. But she had some fabulous accessories. In fact, I saw a cocktail hat I think you'd love. It's a molded cap of blue-black feathers. The veil's studded with rhinestones."

The bartender eyed the chair next to Apple, but one of the men at the bar tapped his empty glass against the counter. "I'll be with you in a second," she shouted across the room, then turned back to their table. "Food?"

"How about the hummus plate?" Apple said.

"Forget about being healthy. Let's do cheese fries," Joanna said. If they were going to celebrate, they might as well do it right. "I can't wait until you see the dresses. A real Dior Bar suit, can you imagine? The jacket is amazingly constructed. The hips and shoulders are so padded they could almost stand on their own."

"Nice."

Joanna twirled the stem of her glass in her fingers. "You should have seen Vivienne North at the auction. Wide cheekbones and long fingers. She could still model, if she wanted." Joanna imagined Vivienne and Apple shaking hands. Vivienne, elegant and spare, and Apple's Indian bracelets dangling. Apple would undoubtedly have a lengthy commentary on Vivienne's aura or a few psychic hits to share afterward.

Apple poured champagne into the wine glasses. She nudged the bottle back into the margarine tub. "Cheers."

"Cheers." The cool wine fizzed against her tongue. With Tallulah's Closet's new website, the remodel — well, at least a new paint job — and now these clothes, the store would be reborn.

As usual, Apple seemed to read her mind. "Maybe we should paint the rear wall near the dressing rooms dove gray, like Dior's salon."

"Once we sell a few pieces." Joanna took a long sip of champagne and let her focus relax.

"We could even get a laptop for the store to track inventory. I know, we could stream music off the web. No more changing records."

Joanna's attention snapped back. "What?" She referred to her ledger books and record-keeping as "hand-crafted," and they'd have to pry her turntable out of her cold, dead hands. When she'd bought it at a yard sale, the seller had lovingly patted its side and said, "I listened to Abbey Road for the first time on that hi-fi."

"Just making sure you're awake," Apple said. "In any case, we should expect a boost in business. I didn't want to say anything earlier, but the landlord stopped by again."

"He usually gives me until the tenth, at least — "

"I know. But he might be looking for the chance to break the lease. Rents have gone up around here." She leaned back into the red Naugahyde. "Not that we have to worry. Not now. Maybe you can sell a few of the dresses to the NAP auction crowd."

Oh yes, the Northwest AIDS Project auction. Joanna had promised to dress the event's hostesses in vintage evening gowns. Lots of potential for new business.

The bartender drifted to the window behind them. "It's raining again. Just in time for Rose Festival."

The old saying went that, despite taking place in June, "it always rains during Rose Festival." They could look forward to two weeks of parades, concerts, and sailors on shore leave. "Maybe we'll sell some vintage evening wear to the Rose Princesses, too," Joanna said.

Apple raised her glass. "Another toast. To the new Tallulah's Closet."

Joanna touched her glass to Apple's. Bubbles rose in giddy ribbons.

*
**

That evening in the auction house's parking lot, Joanna hummed "La Vie en Rose" under her breath as she shut her decrepit Corolla's door. Even the rain couldn't dampen her happiness that evening.

"Il m'a dit des mots d'amour," she sang and pulled open the warehouse's front door.

She stopped in her tracks. "Poppy?"

The loading docks were open, and men hauled crated goods into trucks marked with police badges. Toward the rear of the warehouse, three cops, their breath hanging in the cool night air, worked under portable lights.

"What's going on here?" Joanna asked.

Poppy took a drag from a cup of coffee. A take-out container of Thai food sat on the counter next to her. "Oh Joanna." Her voice was more raspy than usual. "Didn't you get my phone messages? I'm afraid you're not going to get the clothes after all, at least not any time soon." She rubbed her eyes.

"What happened?"

"The police are here. They're taking everything. Vivienne, that lovely woman — I can't believe it."

Joanna set her purse on the counter. "Poppy, slow down. Tell me. What happened?"

"She died. Vivienne did, tonight. They think she was murdered."

Joanna stood, frozen. "I can't believe it. Vivienne—?"

Poppy pushed away her coffee. "It happened sometime tonight. The police showed up a couple of hours ago, and it's been like this ever since." She glanced back toward the loading dock.

"Here? She died here?"

"Oh, no," Poppy said. "At home. At least, that's what the police told me."

Joanna slumped onto the counter in disbelief. Vivienne North, dead. She'd seemed so vital, so full of life only that morning. "What happened?"

Poppy shook her head. "I think—" She picked up a paper clip already twisted into a knot and bent its ends together until it snapped. She tossed the pieces on the counter. "Never mind what I think. Bottom line, I don't know. The police told me they suspected homicide, they closed off the warehouse, and that's it."

"Poppy, something else is wrong, isn't it?" Sure, Vivienne North's death was a shock, and who knew what the police were up to, but it wasn't like Poppy to worry so intensely. She always seemed so capable, so able to see the bright side. Once, at an auction Joanna attended, from her podium Poppy had seen a bidder suffer a stroke. She'd managed to summon an ambulance, keep the crowd calm, and finish the auction without batting an eye.

Tonight, Poppy's eyes were bloodshot, and she avoided looking at Joanna directly. "I'm fine. I just have to get in touch with the people who bought things at the auction. Not looking forward to it."

Joanna leaned forward. "Is that all? You'd tell me if something else were wrong, wouldn't you?"

"Everything's fine."

Joanna picked up a hint of defiance in Poppy's voice. If she didn't want to talk about it, there wasn't much Joanna could do. "What about the police? Did they say when they might be finished?"

"Not sure. They might—"

"Miss," a deep voice rang behind Joanna. "What are you doing here?"

Joanna turned to see a uniformed policeman. "I bought the trunks of clothing in today's auction. I came to pick them up."

"Name, please." The policeman consulted a clipboard.

"Joanna Hayworth."

His finger ran down a list and stopped. "How long have you known Ms. Madewell?"

"Poppy? Nearly four years, I guess." She glanced at Poppy, who nodded briefly. "I met her just before I opened Tallulah's Closet, my vintage clothing boutique."

She'd been on the verge of tears that night trying to secure one clothing rack that just wouldn't stay put. The store was due to open that weekend, but all around her heaped bags of unpressed clothing. The store's fixtures were pushed to the center of the room while paint dried on the walls.

"Well," Poppy had said from the door. "This place has come a long way from the bike mechanic's shop that was here before."

Joanna set the screwdriver aside and wiped her hands. "Can I help you?" She recognized Poppy from excursions to the auction house, but they'd never talked. She looked so small off the stage.

"Poppy Madewell." She extended a hand. "You bought the oak counter display case, right? Yep, there it is. God" — the word came out "Gawd" in her Jersey accent— "that thing's a monster. Anyway, it came with tassels for the knobs. Must not have been in the cabinet when you picked it up. Thought I'd slide them through your mail slot, but you're here."

"Oh," Joanna said. Tassels hardly seemed important with the disaster around her. Although, as Poppy had pulled one from its envelope and dropped it in her hand, she saw that the tassels were lovely, woven of gold silk. They'd add a luxurious touch to the cabinet.

"Let me give you a hand with that clothing rod," Poppy had said. "That's a job for two." They'd been friends ever since.

Not that the policeman tonight would care about all that.

"This is a crime investigation. You'll need to leave," he said.

"But I'll be able to take the clothes, right?" Beyond Poppy, the police crew methodically sorted through boxes.

"No, miss," the policeman said. "They're evidence. We're writing up a receipt now. We'll let Ms. Madewell know when they're ready to be released. She'll be responsible for contacting her clients."

"I'm sure Vivienne North hasn't worn those clothes for years. You think she's been swanning around in fifty-year-old Fath evening dresses?"

"Look, these guys aren't fashion mavens," Poppy said. "I don't know what they want with the clothes. I'm sorry. Hopefully it won't be too long."

Poppy almost seemed to side with the policeman. Joanna raised an eyebrow at her, but Poppy's expression remained impossible to read. Joanna turned to the policeman. "When you test the clothes, you don't cut them up, do you? Or pull fibers from the fabric?"

"Ms. Madewell will be in contact when we're finished with the items," the policeman said.

Lost in thought, Joanna pulled her bag onto her shoulder. "What are you looking for, anyway? Vivienne North didn't die here." She glanced toward Poppy again, who shook her head helplessly.

The policeman ignored her. "I'll see you to the door."

Chapter 4

The slant of the light confused her. And she was on the wrong side of the bed. As Joanna opened her eyes, she stretched out a hand and felt fur. Gemma the Beast. She was at Paul's. The German shepherd mix thumped her tail against the bed and G.I. Joe'd a few feet closer. She laid her head on Joanna's chest. The fragrance of coffee mingled with wood dust rose from the shop floor to the small sleeping loft.

"Hey, sleepyhead." Paul's head popped above the banister. "Here's coffee." His smile revealed the tiny gap between his front teeth. Warmth shot through Joanna.

She pulled the sheet up and leaned forward to take the mug. "Thanks. I'll be down in a second." Gemma jumped off the bed to follow Paul.

Joanna set down her coffee and yawned, then pulled back her arms mid-stretch. The auction, Vivienne North's death. The image of Vivienne's faint smile appeared. How could she be dead? Joanna's chest tightened. And Poppy. Something was up with Poppy, she was sure. Something more than the admittedly huge stress of having the police gum up the auction.

Joanna let out a long breath. All those gorgeous clothes, lost now. She imagined ham-handed policemen rifling through the dresses, smearing everything with fingerprint dust. With a groan she tossed back the blankets and found the old robe of Paul's she'd been using.

Its scratchy wool slid over her skin.

In the kitchen, Paul slid one arm around her waist and kissed her cheek while the other hand held a pancake turner. "How'd you sleep? You didn't worry too much about the auction, did you?"

"Not too much. A little, I guess." The dresses were going to save Tallulah's Closet. Maybe they still could.

She took her coffee to a worn armchair. On the nearby worktable lay two pieces of birds'-eye maple delicately joined to form a corner of dovetails. Last night he had shown her how he worked them by hand, patiently fitting each slat into the other and shaping their edges to a finish so smooth that if she'd felt the join with closed eyes she wouldn't know they were two pieces.

For most of his youth, Paul had spent his after-school hours at his uncle's wood shop. The shop turned out to be cover for a jewel-theft operation that rivaled the Pink Panther's. When his uncle went to prison, Paul ended up with the shop and a career in woodworking.

"Here you go." Paul slid a plate onto the kitchen table.

Joanna laughed. Paul had made her a pancake shaped roughly like a dress, complete with blueberry buttons. "Not bad," she said. "With the prim collar and all, it could be an early Chanel. If you get tired of woodworking, you could go into fashion design."

"I figured you needed a special dress to tide you over until you get the clothes you bought yesterday." He put another plate of pancakes, these round, across the table and sat down. "Seriously, though, it's good to see you laugh about it. The paper has a story about Vivienne North's death. I guess her family's a big deal around here. They're saying she was poisoned."

Joanna cupped the coffee mug in her hands. "Poisoned? It's so hard to believe. I had just seen her, too. She must have been in her eighties, but she looked strong to me. Really elegant. Full of personality. You know what I mean?"

She pulled the newspaper toward her. Below a story about a recent flurry of jewel thefts was Vivienne's photo, taken at a gala the year before. Joanna couldn't quite summon the image of the regal woman on the medical examiner's table, her vibrancy gone. "She didn't strike me as someone who would have a lot of enemies," she said. "Although I guess you never know." She remembered Vivienne's focused gaze from across the auction hall. There probably wasn't much she missed.

"Why was she auctioning off all her stuff before she died?" Paul rose to tend to the pancakes.

"Can't say. Maybe she was downsizing." She remembered Vivienne's crisp dismissal of Eve and smiled. Her smile morphed to a frown. "Poor Vivienne. I wish I could have known her. She moved in completely different circles, but even half an hour and a coffee with her would have been fascinating." She absently drew a heart on the table with her finger. "I wonder if I'll ever get those clothes now."

She'd never even touched a Mainbocher suit before, and she nearly had two she could have spent hours examining. The clever cut of the stand-away collar of the Givenchy. Gone. Besides that, without them she couldn't begin paying back the credit line the bank had extended her for the auction.

She shifted in the chair. It was still a little early to call Poppy for more information. It wouldn't hurt to check on her mood, either. She'd seemed so out of it.

Paul lifted two pancakes to a plate and poured more batter in the pan. "I don't understand why the police took her things away. Doesn't make sense to me. What would vintage clothes and furniture have to do with a homicide investigation?"

Joanna toyed with her fork. "I don't get it, either."

You're worried about the money, aren't you?"

"Yes. A little."

He set the plate of pancakes on the tiny kitchen table. Gemma trotted over, clearly hoping for a scrap. "Do you know if the clothes are actually still yours? I mean, you didn't take possession of them before the police carted them away. If the clothes aren't really yours, the auction house will have to refund you the money, and you won't have the bank to think about at all."

"No way. They're mine. I have the receipt and everything." She shook her head. "I want those dresses even if I have to sell a kidney to get them."

"That's my girl," he said. "Undaunted. We'll work out the money angle one way or another."

"In the meantime, more coffee, please." She reached up to scratch where the rough wool brushed against her shoulder.

"You bet. That robe itches, doesn't it? Why don't you bring over one of your own?"

"Maybe I will." Embarrassed, her gaze slipped to her plate.

"Not to rush you. It took long enough to get you here in the first place." He rose and kissed her ear, and she laughed. "Not that I'm complaining."

"You're a patient man," she said. "A patient man who could use a shave."

"Still a little shy, but we're making progress." He reached over to refill her cup. "Now, if I could just get you to bring over a robe — "

"Yellow light," she said, their pet term for "caution," but she smiled when she said it. Her smile faded. "Something is wrong with Poppy, too. I'm sure."

"From what you told me last night, she doesn't want to talk about it." He dropped a hand to scratch Gemma. "Do you want to give her a call? You can borrow my phone."

"Thank you."

"You must be the last person in the country without a cell phone," he said with affection. "You and some Amish people."

Joanna took his phone from the counter and punched in Poppy's number with her thumb. Cellphones felt so flimsy, not like the solid princess phone she had at home.

Poppy answered on the first ring.

"I hope it's not too early to call. I thought I'd see if the police gave you any updates when they left. I mean, they left, right?"

Poppy sighed. "Eventually. They let me keep the furniture, but they practically took it apart first. They hauled out Vivienne's wardrobe, though."

"They didn't give you any idea of when they'd release it?"

"No." Poppy's voice was flat. Tired.

"How are you holding up? You looked pretty stressed last night. Is there anything I can do? Maybe help you call clients?"

"I'm all right. Ben's here to help me." A pause. "I'll see you at the NAP auction meeting this afternoon, right?"

"Right." Damn. She'd forgotten about the meeting. Gemma wedged her body under the kitchen table and laid her head on Paul's foot. It was so warm here, so cozy, but it didn't look like she'd have time to enjoy it.

Chapter 5

"That's everyone." NAP's events coordinator, Jeffrey, closed the door to the conference room. Rain streaked the ceiling-to-floor windows. The room's fluorescent light cast the group's reflections against the glass. The sharp contours of Portland's tallest skyscraper, nicknamed "Big Pink" for its rosy granite exterior, filled the background.

Jeffrey rested his phone in easy view. "Joanna, I'd like you to meet Clarence and Lacey. They're leading the table host committee. I thought they should look at the dresses before we make any decisions. You already know Poppy."

Clarence rose and offered his hand. "Please call me Clary." Lacey lifted her head from her phone long enough to nod hello. A black Pomeranian squirmed in her lap.

Joanna had run into Clary a few times at auctions and estate sales. He had a rare books boutique in the Pearl District. People called him "Baronet" behind his back because it was rumored he'd bought a title on the internet. He certainly dressed the part with his starched dress shirt buttoned to the neck and small, wire-rimmed glasses. Some might say he acted the part, too. She hadn't met Lacey before, but her blond highlights and puffed lips gave her the look of a dozen other local society women, the sort for whom Clary had probably played the role of walker many times.

Poppy rose for a hug when Joanna crossed to her side of the table and scooted over to make room for her. The clever use of concealer brightened Poppy's eyes, but her usual enthusiasm was absent. A large sheet of paper covered with circles indicating tables, some with names scribbled next to them, lay in front of her. Her job was to know where the big spenders sat and to tailor her pitch to them.

"How are you?" Joanna whispered.

"Okay. Considering."

Jeffrey continued. "I thought we'd start with the outfits. Is that all right?" He looked to Clary for permission to go on. Clary nodded. "Joanna has agreed to lend us a few gowns. I told her we'd take care of dry cleaning, and we'd pay for any damage—not that there'll be any. We'll need five ensembles for the greeters, then another five for the art handlers."

"I don't know about vintage for the hostesses," Lacey said. "Why not something new? You know, nice?"

Joanna sat up. She thought it had been settled that she'd provide the dresses.

Clary swiveled toward Lacey. "Oh no. Vintage is the only way to go. We want something unique. Hollywood glamour, you know."

Jeffrey nodded. "Hollywood glamour. Yes, yes. Definitely."

Clary leaned forward. "But, of course, we'll need to make sure they fit in. We'll have very high-end donors. They expect excellence. The aesthetic must be perfect."

Jeffrey swiveled his head toward him and nodded faster.

Poppy crossed her arms defensively. "Joanna has terrific taste. I see these donors, too, you know, at all sorts of charity auctions I work. I guarantee the volunteers will look better at the NAP art auction than they did at the art museum's gala."

"Thank you, Poppy." Joanna pulled an envelope from her bag and slid out a sheaf of photographs. Apple had offered to make a slideshow on the laptop, but Joanna loved the old-fashioned permanence of a photograph with its glossy surface, even though she had to have one of her customers, a photographer, develop for the film for her. "It wasn't easy finding the larger sizes—so many vintage dresses were made for smaller people—but I think I came up with a good selection."

The first photo showed a floor-length 1940s gown with a black and white plaid taffeta bodice and a black crepe skirt. Its vee neck was ruffled, and a plaid sash encircled its waist, culminating in a large bow at the back. "I kept the palette to black and white. This dress is a modern size eight, but there's room at the hips and the waist if we tie the sash looser."

"I see the references in late '90s Prada," Clary said. Spot-on fashion knowledge, Joanna noted. Impressive. "I don't want to be insulting, but how does it smell?" he added.

"Yes, the smell," Jeffrey said and nodded twice, his attention on Clary.

The Pomeranian yapped and leapt from Lacey's lap. "Porsche, get over here."

"Portia?" Joanna said. "Like in *The Merchant of Venice*."

Lacey retrieved the dog. "No, like in the Boxster."

Joanna swallowed a grimace, then turned to the table. "As for the dresses, I dry clean everything. I'm wearing vintage now." She plucked the collar of her Mugler dress. "Hopefully it smells all right to you." She suppressed her irritation and withdrew the next photo, another 1940s dress with strong shoulders and a drape of fabric at the waist. "Plus, I put a few drops of lavender oil in the steamer water."

"That one looks like it could be in a Humphrey Bogart movie," Lacey said, having corralled the Pomeranian again. "Very film noir." She frowned. "In fact, maybe too film noir. Are they all like that?"

"A lot of them are." Joanna pulled two more photos from the stack, this time tea-length black cocktail dresses from the early 1950s. "The fabric absorbed a lot of light in this photo. It's hard to see the ruching on the bodice."

Lacey wrinkled her nose. "I don't know. Clary, what do you think? War-era dresses are just so — so depressing."

"They're gorgeous," Poppy said, always loyal. "They make me think of dancing to big band music."

Clary straightened in his chair and crossed his legs, revealing a polished calf loafer. "I agree. I don't find them depressing at all. If you ask me, these are the real hourglass dresses. But I get your point. Couldn't we have something a little more — I don't know — grand, maybe? You know, more Academy Awards, more satin and décolleté?"

Jeffrey's head darted from Lacey to Clary to Joanna.

Joanna pondered her stock. She could probably pull together four or five dresses that weren't too small, although it would wipe out her collection in that era for a few weeks. It would be worth it, though, just for the exposure at the auction. She'd need another five, too. She glanced at Poppy. If only she had Vivienne's dresses. They would be great advertising for the new, higher-end direction the store was taking. Then again, maybe the dresses were too fine to lend for a charity auction. Not worth the risk of an accidental Merlot stain.

"I do have a handful in the store that might work, although most of them are awfully small. Size twos and fours."

"Why don't we ask Eve at Eve's Temptation what she has?" Clary said. "I know her pretty well. I bet I could convince her to lend some dresses for the auction."

Eve? Never. "No. I can get them." Joanna was surprised at the force of her voice. She'd be damned if Eve ended up making money over this. "I mean, I've also bought some gorgeous dresses at auction, lots of them, but the police have them right now. I'll look into getting them returned."

"From Vivienne North," Lacey said. "They're her things, aren't they? Oh, that would be marvelous. Once I went over for tea and she showed me a few. I'm not a huge vintage wearer, but I admit they were pretty impressive." She leaned forward. "But you said the police are holding them? Does it have to do with her murder?"

Joanna marked her interest in the dresses and noted her as a potential buyer—if the police ever released them.

"I'm afraid so," Poppy said. "Although I'm not sure why. I can't imagine she'd worn most of the clothes for years. Decades, even."

Clearly excited, Lacey turned to Clary. "You know Helena Schuyler North, don't you? Vivienne's daughter-in-law, the sociology professor? Vivienne was living with her. Maybe she has more dresses that she kept."

Clary shifted in his seat. "Yes, sure, I know her. With all the talk about her mother-in-law's death, she might not want to be opening Vivienne's closet to the world just now—"

"The police probably have everything of hers, anyway," Joanna said.

"Why? I've never heard of the police taking someone's wardrobe—clothes they haven't worn forever—in a murder investigation." Lacey put a hand on Clary's arm. "You could convince Helena to lend a few dresses, I know you could. Besides, Helena's going to the NAP auction. Her husband has a painting in it."

Joanna watched intently. If she could talk to Vivienne's

daughter-in-law, maybe she could get more information about when the police would release Vivienne's clothes. "I'd be happy to visit her daughter-in-law, take a look at the dresses. If there are any." She shot a look at Lacey.

Clary fidgeted. "I don't know if she's taking visitors right now. Even if she is, she might not feel up to meeting with a stranger. I mean, she and her husband were the ones who found Vivienne's body."

"I can understand she'd be upset." The thought of Vivienne sprawled on the floor gave her a momentary shiver. Her death still seemed unreal. "But I'm used to dealing with people who are taking care of their family's estates. Sometimes it's a relief for the family to be able to talk about business for a change. Talking to a stranger, like me, makes it even easier."

Clary stared vacantly at the image of a black rayon dress still in his hand. "I guess I could give her a call."

"Do it," Lacey said. "Call her now."

"It would be nice to have this part of the event taken care of," Jeffrey added with hesitation, as if he were unsure whether he should be siding with Joanna and Lacey or with Clary.

"My schedule is open," Joanna said.

"All right. Just a moment." Clary reached inside his jacket for his phone and walked to the far end of the conference room.

Joanna raised her eyebrows at Poppy. Surely, if anyone knew what was going on with the police investigation, it would be Vivienne's family. And, who knows? Maybe Vivienne did leave a few dresses her daughter-in-law would be willing to part with.

Clary returned, sliding his phone again into the pocket and withdrawing a gold pen. "She's not sure what Vivienne has, but she can meet you tomorrow morning. Here's her address," he said, scrawling the name of a street in the West Hills in an ornate script. "Be careful with her. She's, well, she's fragile."

Joanna looked up in surprise. Fragile? What did that mean?

"Don't be ridiculous, Clary," Lacey said. "She'll do just fine."

Before ringing the bell next to the police warehouse's metal door, Joanna fluffed her hair and adjusted her skirt. She hoped the Thierry Mugler dress with its space age, curve-hugging fit and spritz of Balmain's violet-leather Jolie Madame perfume would work some magic. She needed Vivienne's dresses, and the sooner the better.

"Yes?" The door cracked open, revealing a man in a white jumpsuit with an ID badge clipped to its pocket. He chewed gum as he examined her. He didn't appear as impressed with the Mugler dress as she'd hoped.

"Hi." She gave her best smile. "I think it's starting to rain out here — you know, it's Rose Festival, and like they say, it always rains during Rose Festival." She laughed nervously. "Could I come in?"

The man looked behind him. "I guess. Just inside." His jaw continued to work the gum.

The warehouse's exterior, dingy aluminum siding unbroken by windows, didn't prepare her for its vast, fluorescent-lit interior. Rows of tall metal shelves, each numbered and sheathed in plastic, took up a third of the space. An open area with larger objects, including, to her surprise, an SUV, filled the rest. A few desks and a stained Mr. Coffee were near the door.

The man in the jumpsuit stepped between her and the room. "What is it you want, lady?"

"Oh." She laughed again, then stopped at the sight of the man's unmoved expression. This ingénue business wasn't getting her anywhere. "My name is Joanna Hayworth." She extended her hand.

"Yes?" His hands remained in his pocket.

So that's how it was, was it? She withdrew her hand and pulled her cardigan tighter. "I bought some vintage clothing at an auction yesterday. Vivienne North's estate. You guys took them."

"And?"

"The clothing—"

"Evidence, you mean."

"—Is very delicate. Valuable, too. I need to make sure you know how to store it. Old fabric is sensitive to temperature change, and—"

"How did you find the warehouse?" With an air of long practice, he spit the gum into a wastebasket an arm's length away.

"Just a quick call to the police station." In fact, she'd spent nearly an hour with Kimberly at the Central Library's reference line, who'd scoured city databases until she'd located it. The reference team had long been Joanna's substitute for a web browser. Kimberly was a new hire, but she was top notch, and Joanna always requested her. She'd have to ask the library's team lead how Kimberly might feel about a vintage charm bracelet for her trouble.

"Really." He folded his arms in front of his chest and widened his stance. "Look. I have work to do. I can't stand around talking."

"But what about the clothes? When will you be done with them? I can bring down some acid-free tissue—"

"You seem pretty eager to get the clothes back."

"Yes." At last he was listening. "I need those clothes for my store. I've already bought them, and I need to sell a few pieces to pay some bills."

"So the clothing is valuable."

"Very valuable. Those pieces are ridiculously rare nowadays. People would kill to own just one of the dresses." She clapped her mouth shut. Bad choice of words.

The man nodded. "Including you? Is there something we ought to know, Joanna Hayworth?" He stressed each syllable of her name.

She felt a chill. "No, it's just—"

"Then it's time for you to go." He opened the door behind her.

It was really raining now. She backed up a few inches. He moved forward and her feet hit the gravel of the parking lot. He took a fresh stick of gum from a pocket in his jumpsuit. "Did it occur to you that a major crime was committed? We're doing all we can to find out what happened. I'm sure a few dresses can wait."

The door shut with a thud.

Chapter 6

In most Portland neighborhoods, the North home would have stood out as a mansion. In this older part of the West Hills, it was merely a modest Tudor-style home with a stretch of velvety lawn and a protective ring of old rhododendrons, their hot pink and pale purple blossoms just starting to fade. The rain had stopped during the night, and cool sun bathed the yard.

Joanna left her Corolla, nicknamed "Old Blue," on the street and walked up the brick path to the door. The brass knocker was heavy in her hand. No one answered after a few, tentative raps, so she knocked again, this time harder. The June sun warmed her back. Vent Vert, the crisp, mossy-green perfume she'd dotted on her wrists, was perfect for the day.

Just when she had turned toward the street to leave, a woman in a dirt-smeared Trail Blazers sweatshirt opened the door.

"I'm sorry," she said. "You must be Joanna. I was working in the garden and didn't hear you. Come in."

"Thank you. I'm here to see Helena Schuyler North." She stepped into an entry hall with oak-paneled walls fragrant with lemon and beeswax. The entry opened to a larger central hall with French doors at the far end, giving out to a broad stone patio and a large garden hidden from the street. No sign of anyone else. Hopefully Vivienne's daughter-in-law remembered their appointment.

The gardener slid off a glove and proffered her hand. "I'm Helena. Sorry I wasn't quite ready for you. The garden really needed some work. I'm afraid I let it go during spring term." Now Joanna noticed the precisely cut bob, no Super Cuts job, touched with gray. A lot of women with her money would have dyed their hair blond. Helena's mouth widened into a smile, revealing a few lines around her almond-shaped eyes. With her eyes and straight nose, her profile could have been lifted from a Greek coin.

"If it's not too cold for you," Helena said, "would you like to sit in the back for a few minutes? I want to run upstairs and change." She led Joanna to the patio and gestured toward a chair at a small metal table in the sun. "You can sit here, if you'd like. Or feel free to wander the garden. The Paeonia delavayi are blooming. Would you like some tea?" The words came out in a girlish tumble.

Joanna smiled and nodded. "Thank you."

The back garden was beautiful enough for a spread in *Town and Country*. Roses were only starting to open, but rhododendrons bloomed profusely. A hummingbird whirred by and hovered at an azalea before darting on. A fenced-off vegetable garden filled the far corner of the yard.

Joanna took the slate-paved path to check it out. Vegetable gardening had to be a rarity in this neighborhood, but here a row of peas crawled up string, and French breakfast radishes broke through the black soil. Just beyond the vegetable garden were two stacked, white boxes on stands. Joanna stepped off the paved path, her 1940s sandals sinking into the damp grass, to look more closely at the boxes.

"I see you found my beehives," Helena said.

Joanna whirled around. She sure had changed her clothing fast.

Now she wore loose pants and a linen tunic. Nothing flashy, but not cheap, either. "Just looking at your vegetable garden."

"I'm sorry if I startled you. Change in plans. Let's go into the house. It's cooler than I thought out here." She lifted a tray with tea things from the small table and carried it in. "Clary said you wanted to talk about Vivienne's clothing."

"Yes. But first, let me say how sorry I was to hear about her death. This must be a difficult time for you."

"Thank you," she said simply. "People have been very kind." She nodded toward a vase of lilies of the valley on a side table. "In fact, Clary sent those. Such a nice man. Magnificent taste, too."

Joanna thought of his creased trousers and nodded. Most Portland men couldn't operate a steam iron if threatened at knife point. "He helped come up with this year's theme for the art auction, Hollywood glamour."

"I've got the evening blocked out in my calendar. One of my husband's paintings was selected for the live auction." At the mention of her husband, Helena's face lit up.

"Is that one of his?" Joanna nodded toward a small canvas of a nude. The painting looked competent, but not unusual. But who was she to judge?

"An earlier work." She looked at the painting with obvious pride. "Two galleries in town and one in L.A. want to represent him, but he can't decide."

"Maybe being at the auction will help. I'm pulling together some outfits for some of the people volunteering that evening. I know most of your mother-in-law's clothing was sold, but we wondered if she might have held back a few dresses that you'd be willing to lend us." She'd wait until she saw what Vivienne might have left before mentioning that Tallulah's Closet was always looking for new stock.

Helena led her into a large room overlooking the front yard, just off the entry hall. She rested the silver tray on a coffee table. Sun pooled on the coral and pale green tones of the oriental carpet, and bunches of white tulips, big as fists, sat on the fireplace. "To tell the truth, I'm not completely sure what Vivienne kept and what she sold."

"You probably haven't had time to go through her things since her — since she died. I hope I'm not causing too much trouble."

Helena's expression remained calm. "She'd been living with Gil — my husband — and I for only a few months now." She lifted the teapot's lid and stirred the leaves. "She'd decided on a change of lifestyle and sold her house and moved into ours. She auctioned off most of her furniture and wardrobe. You'd be amazed at the clothing she'd kept over the years."

Joanna thought longingly of the trunks of beautifully crafted dresses. "I bought some of it at the auction — I have a vintage clothing store. They're gorgeous pieces." She glanced out the window to catch an elderly woman walking a King Charles spaniel. The woman cast a disgusted look at Old Blue as she passed.

Helena followed Joanna's gaze and laughed. "That your car? Don't mind her, the old snob." She poured tea for each of them.

"It does look a little out of place." She eyed the brand new Range Rover parked across the street.

"We've been living here for almost ten years, and sometimes I still feel a little out of place, too." Helena touched Joanna's hand briefly. "Don't worry about it."

Joanna set down her tea cup. "The police seized the clothes I bought from Vivienne at the auction house. Did they take her things here, too?"

"Oh, they had a whole team here taking photographs and nosing around, but they didn't take anything away. At least, I don't think so." Helena's gaze lost focus.

"I can't imagine how you feel." Why had the police, then, hauled off Vivienne's auction items? It didn't make sense.

She shook her head. "Someone came in here, in this room, and killed Vivienne." She grasped a throw pillow and pulled it into her lap. She drew a deep breath. "It wasn't the first time someone broke in, either."

Joanna inhaled sharply. She passed her gaze once again over the carpet's soothing tones, the tulips on the mantel. "I can't imagine."

"The house was broken into a few weeks ago, and my jewelry was stolen. It wasn't much—a tennis bracelet and a pendant. But Gil had given them to me. Vivienne's jewelry was all in her safe deposit box. She was going to send it to Sotheby's." Helena gave a bitter laugh. "Not that it mattered in the end."

"I'm sorry. I've heard about all the diamond thefts lately." Joanna wondered if Clary had been right. Maybe it was too soon to be visiting the Norths. After all, it was just a few dresses. Not worth stirring up all this pain.

Helena pushed back the tea tray. "I'm sorry for burdening you with this. Why don't we go upstairs and see what she had?"

Joanna rested one hand on the polished banister as they climbed the stairs to the second floor. The hall darkened as they reached a closed door at its end. Helena pushed it open.

"This part of the house extends over the garage. It was originally a nursery. We didn't use it much until Vivienne came to live with us." She moved the windows and pushed open the curtains. She ran a finger along the windowsill. "I need to get up here and dust."

Sunlight illuminated a suite of simple blond wood furniture. The room looked like a cross between a sitting room and a chapel, with a small fireplace and bookshelves on one end and an oil painting of the Madonna and a prayer bench with a purple velvet knee pad on the other. Joanna knelt and touched the pad. Silk velvet. They didn't have silk velvet kneelers at the church where she grew up, that was for sure.

"It looks practically — monastic," Joanna said.

Helena sighed. "Vivienne had recently become quite religious. That's part of the reason she arranged to sell everything and move in with us. She didn't think it was right to have so much when so many people have so little."

Joanna remembered the furniture sold at the auction and the dizzying bids for some of it. Her estate must have collected a real packet.

Helena shook her head. "I can't explain it. Since we don't have children, she left most of her estate to the convent." Seeing Joanna's puzzled expression, she added, "Sisters of Saint Mary Salome the Myrrh Bearer. She knows the Mother Superior."

"That's an unusual choice."

Helena moved to the window and picked a piece of lint off the curtain. "Yes, but it's all right. We're doing fine. Obviously." She looked shy for a moment. "Maybe she didn't see the need to put us in her will. Then there was the convent. But that's more than you want to know, I'm sure." She gestured toward the other side of the room. "The bedroom is through there."

The bedroom, facing the back garden, was as simply furnished as the sitting room. A twin bed occupied one wall, and a dresser with a framed painting of the Virgin Mary hung on the other. Yellow roses, now limp and scentless, filled a red glass vase next to the painting.

Helena opened the closet. "She did save her wedding dress, but that's in a cedar chest downstairs. This is what's left."

A trace of the rich tuberose of Fracas perfume still clung to the few clothes in the closet. A pale blue, quilted bathrobe hung from its door. Not exactly a nun's habit. Joanna felt its charmeuse lining and imagined the buttery texture on her skin as, warm and damp from a bath, she slipped into it. On the floor was a pair of mules with beaver trim. "Vivier" in gold script ran down their lasts. Joanna glanced back at the bed. From a distance, the pillowcases had only looked like cotton muslin. Now she realized they were linen, probably Italian.

"Everything is so simple here — stark, really — but so beautiful."

"Oh, even after she found religion, Vivienne liked her luxury. She had to have flowers, and she insisted on sterling flatware. Said it was softer in the mouth." As she spoke, she opened and closed drawers, lifting stacks of pristine white blouses and loose pants. "Every evening before dinner she went to the den and put on classical music. Debussy, lately. She had a special set of Baccarat cocktail glasses, and she'd make herself a Bee's Knees."

Heaven, Joanna thought, wishing she'd known Vivienne in life. "A Bee's Knees?"

"Some kind of gin cocktail she'd first had at a bar in Paris when she met Dad." Joanna noticed Vivienne's husband earned "Dad" while her mother-in-law was still "Vivienne." Helena turned from the closet. "Anyway, as you can see, I guess there's not much here for you. Just her everyday clothes. I'm sorry. I should have looked before I had you come over." She stopped. "You know, though, Vivienne did give a few dresses to the convent for a fundraiser. I think they were having some kind of sale. I don't know if the sale is over or what, but you could check with them. Maybe they'd lend them to you."

As she passed through the bedroom, her eyes were again drawn to the backyard's vivid shrubbery. Helena had turned out to be a lot nicer than she'd anticipated. She'd been through so much lately, too, with Vivienne's murder.

"I know the words must sound empty right now, but I'm so, so sorry for everything you've been through. I imagine you'll be glad when the police investigation is over and you can get back to normal."

"Normal? What's normal? I don't even know anymore."

Chapter 1

After spending the morning at Helena's, Joanna's home felt like a shack. Her neighborhood was slowly gentrifying — the sewage treatment worker next door had retired to the coast to be replaced with a graphic designer who held backyard parties where guests cooed at his Taj Mahal of a chicken coop stocked with Araucanas. But the houses, including Joanna's, were mostly small, postwar affairs, as simple as if they were drawn by children.

"Hello, Aunt Vanderburgh," Joanna said to an amateur pastel of a stranger with thin, pursed lips and horned-rimmed glasses. The portrait bore a crease across its middle from where it had almost been destroyed when her house was broken into the year before. Now the portrait was back on duty as a sounding board. "It turns out that not all rich people are tasteless. I was just at a fabulous house." She put her hands on her hips and looked at Auntie V's disapproving stare. "I'm afraid you'd be tossed in the dustbin over there."

The midday sun radiated through the Schiaparelli-pink rhododendron outside to fill the living room with rose-inflected light. Pepper, Joanna's cat, lay partly under the coffee table in a sunbeam's path. His black fur was warm, and his tail curled up when she reached down to pet him. She set her purse on the chaise longue by the front window and leaned against the window frame.

Her life had taken such a dramatic turn during the past nine months. Just last summer she was moving in on her fourth year of owning Tallulah's Closet and had found a quiet, comforting routine. Work, scout for more stock, home, hot bath, bed. Then Marnie — someone she regularly bought clothes from — turned up dead in the store. Thinking of Marnie, she took a deep breath. What she wouldn't give to be able to share a Martini with her at the store after hours again some evening. Joanna had met Paul at about the same time. And Eve's attempts to open a rival vintage clothing store down the block had sparked Joanna to upgrade Tallulah's Closet with higher-end dresses and clientele. The peacefulness of Helena's sun-filled den felt far away. Joanna sighed and turned back toward the living room.

"Pepper, have you been good today?" She opened the mail slot that fed into the dining room and flipped through the envelopes. Mostly bills, including one from Puddletown Plumbing and an even larger bill from the designer who did her website and never seemed to get it right. Joanna's resolve to take Tallulah's Closet to the next level was getting expensive, but selling just one of Vivienne's items would pay this bill at least. If she ever saw those dresses again. And then there was the NAP auction. Really, all she needed were five more gowns. She tossed the mail on the table.

Maybe it was time to go visit some nuns.

The Sisters of Saint Mary Salome the Myrrh Bearer convent was a two-story colonial house not far from the Saint Philip Neri Catholic church and a short walk from Tallulah's Closet. Joanna wasn't sure of her reception as a drop-in. What were the ways of nuns, anyway? She figured an early evening visit might be best — the sisters probably weren't night owls.

It wasn't hard to convince Apple to come along. Although Apple wasn't much a fan of the pope, she saw the convent as a sister institution to a coven and was just as curious as Joanna to check out its interior. Joanna shut off the store's lights and flipped the sign to "closed." They crossed Division and entered shaded streets of bungalows.

The convent's grounds spread across the end of a short city block. Roses beginning to open in garish coral and lipstick red lined the parking strip. A tidy lawn sloped up the hill to the house, interrupted by a rusted arch announcing Sisters of Mary Salome the Myrrh Bearer. A curtain rustled on the second floor as a figure pushed it aside, then let it drop.

Joanna and Apple mounted the path through the lawn, past a cement Madonna. "I hope we're not catching them at dinner." She pictured an antiseptic kitchen with buzzing fluorescent lights and institutional food. Or maybe the nuns were reading the Bible and knitting caps for orphans.

Apple appeared not to hear her. "Haint blue."

"What?"

"The shutters and door are haint blue. It's a color people in the south use to keep bad spirits out."

The convent's trim was a shade of flat sky blue Joanna associated with 1960s park-at-your-door motels. A cut-out of a cross pierced each shutter, and paint peeled off in spots. "Good one, Apple. Maybe they do voodoo, too. Come on." She rapped the brass door knocker.

The door opened quickly, as if someone had been waiting, hand on the knob, for their arrival. A middle-aged woman in a powder blue habit with navy trim smiled. "May I help you?"

"My name is Joanna Hayworth, and I was hoping I could talk to you about some old dresses Vivienne North might have given you."

"Vivienne. One of our favorite donnés." The nun smiled again. Her face fell just as quickly. "So sad about her death. Come in and I'll fetch Sister Mary Frances. I'm Sister Mary Carmen. Have a seat." She gestured from the entry hall to a living room to the right. "Just let me move this bag from the couch."

Joanna raised an eyebrow at the shopping bag brimming with pink-wrapped condoms.

"We're making safer sex kits for the high school's youth group. Of course, we don't condone sexual relations outside of marriage. But you know what they say about an ounce of prevention." Mary Carmen was already turning toward the hall as she spoke.

Joanna and Apple traded glances as they settled on a low couch in the living room with a view down the lawn, past the Madonna, to the street. Joanna pulled her sweater closer to ward off the chill. The scent of dank carpet competed with an armload of lilacs in a chipped vase on the mantel. Above it loomed a lurid print of Jesus with a bored stare despite his open chest cavity and thorn-wrapped heart. She was busy mentally ripping out the false ceiling and replacing the carpets when Mary Carmen returned, accompanied by a steel-haired woman with a sharp nose.

"Joanna and, I'm sorry, I didn't catch your name—"

"Apple, pleased to meet you." She rose and extended a hand.

"And Apple. This is Mary Frances. She's our money manager and the one handling Vivienne's donation. Sister Mary Frances, Joanna is interested in talking about Vivienne's dresses."

The Sisters Mary took the love seat across the couch. Meanwhile, another, heftier nun settled into an armchair behind them. She put on reading glasses and opened a magazine. It wasn't *Vogue,* was it?

"I'm sorry about the temperature in here. Heating oil costs money, and, well it's June anyway. How can we help you?" Mary Frances folded her hands in her lap.

"I'm helping with the Northwest AIDS Project's gala. NAP — we call it NAP — is holding its annual fundraiser, a dinner and art auction. We're dressing some of the volunteers in evening dresses from the 1950s. I have a vintage clothing store, but my stock of evening dresses is thin right now, so I visited Vivienne's daughter-in-law — "

"Helena," the younger nun said.

"Yes, and she mentioned that her mother-in-law had given you some of her gowns. I was hoping I might borrow them for an evening. Of course, I'd have everything cleaned before I returned them." The nuns' expressions were friendly but blank. Then Joanna had another idea. "If you'd like, I could sell the dresses in my store for you. That is, if you're not going to keep them."

The nun reading behind them perked up and lowered her magazine.

"That's a very generous offer, Joanna. But I'm afraid we aren't able to lend the dresses to anyone. We're putting them on the, um — "

"Etsy. We have an online store," the magazine-reading nun finished.

"You see," Mary Frances glanced at the younger nun, then blurted, "We've been having some financial troubles."

Joanna wasn't surprised. "I'm sorry."

"We own the convent outright, but the house needs several thousand dollars in repairs, including a new roof. The county is threatening to condemn us. Vivienne, bless her soul" — she made the sign of the cross — "knew we were having trouble and put her things to auction. The proceeds all go to us."

"You should be fine, then. The auction must have raised quite a bit of money. In fact, I bought Vivienne's wardrobe."

"Then you know the police are holding everything in custody until the question of her death is cleared up. We were due to receive a generous check from the auction house, but everything is up in the air now." She clasped her hands in her lap. "So we're no better off than we were."

Suing a convent seemed a little harsh to Joanna, but she wouldn't put it past some people. "Surely the church will help you?"

Mary Frances looked at Mary Carmen, then at Joanna and Apple. "We, well, we haven't had a completely cooperative relationship with the Church. Some of our methods are, uh, unconventional, dear. They said they'd pay the bill if we moved, and — "

" — Then they'd raze the convent and divide the land into lots," Mary Carmen finished.

"And what would happen to you, to the sisters?" Apple asked.

"I'm afraid we'd have to split up. The convent would dissolve."

The women sat in silence for a moment as a clock ticked in the background.

"So you understand why Vivienne — God rest her soul — Vivienne's estate is so important to us."

Joanna glanced through the living room. The place did need a lot of work, and that was just the part she saw. It hardly seemed fair, though, that a group of harmless nuns could be kicked out of their home. And no dice on Vivienne's clothes. Where was she going to find five more dresses?

The nun in the armchair heaved her body forward, reached under her chair, and withdrew a silver laptop. Without speaking, she settled between Apple and Joanna on the couch. Apple grabbed an armrest as the sofa's springs caved. The nun opened the computer on the coffee table in front of them.

"Pride goeth before a fall, Sister Mary Alberta."

"Yes, Sister Mary Frances. But these ladies are vintage clothing professionals. Maybe they'll have some ideas to help us."

Mary Carmen, Mary Frances, Mary Louise, and now Mary Alberta. "Are you all named Mary?" Joanna asked.

Mary Frances raised her eyebrows. "Of course."

The laptop whirred to life. Mary Alberta's thick fingers typed a few keys, and a pink tableau filled the screen. "Sisters Vintage" it said in gothic letters next to an image of a church. "It's not live yet, but here's what I have so far."

"Nice," Apple said. "Wait— is that part of Saint Philip Neri?"

"We clean the rectory for the priests. We were sure they wouldn't mind if we took a few photos while they were at mass."

Mary Alberta pressed "enter" and the screen broke into squares. Hovering the mouse over one square filled the screen with a young blonde wearing a slender navy cocktail dress and leaning against a stone fireplace with a crucifix mounted over it.

"Is that a Givenchy?" Joanna asked.

"Dan Millstein copy from Boston," Mary Alberta answered promptly. She moved the mouse, and a handful of other items, all worn by the blonde in different poses in the rectory, popped forward. "What do you think?"

"Impressive." The clothes weren't as valuable as those Vivienne put up for auction, but they would thrill any vintage clothing collector. And they'd be perfect for the NAP auction. Joanna looked at Mary Alberta with fresh respect. She only wished her own website were as nice, especially for all the money she'd already laid out for it. Her heart dropped as she thought of the bill at home. "I wouldn't change much. It might be useful to have photos of the labels for collectors, but, really, the site looks great and things seem priced fairly."

"Sister Mary Alberta did all the design herself, including the styling," Mary Carmen said. "And the model is Sister Mary Louise's niece."

"We only have a dozen items for sale, but we wanted to do it up right, you know? Attract a higher level of clientele."

Mary Frances rose. "I'm sorry we can't help you. I wish you the best of luck with the fundraiser."

A sharp rap on the ceiling drew their attention. The Sisters Mary exchanged glances. The rapping started again. "Just a moment, Mother," Mary Frances said in a singsong voice, looking toward the second floor.

"The Exalted Mother. She's bedridden, unfortunately," Mary Carmen said. "Can't come down."

"Who's there?" a gruff voice yelled from upstairs. "Bring them up."

Mary Frances looked alarmed. "But Mother—"

"Bring them up, I said."

Apple kicked Joanna's foot, and she flashed her a glance. There was no way Joanna was going to miss this. "We'd love to meet the Mother if she's up to receiving guests."

"This is highly unusual—"

"And be quick about it," shouted the nun from upstairs.

"This way." Mary Frances sighed and led Joanna and Apple back to the entry hall and up the stairs. If anything, the second floor was more dingy than the first. Strips of paint had bubbled yellow from the ceiling. A water mark stained the edge of one wall. Mary Frances stopped at a door and knocked twice before opening it.

The scent of humid soil greeted Joanna's nose before she even entered the bedroom. Once inside, she saw why. Orchids as brilliant as parrots perched on nearly every surface. In the center of the cacophony of sword-like leaves and frilled petals stood a double bed made up in crisp white sheets. In the bed lay the Mother.

This was the room from which Joanna had seen the moving curtains outside, but it must have been someone else at the window since the Mother Superior clearly couldn't walk on her own.

"Mother, I'd like you to meet Joanna and Apple. They stopped by to ask about Vivienne's clothes. I told them we'd put them up for sale already."

The Mother first examined Joanna, then shifted her eyes to Apple, where they rested longer. Leaning against the wall on the other side of the bed was a folded up wheelchair. A porcelain tea cup painted with violets sat empty on the bedside table next to a half-eaten macaron — where did she get such good-looking macarons in Portland? — and a gold and green Cattelya orchid.

"You can go now," the Mother said to Mary Frances. She turned her head toward Apple. "You. What do you know about it?"

Joanna raised her eyebrows. What was she talking about?

Apple returned the Mother's stare. "Nothing really. Some strange music, but that's all."

Joanna's gaze shot to the bedridden nun. What was going on?

The mother nodded. "The police have it all wrong. They'll never figure out who killed her if they keep this up."

"Are you talking about who killed Vivienne North?" Joanna said. The Mother must have been able to hear them downstairs.

"Of course. You want your clothes, don't you, the dresses you bought at the auction?"

"Well, yes."

"Then you're going to have to help keep the police on track. I can't get out like I used to. Vivienne was a dear friend to us, and to me in particular." The old woman shifted in her bed. "Besides, we need that money."

Joanna shook her head. "Look, I'm happy to call the police and ask when they'll be finished with Vivienne's things, but as far as the investigation goes, it's in the police's hands." She remembered the murder investigation she'd been sucked into the summer before. No way she was going down that road again. "I mean, have you talked to the detective in charge yet?"

"Mary Frances," the Mother bellowed. Quick steps sounded on the stairs. "Here's the deal. You look into Vivienne's death, and I'll make sure you have Vivienne's clothes — the ones we have up for sale — for your charity auction."

"But I don't even know where I'd start."

Sister Mary Frances stood breathing hard at the door. The Mother said to Joanna, "You'll make do. She'll help." She nodded at Apple. "But don't do anything stupid. And report back." The Mother fell back into her pillows, her face whiter than before. She closed her eyes.

"This way," Mary Frances whispered.

On the street, Joanna was grateful for the cool air. "What was that all about? Did all that really just happen?" Or had they somehow stepped through a tear in reality and ended up on the set of *The Sound of Music?*

Apple didn't reply, but glanced back at the house.

"And what's up with the way she looked at you?"

"She's psychic, too." Her voice was thoughtful.

"For God's sake," Joanna said. "I have a headache."

Chapter

"What are you thinking?" Paul asked. Holding a hand plane in his fingers, he stood over his workbench and contemplated the leg of a table. Its curve, in raw mahogany, approximated the calf of a tall dancer. Cyd Charisse, maybe.

Joanna leaned back in the armchair and rested her leg on a box. Not quite Cyd Charisse, but could be worse. Cyd would have liked her shoes — pale green satin closed-toe sandals, although the fabric was frayed and soles scuffed. "When I was a kid, I used to climb fir trees. The big ones have good footing. You can get pretty far up, but spiky little branches poke out everywhere. The bark's sappy, too. I can't tell you how many times I got up a tree then realized it was going to be a painful scrape down." She let out a long breath. "That's how I feel now."

"You mean with Vivienne's clothes, or the nuns?"

"All of it." Joanna longed for a Martini. She wished for the hundredth time Paul drank. "I guess I could try calling the police station at a different time. Maybe I'd get someone who would tell me something I could use for the nuns. I need to borrow those dresses." She imagined Clary looking at her with a "What did I tell you, she'll never come through, we should have gone with Eve to begin with" look.

"I have to admit I'm kind of worried about money, too," Joanna added.

Paul put down the hand plane and plucked a piece of sawdust from her hair. "Why don't you let me help you?"

"You? You're as broke as I am."

He returned to the workbench and picked up a sheet of sandpaper. He focused on the table leg. "Money isn't everything. Besides, we could move in together. I could set up my shop in your garage."

Joanna lifted her head. This was new. Paul smoothed the angle of the table leg and turned it slightly. Her house was no palace but plenty big for two people. And he was right about the garage—it was large, and with some insulation and a little more electrical work it might make a decent workshop. This was a lot to take in.

"You surprise me," she finally replied.

"Just something to think about." He didn't seem bothered by her lack of an immediate "yes." He set the table leg down and wiped the sawdust from his hands. "I might be able to help you with money, though. It looks like I'll be starting a new project soon, a big one."

"Oh, really? Doing what?"

"Building some cabinets for an office. The woman running the project wants it really high end: a built-in desk, some bookshelves, and a full-wall wardrobe—plus all the trim in the room. Lots of Myrtlewood. The wood alone is going to cost a fortune, but it will be great to work with. Should keep me busy for at least a month."

"Sounds perfect. What kind of office?" Trim and cabinet work were Paul's specialties. He loved restoring older pieces, but it was rare he had the chance to build fine cabinets from scratch.

"She said it's some sort of consulting business where she finds things people want. Sounds like she's done a lot of scouting for people in New York already. You know, first edition books, fancy lamps, whatever. She even scouts for vintage clothes. There's one thing, though."

"What?"

He picked up his file again. "It's Eve Lancer."

Joanna's leg dropped to the floor. "You can't work for her."

"Why not?" He drew the file along the mahogany. "She's not selling vintage clothing anymore—well, not exclusively vintage clothing, anyway."

"You know my history with her. She tried to run Tallulah's Closet out of business last year. Remember? She tried to buy Vivienne's clothes out from under me, too."

"But she never did open that store. And as for the auction, the idea is that people compete with each other to buy things, right?"

"Yes, but—"

"You don't think she'd skip out on paying me or anything?"

"No, she has plenty of money, but—"

"But what?"

Joanna fidgeted. What could she say? That Eve had something personal against her? That maybe she'd even enjoy stealing Paul away?

"You're jealous," Paul said. Joanna stared in reply. "You don't have any reason to be. You know that." He strode to the far end of the workshop near the kitchen. He placed his hands on the counter, then turned to face her. Joanna watched nervously. "I need the money and Eve needs the work. I have to take this job, Joanna. You get that, right?"

She opened her mouth to reply, but thought better. "Yes. I understand."

The room was silent for a minute except for the clicking of Gemma's toenails as she crossed the cement floor to her water dish. Joanna stood and put her arms around Paul. He kissed the top of her head. His chest smelled of clean cotton and wood. Damned Eve.

"I don't want to take your money, but how would you feel about doing some work for some nuns? One of them seems to have a knack for web design. I bet she'd finish the Tallulah's Closet website for me if you helped shore up the convent a bit."

"The nuns you saw today?"

"They're a quirky group. I think you'll like them." She filled him in on the Mother Superior's offer to trade the dresses for information on Vivienne's death.

Paul pulled a wavy section of hair gently and released it. "I could do that. At least give them an idea of how much work needs to get done."

"What are you going to do about the police investigation?" he asked.

Joanna felt his arms tense. She leaned into him. "I don't know. I guess I'll call Helena Schuyler North, Vivienne's daughter-in-law. She was friendly. The police must keep her up to date with what's going on."

"All you're doing is asking, right? And telling the nun? No digging around on your own." He strung his fingers in her hair. "Remember last year," he murmured. "How dangerous it was."

"I know," she whispered. God, she was lucky to have him. "I'm just passing along information. That's all."

His arms relaxed. "Helena Schuyler North. What a name for a rich lady. Too perfect."

"Mm-hmm." Joanna only half heard him. Crisis averted. For the moment, at least.

Chapter

"It's so nice of you to come down to the store." Joanna rose from behind the bamboo-fronted tiki bar that served as the cashier's table at Tallulah's Closet.

Helena closed the door behind her. "I enjoyed talking with you yesterday. Besides, I was having lunch just up the street and thought it would be nicer to stop by rather than just return your call. I wanted to see your boutique, too."

Her blunt-cut bob and earth-toned ensemble contrasted with the rack of pastel cocktail dresses beside her. Her diamond wedding ring caught the light from the front window and flashed watery brilliance on the opposite wall. "I've never been in a vintage clothing store. It's fabulous."

"Thank you. Against that wall are all the black cocktail and evening dresses. In the middle, in front of the bench, is casual wear — mostly house dresses and cotton sundresses — and over here are the color cocktail dresses. The dressing rooms are in the back."

"What are you doing there?" She pointed toward the tiki bar, covered in papers.

Joanna had been making a list, and some of the papers had half-sketched dresses on them. "Oh, counting my chickens before they hatch, I guess. If the police ever release Vivienne's clothes I want to have a fashion show, invite the press and some of my regulars. These" — she tapped her pen on a drawing— "are some ideas for an invitation."

The sunlight into the store darkened for a moment as a familiar figure passed the front window. He paused for a moment and looked in, then seemed to think the better of it. "Was that Clary?" Joanna asked.

Helena turned to follow Joanna's gaze. "Yes, I think it was. I had lunch with him just now."

She placed her purse on the glass-topped jewelry case and fingered a pair of crystal Eisenberg earrings. "You said on the phone you wanted to talk about Vivienne." She unclipped one of the earrings from its post and held it up to her ear, turning her face to the mirror.

A girl, not more than twelve years old, strode into the store. Wearing designer jeans and sandals with heels, she was dressed more like a co-ed than the middle-school student she must be. Joanna glanced behind the girl to see if her mother followed, but she was alone.

Joanna waved. "Let me know if I can help you find anything."

"Just looking, thanks." The girl's heels clicked toward a display of reptile box bags from the 1930s.

Joanna returned her attention to Helena. "I'm sorry to bring up Vivienne again. I know it can't be easy for you." Helena nodded but turned toward the girl. "I went to the convent, like you suggested, to see if the nuns would lend me a few of her dresses, the ones she didn't auction off. They said they would, but the Mother Superior put a condition on it." Joanna looked up to see if Helena was paying attention. She seemed to be listening, but was still turned away.

"Anyway," Joanna continued, "She wanted me to find out what I could about Vivienne's death. I guess the police won't tell her anything. That's why I called you."

"Watch her," Helena murmured.

"What?"

"The girl." She raised her head. "You," she said to the girl. "Give it over."

"Really, she's okay," Joanna said, surprised at Helena's harsh tone. "I don't mind if people want to look around. They don't all have to buy."

"I saw you put that scarf in your bag. Give it over."

"I don't know what you're talking about," the girl said.

"The scarf. Now."

The girl pulled a vivid green and blue Vera scarf from her bag and tossed it on the bench. "Take your stupid scarf." She edged toward the door and left without speaking.

"Sharp eye. Thank you," Joanna said and retrieved the scarf.

Helena shook her head. "Gypsy kid. Probably here because of Rose Festival. Take my word for it — you don't want her type in here."

"But, surely, just because she's a gypsy doesn't mean she steals." Any girl might be fascinated by old things and drawn in by the window display.

"True. Not always. But there was something about her — " She didn't finish her thought.

"I had no idea there were gypsies around here," Joanna prompted, fascinated.

"Oh yes. You'd be surprised." Helena returned to the counter. "But you were telling me about the nuns. About the Mother Superior wanting to know about Vivienne."

"I thought gypsies lived in caravans and read fortunes."

"Not American gypsies. Not these days. For one thing, they drive

RVs. Nice ones, too." Helena must have picked up on her surprised expression. "Sociology professor, remember. I did my dissertation on travelers — that's what you call them in this country. But about Vivienne."

"Yes," Joanna said, still thinking of the girl. She'd have to tell this story to Apple. She'd love it. "If you don't mind filling me in on what you know about the police investigation, it would help me out."

"I'm happy to. I don't have a lot to share, though. The detective hasn't come by or called since they searched Vivienne's room. I don't know if that's good or bad. Gil has called them a few times."

"Did they give you any hint as to how Vivienne died?"

"I wish they did. But we know no more than the papers said. Poisoning. The police aren't even sure what exactly was poisoned. They tested her liquor and came up dry. Gil and I were out that night at the biennial art awards ceremony. When we came home, we found her. In the library."

"She was reading?"

"She'd had a guest. There were two glasses — Vivienne's and a tumbler, like for Scotch. She'd had her usual apéro as she called it, at five o'clock, before we left. She must have decided on another when the guest arrived. I imagine she made herself a drink, then sat by the fire. The coals were almost burned out. A few things were knocked off the coffee table, but the doctor said that would have been normal if she'd had a seizure." Her eyes had a faraway look. "She was just lying there. She'd always had so much dignity, but — " She seemed unable to finish her thought.

Joanna's stomach turned at the grisly image. "But no sign of the guest."

"No. We don't know who it was. The police have questioned all the neighbors. One of them saw someone — a man, she thinks — hanging out in the front in the early evening, but she didn't see him go in."

Joanna waited for her to say more.

"I wish I could say I was more attached to Vivienne, but I wasn't. I feel kind of guilty about it, actually. I let her down in so many ways. For one thing, we never had children. But I really don't see the need to bring children into the world. That was a huge disappointment to Vivienne. Also..." Her voice trailed off. "Is that your husband?" she asked suddenly.

Helena's gaze had caught a small photo of Paul that Joanna had taped to the inside of the tiki bar along with a bent bobby pin. "Oh, my boyfriend," she said. "It's a long story, but once we were stuck together on a boat, and he used that bobby pin to pick the lock to get us out."

She remembered the night before, when Paul had suggested they move in together. This talk about death made her regret she hadn't said "yes" right away. Waking up next to him every day, coming home to him every night — what could be better than that? And yet, it was still a little soon. She couldn't explain it.

Helena nodded. "This whole thing has been hard on my husband." She paused. "It's created some — well, strain, and I don't know what to do."

Her intimacy surprised Joanna. She wasn't sure how to respond. Then again, just in their two meetings they'd talked about death and loss — subjects perhaps even more intimate. "That's natural. His mother died a horrible death. He's probably traumatized."

"It's more than that. He never had to work, so I was glad when he took up painting. But now he's even lost interest in that. His medal from winning the art biennial seems to mean nothing to him. He's so anxious. All the time. It's like he expects more disaster." She searched Joanna's face, looking for some kind of comfort.

"It must be hard for you both. I can't even imagine."

"Maybe it's all the stress, but I keep having this feeling that —" A few seconds passed in silence.

"Feeling that what?"

"Well, I know it sounds strange, but I don't feel safe yet. I feel as if — as if someone is watching me." Helena bit her lip.

"Oh," Joanna said. "Have you told the police?"

She shook her head. "It's just me. Out of sorts. We have a new security system, I'm safe. At least, I should be safe."

"Maybe family should come stay with you for a while."

"I don't have any. I was an only child, and my parents are dead now. Gil is it for me." She started to play with the earring again. "I have friends, of course."

"Of course." Money didn't necessarily make everything better. Although Apple was like a sister, Joanna knew what it was like not to have family near.

Helena seemed to be near tears, but she managed a short laugh. "I know we just met. You've been so kind. It's kind of a rough time right now, and I don't want to burden you with it. Thank you for asking about Vivienne and for telling the nuns. Vivienne would have liked that."

"It's all right. I hope you'll think of me as a friend." Joanna remembered Clary's warning that Helena could be "fragile."

Helena drew a deep breath. "Thank you. I appreciate it."

"I wonder when it will all be over? The police have had Vivienne's things for a few days now," Joanna said.

"Hopefully it won't be long. Gil says Detective Crisp told him they're following up something big. He thinks there'll be a break in the case soon. I hope to God so."

"That's great news." For both of them, since the police might release the clothes. And Detective Crisp—that was a stroke of luck, too. Joanna knew him from his investigation of the murder the summer before. She touched the sketched invitation on the tiki bar. Maybe she'd hold that fashion show yet.

Blossom Dearie's baby-like voice sang from the record player. One of the Rose Festival princesses, accompanied by her official chaperone, had just bought the expensive pink tulle dress that had been on display. Its pale rose set off the princess's creamy Asian skin and dark hair. Joanna dropped a few business cards in her bag, hoping she'd tell the other Rose Princesses about Tallulah's Closet. Couldn't hurt.

Despite the sale, she couldn't help but feel uneasy. Twice she'd had the sensation that someone was watching her through the store's front window, but when she looked up, no one was there. She chalked it up to the strange interaction with the gypsy girl earlier in the day. That and the landlord's impending deadline must have made her edgy.

The shop's bell startled Joanna, nearly causing her to topple the mannequin in the front window. She'd been fastening a strapless daffodil-yellow satin gown around it.

She turned to find Clary next to her. "Whoa, let me help you."

With one hand, he reached for the mannequin to steady it. He had three book-shaped packages under his other arm, each wrapped in brown paper. Today he looked professorial in khaki trousers and a tweed jacket, complete with leather elbow patches. The gentle wear on his Belgian loafers and a wrinkled corner of handkerchief poking out of his breast pocket kept him from coming off as too self-consciously put together. No wire-rimmed glasses today, either. His eyes were gray flecked with amber.

She stepped down from the platform at the front window. "Thank you. How are you?"

"I was just at the bookstore around the corner." He set the packages on the counter. "Thought I'd check in on how you're coming along with the dresses for the art auction."

Wouldn't he already have this information from Helena? "I might have seen you pass by the store earlier."

"What? Oh, yes. I was getting these books." He patted the package.

"I visited Helena." She glanced up to see if his expression changed, if he would volunteer that they'd had lunch. Nothing. "Vivienne didn't have any other vintage pieces at home. Helena did give me a lead to a group Vivienne had donated gowns to, though. Should be no problem."

"Eve is pretty excited about some dresses she could lend. Really, if it's any trouble at all for you to — "

"No. Not a bit of trouble. In fact," Joanna faked a laugh, "it would be more trouble for me not to donate them at this point. Everything is worked out." Shoot. She'd better get in touch with the Mother Superior right away.

"If you're sure," Clary said absently.

"Oh, I'm sure all right."

He didn't reply. He seemed absorbed in looking at the store. "You like it?"

Clary nodded. "I was just marveling at all the colors. They don't make blue like that anymore." He touched the sleeve of a mid-century swing coat. "Did you go to design school? Parsons, maybe?"

"No. Law school, if you can believe that. But I always loved vintage clothing. The world it evokes is so glamorous, so Golden Age. Maybe it's from watching a lot of old movies, but I can't help but think that someone wearing a Grace Kelly-style dress will surely lead — I don't know — a charmed life full of roadsters and Manhattan penthouses."

When she was in high school, at a church bazaar Joanna had picked up a cardigan in a saturated lavender color she'd never seen before. "Pringle" its label said next to a small crown. The cashmere was soft as a kitten's paw. She'd buttoned it over her blouse and admired the form-fitting cut and sleeves that stopped just below her elbow.

"You like that?" the woman minding the table had said. "Used to be my aunt's."

The sweater had felt so right, so her. She was ready to leap on a Vespa as she'd seen Audrey Hepburn do in Roman Holiday, although the church's Bible study room in the backwoods of the Pacific Northwest was about as far from mid-century Rome as you could get. "I love it."

"Come to my house later in the week, and I'll show you a few other things she had."

At first Joanna only wore the older clothing at home. But little by little she ventured out in full-skirted cotton day dresses from the 1950s and wild-patterned blouses from the sixties. She showed up her first day in college in a broad-shouldered rayon suit that had undoubtedly been worn by a secretary during World War Two. She'd haunted thrift stores and yard sales for vintage fedoras, coats with fox fur collars, and Pendleton plaid skirts.

The record player's arm bumped at the end of the album. She flipped the record and lowered the needle at the beginning.

"Law school, huh? Funny," Clary said. "I went to law school, too, and even worked a few years in one of the big downtown firms. Finally couldn't take it anymore. Only it wasn't old movies that lured me to antique books, it was history. Even as I kid I used to chart the royal families of Europe. I could tell you every Hapsburg back to when their first castle was built in one-thousand-twenty." He laughed. "I'm embarrassed to say I even bought a Baronet title on the internet." He raised his eyes. "Maybe you heard? I get teased about it sometimes."

"No, never," Joanna lied. Clary was a lot more likable than she'd anticipated. Charming, even. A quick vision of being with someone like Clary—he in his place across town and she in her house here, of course—flew across her brain. No sawdust, no stubbornness, no over-protectiveness. Maybe even the occasional nightcap.

The bell at the door rang as Paul strode in. His tool box clattered to the counter beside Clary's books. "Hi Jo. Here and ready for duty. Where's that loose clothing rod?"

She couldn't help smiling at the sight of him. Maybe being with a man like Clary would cut down on the sawdust, but she'd rather sweep up pounds of it a day than lose out on Paul.

Clary nodded at Paul and picked up his books. "I'll see you at the NAP auction," he said to Joanna.

When the door shut, Paul turned to Joanna. "Who's the Poindexter?"

"No one you need to worry about." She pulled his palm to her lips.

Later that afternoon, Joanna was arranging a pair of sage green suede pumps next to their matching purse when the phone rang.

"Poppy's been arrested." Apple's voice over the phone was agitated.

Joanna set down the pump and focused on the phone in her hand. "What? Poppy?"

"Gavin saw it on TV at work and called me."

Joanna's thoughts whirled. Poppy couldn't be in jail. She's not a criminal. "Why did they arrest her? Not Vivienne's death?"

"They said she was selling stolen jewels. I don't know if it's connected to the murder or not."

Jewel theft? Absolutely not. "No. Poppy wouldn't do that. There's no way." She paced to the front of the store as far as the phone's cord would let her, then back to the counter.

"That's what the police say. You know all those diamond thefts this past year?"

Helena's diamonds had been stolen, and she'd seen news reports of other break-ins. But still, it couldn't be Poppy. Impossible. "Did they say anything else?"

"That's all I know. I wanted to tell you right away."

Joanna hung up and hurried outside to drag in the sandwich board. Poppy was no diamond smuggler. This was all a big mistake. There had to be some other explanation.

Joanna flipped off the store's lights and reached for her keys.

Chapter 1

The Justice Center's visiting room was small and gray. Gray linoleum floor, dull gray walls, and a gray, formica-topped table. A slab of smudged glass separated rows of visitors and inmates, and emotional chatter filled the air. Poppy was already seated when a guard chaperoned Joanna to her seat.

"You've got thirty minutes," he said.

"Oh Joanna, it's all a mistake." Poppy's skin was almost translucent with dark circles under her eyes. Mug shots were always hideous, and now she knew why. Nobody looked good in this place. If only Joanna could stretch a hand through the glass to comfort her.

"Are you okay? Do you have a good lawyer?"

Poppy nodded, her eyes tearing.

A baby cried and was shushed somewhere down the long table. Nearer, a young woman said urgently, "I told you, Goldie don't want no dog." The stuffiness was almost unbearable.

Joanna focused on Poppy. "What happened?"

Her right hand trembled. "They say when they were checking Vivienne's things they found stolen diamonds hidden in a lamp. They say I was getting them from somewhere and reselling them. It's not true!" A guard raised her eyes from examining her fingernails. "It's not true," Poppy repeated more quietly.

"I can't believe it."

"I was at the warehouse when they came. I figured — " She closed her eyes a moment and regained her breath. "I figured they were coming to tell me they were through with the North lot. I had no idea they suspected me of selling stolen jewels."

"I know you're innocent. The charges are ridiculous. But they found the diamonds in Vivienne's stuff." That had to explain why they seized everything from the auction. "Somehow, they suspected you."

"I had no idea." Both women sat in silence a moment.

"How do you think the jewels got there?"

"Don't know." Poppy's voice was emphatic. "It's only me at the auction house. Me and the guys."

This put a whole new spin on things. The fact that the police had held Vivienne's auctioned goods made a whole lot more sense now. They weren't looking for evidence in a murder case — they were looking for stolen jewels.

"Okay, let's examine the facts. The police found diamonds at the warehouse. You didn't put them there, but someone at the auction house must have. Besides you, there's Ben. Anyone else?"

"We have someone who comes in for cleaning twice a week, and the catalog writer stops by sometimes. Appraisers, too." She knitted her brow. "Most auctions, I pick up temporary workers for load in. Then there's the trucking company. Been using them for years. Depending on how big the auction is, I might pull in a few more spotters. That's it."

"Nothing has seemed out of the ordinary?"

She stopped as if remembering something. "Travis has been a little — well, no, I don't think he'd do anything as stupid as to steal diamonds. But — "

"But what?" Joanna remembered Travis as a stringy-haired teen, one of Poppy's warehouse hands.

"Ben was at the warehouse after hours a few weeks ago and caught Travis there. It was the night Vivienne's shipment came. I'm not sure how Travis got in, but no one except Ben's supposed to be there after I lock up. We have to keep everything secure for the clients. He's a good kid, but we had to let him go. Now I wonder—"

"What was he doing?"

"That's the strange thing. It's not like he was hauling out sterling platters or anything. He was going through the files in my office. Every shipment that comes in has a manifest that lists all the items on the truck. When we unload, we compare the manifest to an inventory of what the customer has given us to put up for auction."

"And Travis was going through the file."

"Ben said he didn't have a good excuse for being there. He knows the rules."

"Poppy." Joanna put her hands flat on the table and leaned forward. "Vivienne's daughter-in-law told me her diamonds were stolen. I mean, the diamonds in the furniture—could Vivienne have put them there?" Travis may have caught onto it.

"You think Vivienne was a jewel thief?"

"I don't know. But someone did it."

Poppy glanced at the guard. "Something was going on with Vivienne. The night she died—" Poppy paused for a breath. "She telephoned me. She said someone was trying to kill her."

"Oh my God, Poppy." Helena hadn't told her any of this. Maybe she didn't know. But it partially explained why Poppy had been so out of it the night Vivienne died. "What did she say?"

"Not much. I could barely understand her. She sounded—frantic.

Kind of confused. At first I thought she was returning my call from earlier about the lots. Sometimes clients call after business hours, they don't always think you might have a life. So I picked up the phone. All I got out of her was that she thought someone was trying to kill her, then a bunch of nonsense."

"Nonsense?" Joanna remembered Vivienne the day of the auction. She'd been so cool and deliberate.

"Her voice was shaky, and she was almost panting. She didn't make any sense, Jo."

"Could you make out anything? Even a word or two?" Helena said Vivienne was having a cocktail when she died. Perhaps she'd had more than one.

The young woman's voice nearby rose again. "If Goldie don't want him, I can't force him. I don't care if he is your brother, Goldie don't want no dog!"

"Keep it down," came a warning over a loudspeaker. "If I have to tell you again, you're out."

Poppy was oblivious to whatever dog trauma plagued Goldie. "She might have said 'voyeurs.' But I'm not sure."

Voyeurs. Someone looking in. The police had said there were two glasses. "You told all this to the detective, right?"

"Of course." The musculature of Poppy's face tensed under her skin. "Vivienne's call scared me. I made the call on their anonymous tip line." She looked up, her eyes full of guilt. "At first I didn't want to mess up the auction, you know? I was afraid her son would find out about the call and think I was meddling. So I waited before I called the police. Probably an hour." She put her face in her hands. "They'd found the body by then. The police must think somehow Vivienne found out about the diamonds, and I killed her to shut her up. Oh

Joanna, it's all so — unbelievable."

"But the police should be able to find out easily enough that a call was placed between Vivienne's and the auction house. That would prove you weren't at her house, that you couldn't have done it."

"Or that I knew she was home alone." She took a deep breath that seemed to rattle as she inhaled. "I've had nothing else to think of all night."

"I'm so sorry." Joanna clenched her hands in her lap. There had to be a way out of this somehow.

"Goldie Goldie Goldie. That's all you want to talk about." A guard lifted the young woman from her seat. The room quieted as the woman shrugged off the guard's grasp and marched toward the exit on her own. Hand on the doorknob, she swiveled her head toward the room. "Well, Goldie can go to hell."

Joanna turned back to Poppy and bit her lip. A few people tittered, and conversation resumed around them. "We'll figure this out. We will."

"I don't know."

"I wonder if the diamonds were hidden after something sold? The buyer would have paid whatever it took to make sure he got the item," Joanna thought aloud.

"So the item probably wouldn't be anything very popular."

"And the lamp the police said they found the diamonds in?"

"Nice, but nothing special."

Joanna tapped the table. "Or, the diamonds arrived at the warehouse already hidden." So many possibilities.

Poppy shook her head. "How could that happen? We get things from all over."

"I'll do a little digging around. See what the police know. I'm sure you won't be here for long, Poppy. You're innocent. At some point they'll figure that out." Joanna's heart sank. She tried to sound convincing, but the evidence against Poppy didn't look good.

Poppy leaned back. Despite the room's stuffiness, the skin on Joanna's arms prickled as if she were cold. "I hope you're right," Poppy said. "I think I'm being framed and I don't know why. Oh Joanna, you've got to help me. Please."

"I'll do whatever I can." This was awful. Too awful, too wrong. "I promise."

Chapter 11

When Joanna arrived home, Paul was sitting in his truck in front of her house. He stepped down from the cab. "What's this about you going to visit Poppy in jail?"

He followed her into the house. Weak sun filtered through the rhododendron into the living room. Paul sat on the sofa, his jeans and work shirt rough against the velvet upholstery. Pepper jumped in his lap and began to knead his paws on Paul's leg.

"You should have seen her. It's horrible in there—" She remembered Paul had a firsthand familiarity with jail thanks to visiting his uncle.

"I know. But it's just the detention center. Much better than state prison," he said. "So. Poppy. What's going on?"

"She says they're accusing her of selling stolen diamonds—"

"Diamonds?" He tensed.

"Obviously she didn't. It had to be someone else at the auction house. She looks terrible. She's totally out of it."

"Wouldn't the police have thought of that? I'm sure they'll investigate everyone who works there." He patted the couch next to him. "Sit down. Relax for a second."

"They might have missed something important." The sofa's springs creaked under Joanna. She swiveled and rested her feet on Paul's lap.

With a "mew," Pepper moved over to make room for a calf. Joanna lay back and put her hands behind her head. Despite lying down, her foot jiggled nervously. Paul squeezed her toes. "Poppy says she was framed."

"Framed? Why her?"

"I'm not sure. There's just too much I don't know." Using Joanna's leg as a bridge, Pepper padded to her stomach and lay down. Paul was right. The police surely talked to everyone at the auction house. But maybe they missed something. Maybe, if they had it in their minds Poppy was guilty, they didn't ask the right questions. Travis, for instance. Poppy said Travis was at the warehouse after hours.

"You need to stay out of it. Let the police do their job."

What was his deal? He didn't order her around like this. He let her do what she wanted, and even seemed to appreciate her occasional indulgences in weekend-long Raymond Chandler reading jags or ragù alla Bolognese cooking marathons. She dodged his question. "I'm thinking of painting the ceiling. Maybe a shell pink? It looks kind of dingy."

Paul shifted on the couch. Even though her head was turned up, Joanna knew he was looking at her. "Promise me you won't get involved in this." His hand was warm on her ankle. "I like your sense of justice, I really do. And I know Poppy is your friend. But let the police handle it."

"Oh Paul, you should have seen her. She begged me to help her. What am I supposed to do?"

"You can help by keeping out of the police's way. And staying safe."

She paused for a moment then decided to say it anyway. "You know that I'm not your sister, right? I won't get killed because you weren't paying attention." His sister had died years before in a car crash after Paul had forgotten to pick her up after school.

"This has nothing to do with her…" His voice trailed off.

"I can't bear to see Poppy in jail like that. Meanwhile, the real thief is going loose."

"It's frustrating for you, but you're letting it go, right? You're already asking around about Vivienne North's death. Don't tempt fate with Poppy." Paul's voice hardened with obstinacy. She knew he wouldn't rest until she'd promised him she'd leave things alone. "Promise me."

"I guess the police know better how to deal with this than I do." Neither a yes nor a no.

"Jo. That's not an answer."

"But she begged me. You should have seen her."

"I'm sure her lawyer will have her out on bail soon."

"It's not just that," Joanna said. "It's her reputation. Think about it. No one will hire her. And how will she feel walking around town with everyone looking at her and talking about her behind her back?"

"And how will she feel if something happens to you because you were nosing around in what should be the police's business?"

Paul's argument was logical, but she knew it was driven more by his stubborn protectiveness than reason. Why, she had no idea. She refused to look at him.

He ran a hand down her calf. "Jo," he said, this time softly. "Look at me. Do you promise?"

She met his eyes. "All right." She relaxed back into the couch again. Pepper's purr reverberated through her abdomen. "I promise."

She knew his urgency that she not get involved came from a good place. After all, he took time away from his work to check on her. If he moved in, in the evenings when she came home, he'd be around—in the house, or working out in the shop. Maybe when he had a big job she'd bring him dinner and watch him work a little. Other nights he might already be in the house listening to one of his old jazz records.

But even these simple pleasures were things Poppy might not experience for years. Not the way things were headed.

"If Uncle Gene weren't locked away, I know where the police would start looking for the jewel thief," Paul said.

"Did you ever see anything he stole?" She imagined piles of diamonds in chamois bags.

He looked away. "Well, it wasn't really like that."

"Like what?"

He hesitated. "You know."

He wasn't telling her something. He would eventually, though. She probed a bit further. "Tell me about his heists."

"Well, his job was to steal the goods. Another guy, a jeweler, took the stones from the jewelry and melted down the settings. That way they couldn't be traced. The bigger, more valuable gems are pretty well documented. So they had to cut them down to resell. It hurt the value, but it was the safest way to go."

Way too complicated. Yet another reason Poppy wouldn't be involved in any diamond operation. She was a spectacular auctioneer, but if it weren't for her manager she'd never keep the auction house afloat. Anger flushed once again through Joanna's bloodstream.

"It gets even more interesting," Paul said. "Some of the diamonds were special enough that they had serial numbers engraved on them. That way if the owner took, say, her ring in for cleaning, a jeweler wouldn't swap out the diamond for a cheaper one. My uncle had to file them off the jewels." He tapped her calf with a finger. "If I were the police, I'd figure out how to flush him out."

Joanna tilted her head toward him. Pepper mewed in protest of being jiggled. "What do you mean?"

Their eyes met. "Don't get any ideas." He pinched her toe. "I mean a kind of sting operation. You know, hold an auction, give the diamond thief the chance to do his thing. Then nail him."

She shook her head and rested it again on the couch. "That's ridiculous," she said. Nonetheless, she was listening. "Whoever's selling the diamonds would be crazy to take a risk like that. Why would he? He knows Poppy's already been arrested."

"But not convicted. This would seal it." Paul paused. "You're fishing for more info, aren't you? Forget it."

"But I — " A sting operation. Hmm. The mantel clock ticked. The NAP art auction was Saturday.

"Jo." Paul interrupted her stream of thought. "I know that look. I was just talking off the cuff. You know, making stuff up."

"You never did answer me about the ceiling color."

"Stop it. You're right, you know. A sting operation would never work. Too risky. I shouldn't have said anything."

"Relax. It's okay. I told you I'd leave it alone, remember?"

He didn't even smile. "I'm serious. Let the police handle it. There's one dead body already."

Joanna rolled over in bed and pulled a pillow over her head. Poppy, pale and anxious in the jail's visiting room, had haunted her dreams. She wished she had accepted Paul's offer to stay, but she'd sent him home instead. He'd hesitated at the door as if he'd had something to say, but had seemed to think better of it and left. She tossed the pillow on the floor.

Today, Apple was working, so Joanna didn't even have Tallulah's Closet to distract her. There was only one thing to do when anxiety whirled: go thrifting. Eighty-second Avenue — the ill-named "Avenue of the Roses" — defined the eastern border of town. A Goodwill, Salvation Army, Value Village, and Deseret Thrift Shop staked outposts along a dingy three-mile stretch also home to used car lots, taquerias, and muffler shops.

An hour later, Joanna eased her Corolla into a parking spot next to a dented panel van. In past visits, this Goodwill had yielded a periwinkle leather jacket from the 1960s, a pair of evening pumps from Henry Waters Shoes of Consequence with tiny mirrored fans adorning the toes, and, to her great surprise, a pair of Manolo Blahnik slingbacks.

Joanna worked a shopping cart free of the two tangled with it and pushed it into the store. One of the front wheels wobbled, but with a strong hand she could keep it from veering to the right. "Wichita Lineman" played over the stereo system. A hipster trolling the T-shirt rack stopped to air-pluck the song's bass solo.

Joanna rolled the cart down the linoleum floor. First stop, women's suits. Because suits usually cost so much, people tended to hang on to them for years, even if they were rarely worn, before finally offloading them to Goodwill. Joanna knew she stood a good chance of finding an old YSL blazer or at least a keenly styled Louis Féraud pant suit from the 1980s.

As her hands flipped through the racks, her brain relaxed into a meditative groove. Thrifting was a slow and laborious way to find new stock for Tallulah's Closet — the store's best things came from estate sales and boxes of clothes people brought to her to sell. But the flip-touch-next of searching a rack of dresses, the rhythm of plastic hanger on metal rod, focused her mind. She trusted her fingers to stop at the tight weave of good fabric and her eyes to alert her to the telltale colors of a 1950s print while her brain worked over what it needed.

Sure enough, her fingers lit on silky wool. She drew a navy blue pinstriped suit jacket from the rack, probably bought in the 1980s *Dress for Success* era and originally worn with a blouse tied at its neck with a fat fabric bow. The suit was department store Dior. Joanna examined it quickly for moth holes or stains, then dropped it in the cart. A Tallulah's Closet customer would likely style it with a vintage rock T-shirt and patent leather loafers. Maybe she'd pin a tattered silk flower to its lapel.

Joanna pointed the cart toward lingerie. Occasionally she found crisp rayon nightgowns and slips whose owners had deemed too nice to wear. The lingerie sat in drawers for decades until the owners died and their children sent it all to Goodwill.

As she sorted through acrylic slips and cheap lace, her thoughts drifted to Poppy. Poppy thought she was being framed, and Joanna agreed. Her fingers trembled with anger and she flipped past a few fleece bathrobes. An African woman wrapped in bright cotton print looked up at the smack of the hangers. Joanna willed herself to calm down. Nothing in lingerie.

Next stop, shoes. Joanna remembered the warehouse full of Vivienne's things. Even if the police thought they could charge Poppy with selling stolen diamonds, it didn't mean they could link her to Vivienne's murder. At least, Joanna hoped not.

Chunky-soled loafers from the 1990s crowded the shoe racks. Among them Joanna spotted a pair of black patent leather Ferragamos with a grosgrain bow at the toe, but their heels were too worn to resell. Besides, they were 10 AAA. Women with long skinny feet seemed to love Ferragamo. A pair of Kennedy-era black satin Daniel Green slippers caught Joanna's attention. Nice and not even worn. Probably a Mother's Day present that didn't quite fit. They joined the Dior suit in the basket.

Paul had said if he were the police he'd try to draw the real diamond thief into the open with a sting operation. Great idea, but Joanna bet that once Poppy was in jail, the police had quit pursuing any other leads. For them, a sting would be a non-starter. Besides, Paul would flip out if he knew she were even considering it. And yet...

The cart's listing front wheel squeaked as she pushed it toward housewares. Tallulah's Closet stuck to clothes, but Joanna liked to look for etched crystal cocktail glasses and Murano ashtrays for home. Three chunky ashtrays sat on her dresser now holding bracelets and earrings.

She considered the sting operation idea. The NAP art auction was just around the corner, and Poppy had been scheduled as its auctioneer. If Paul was right and the real jewel thief would seize the auction as an opportunity to square the blame on Poppy, it might work.

As Joanna pondered the idea, she picked up a black resin pen holder with glittering shells suspended in its base. "Roy Rogers Museum" wound in gold script below the cap designed to hold a now-missing pen. For ninety-nine cents it would look chic on the store's tiki bar. She could stick a feathered pen in it. Customers were always walking off with her pens, but a pen with an ostrich feather, something she could pick up easily at a wedding supply store, would stay put.

As for the police, Joanna knew they'd never even consider a sting operation unless she had evidence pointing firmly away from Poppy. Poppy had mentioned Travis. Maybe Joanna would be able to wheedle information from him the police couldn't. After all, she wasn't threatening. She could find some excuse to talk to him. She'd need to feel out Ben, the auction house manager, too. He might have seen something Poppy missed.

Paul's warning came back to her. "Promise me," he'd said. If he found out she was even considering nosing around at the auction house, he'd be furious. But was she supposed to ignore Poppy, when a quick talk with a couple of her employees could free her? It wasn't really investigating, she convinced herself. Once she had a little information, it would be all in the police's hands, anyway.

It would only take her a couple of hours. Tops. Paul didn't have to know. Her conscience twinged. But who was he to tell her what to do? A year ago, she could have done whatever she'd wanted. Plus, he was working for Eve, and it wasn't like Joanna was happy about that. Once Poppy was free, he'd surely understand.

If she was going to gather evidence to spring Poppy, she'd have to be quick about it. The NAP auction committee met tomorrow. Besides convincing the police a sting was a good plan and that they should release Poppy for the evening, she'd have to talk the committee into honoring Poppy's contract. Joanna shook her head. Finding evidence, getting both the police and the NAP auction committee on board — nearly impossible. But what was the alternative?

Joanna hurried the cart toward the cashier, the cart's wobble and squeak reaching a fever pitch. For Poppy, she had to try.

Chapter 12

If the phone book was right, Travis lived somewhere around here. His address was a 1960s apartment building called the Kari Ann. Some people were fascinated by the names cosmetics companies chose for lipsticks or auto companies for cars, but Joanna loved the names of apartment complexes. The Crown Royal, Princess Judy, Andrew Jackson, and Big John's were a few of her favorites. Despite the buildings' grand names, most sported peeling siding and overgrown arborvitae.

The Kari Ann was typical of its genre. The apartment complex formed an "ell" with the parking lot along the long edge. Two levels of apartments with exterior stairs made up the complex. The whole mess was painted dingy mauve. An industrial-sized dumpster took up the last parking spot next to a handful of misshapen conifers perhaps once trimmed into poodle-like hedges.

On the third bank of mailboxes, Joanna found the name T. Kowalski. She passed under the darkened stairs and rang the doorbell. Crumpled flyers for a housecleaning service lay wadded on the ground. The door opened a crack behind a brass chain, and Travis peered out. A bird shrieked inside the apartment.

"Yeah?" he said. "Oh, it's you."

"Joanna Hayworth," she said, extending her hand through the crack.

He undid the chain and opened the door wider, but didn't invite her in. "Yeah?" he repeated.

She withdrew her hand. "I went to visit Poppy yesterday," she began, watching his face. "In jail. She told me I should get in touch with you about the things I bought in Vivienne's estate. May I come in? It's damp out here." Travis, in a tee shirt and jeans that clearly hadn't seen the inside of a washing machine recently, didn't seem to notice the cold.

"Why me? I don't work there anymore."

"Please. It won't take long."

He shifted his feet and glanced down the hall. Finally, he moved out of the way of the door. "I guess. But only for a minute."

Joanna passed through the entry hall into the living room. A parrot in a cage surrounded by bits of seed occupied one corner. The bird squawked and skittered sideways on his perch, turning his head to point one fishy eye at her.

She lowered herself to the edge of the sofa, not so much to be proper as to avoid the ripe-smelling sweatpants tossed along its back. The morning's quick spray of Nahéma, a peachy rose perfume she'd chosen in honor of Rose Festival, wasn't up to the competition. A video game was on pause on the large, pristine television. Its screen showed a robot crouched on a green-tinted planet. A box in the corner revealed Travis had earned over nine thousand points and five nunchucks.

"Yeah, well I don't know why Poppy told you to see me. Ben is the one who's taking care of everything down there."

"She looked terrible. Poppy, that is. I can't believe the police said she was selling stolen diamonds." She kept her hands on top of her purse in her lap.

Travis fidgeted in his recliner. Its corduroy upholstery was worn to the nub at the head and arms. If he were involved in selling stolen jewels, he was sure getting the short end of the stick, money-wise. "Yeah, diamonds. I don't get it."

"Yet the police said they found diamonds hidden in some of Vivienne's things."

Travis didn't reply. Joanna waited. The bird clucked again.

"Why are you really here?" Travis asked.

Joanna ignored him. "What's worse is they said Poppy killed Vivienne to cover it all up. Poisoned her and left her to die."

"They're saying that? Poppy would never do anything like that." Travis's voice exploded into the room, silencing even the parrot. Joanna tensed. Maybe she'd gone too far with her story. Travis stood. "They said—I know Poppy didn't do anything like that, okay?"

"You sound so sure."

"I am sure."

She really didn't know anything about Travis, she realized. Maybe it was a little rash to come down here alone. She glanced toward the hall to the front door.

"Have you talked to the police?" she asked.

Travis paced the living room. On the coffee table in front of her sat several sheets of paper, folded as if they'd been in a pocket. It looked like some sort of computer-generated list. With Travis's back toward her, she quickly stuck her fingers in the papers and pried a few pages apart. Travis turned, and her hands shot to her lap.

"Sure, they talked to all of us," he said.

"Did they ask about Vivienne's visits to the auction house?" The list looked like some sort of inventory. Could it be one of the manifests Poppy had mentioned?

"Yeah, but I don't know anything about that. Ben's the one who'd know. I saw her once. Vivienne. She was with a nun." Travis pulled at his sleeve and frowned. "I'm telling you, Poppy is not like that."

"I know," she said. "Poppy isn't like that at all." She looked around the room for something to comment on to calm him. An artist's portfolio leaned against the wall. "Do you draw?"

He looked at her with surprise, then followed her glance to his portfolio. "I'm making a story. For gaming. Poppy gave that to me."

"Poppy is so encouraging," Joanna said. "She gave me a lot of advice after I opened my store. I really counted on her."

Travis's face softened. He settled back into his chair. "Yeah. She gave me the job at the auction house, too."

And let Ben fire him. But he didn't seem to hold it against her. In fact, he almost seemed to have a crush on her.

"For her birthday," Travis continued, "I gave her a couple of Jimmy Buffet bootlegs I found online. She was so psyched."

Joanna bet she was. "That was awfully nice." Travis blushed. "But Poppy's in jail now, and we both know she's not guilty." She leaned forward a few more inches. "What happened the night Ben found you at work?"

He looked at the carpet. "Nothing."

"But you were there at night. You knew you weren't supposed to be."

"I can't tell you," he mumbled.

"You had a reason for being there. I know you did. Travis, look at me."

He looked up. Fear filled his eyes.

Joanna's pulse leapt. "You saw something, didn't you? What was it?" Somehow he knew to go back to the auction house after hours. What would terrify him so much he'd let himself be fired without standing up for himself? "Did it have to do with the diamonds?"

"I don't have anything to say, okay?"

In what she hoped looked like a casual gesture, Joanna rested her purse on the coffee table, on top of the list. She stood. With both hands she swept up her purse and the papers, tucking the bundle under her arm, papers in.

Travis's eyes darted through the room but didn't settle anywhere. Safe, so far.

She edged toward the door. "All right," she said. The bird squawked. "I'm leaving. Keep your secrets. But don't be surprised if it ends up making more trouble than you think."

Outside, Joanna filled her lungs with fresh air. A few minutes later, Travis and the Kari Ann were behind her. The list was in her purse's side pocket.

At Tallulah's Closet, Apple counted receipts for the day's sales. "We sold the Weiss brooch and that houndstooth suit with the peplum. Plus, another prom dress is on hold." Apple looked at Joanna. "Not too bad."

"No, not too bad."

"And the landlord came by again for the rent check."

The rent. With all this craziness, she'd forgotten about the rent. Damn. Where was she going to come up with the rest of the cash? If she put off the plumber and web designer she might be able to make it. "Thanks. I'll give him a call."

"He was pretty urgent about getting the money right away." Apple bit her lip. "I've been thinking. I haven't been getting as much painting done as I'd like. Maybe you'd like to take a few of my shifts?"

Joanna set the bag from Goodwill on the bench. "Oh Apple. We're not that bad yet. It's just the money I sank into getting better stock and upgrading the website. And then the plumbing disaster. I hadn't budgeted for that. The NAP auction is coming up. I bet that will draw some new business." God willing, she added silently. "I found a few things at the thrift stores. One's a suit. I'll drop it at the dry cleaners this afternoon. Do you think you could tag the rest?"

"Sure. Any news on Poppy?"

Joanna filled her in on the visit to Travis and laid the list she'd taken flat on the tiki bar. The top was dated and labeled "Vivienne North." "This is the manifest. This is it, I'm pretty sure." She tapped it for emphasis. "I'm going to have to go to the auction house, see if I can find the inventory that matches this. Travis obviously thought something was wrong and went back to try to clear up what he thought was his mistake."

"You stole it?"

Feeling guilty, Joanna folded the manifest and returned it to her purse. "I think Travis forgot he even had it."

"Don't get me wrong. I'm impressed. But how are you going to get the inventory without letting Ben in on it?"

"The thought had occurred to me." If Ben were guilty, he couldn't know about her nosing around.

"You can't do this alone. You need someone to distract Ben. I'll go with you. I'll tell Ben I'll read his aura for him. People love that. I could chew up a good fifteen minutes that way. You could dig around in Poppy's office." She dropped the bag and turned toward Joanna. "It would be fun."

"I don't know. Besides, someone has to stay at the store."

"Please. It's not like it's been super busy lately."

Joanna laughed then grew somber. "Seriously, App. I mean, what would be our excuse? You're right, though. I do need someone else with me."

She absentmindedly stacked the receipts. Who would have a good reason to go? Her hand hovered over a receipt. Helena, that's who. Helena could say she wanted to know if there was any news about Vivienne's things being released. Plus, the way she noticed the gypsy girl? She was observant. Yes, she'd ask Helena.

While Apple sorted through the Goodwill bag, Joanna reached for the phone.

***

Later that day, when Joanna arrived, Helena was already sitting in the bar at the Portland Golf Club. Just off the main lobby, the bar looked over a crewcut-short lawn studded with massive oak trees. A golf cart trundled silently in the distance. The low, late afternoon sun streaked the grass chartreuse.

"Thank you for meeting me out here. I hope it wasn't too much trouble." Helena's face, scrubbed of makeup, glowed from exercise.

Joanna slid into a chair across the table from her. "I'm glad you were able to talk on such short notice." She'd never been to the Portland Golf Club, although she'd heard of it, of course. The club had been around for a century, and membership dues ran in the thousands of dollars — that is, if you were elected to be a member at all. She hoped Old Blue wasn't being towed from the parking lot as they spoke.

"It sounded important."

A small Asian waitress appeared. "Would you like a drink?"

"Yes, Birdie. Thank you," Helena said. "An Arnold Palmer. Anything for you, Joanna?"

"Coffee, please."

"If you want a drink, please, go ahead. I get a little lightheaded after an afternoon on the links, but that shouldn't stop you." She lowered her voice. "Seriously, Joanna, ix-nay on the offee-cay. It's pretty awful."

Joanna smiled at her Pig Latin, then glanced at a clutch of white-haired men drinking Old Fashioneds at a nearby table. "How about an Old Fashioned?"

The waitress left. "Clary always drinks Old Fashioneds," Helena said while she fumbled in her bag for a small, brown bottle.

He would. With top drawer whiskey, too, no doubt. Interesting that Helena brought him up. "Have you known him a long time?"

"He went to Yale with my husband. That's where I met them both. At one point we even dated, before Gil and I got serious, that is. Clary was drinking Old Fashioneds even then. He has a set of Waterford tumblers he uses for his drinks. Even has a cut crystal ice bucket." She unscrewed the bottle's lid and squeezed an eyedropper of green-tinged liquid into her water glass. "Peppermint oil. For energy," she said. "Want to try it?"

Joanna shook her head. Clary was straight? This was news. She imagined him, right down to the satin-lapeled smoking jacket he probably lounged in while he mixed cocktails. She couldn't resist asking, "What's his house like?"

"A restored Victorian in Northwest. Lots of books, of course. Over the sofa is a gigantic oil painting of some minor Austrian count or something like that." She laughed. "He'd make a great sociological study. He's a good guy, really." Her gaze softened. "Good cook, too. He had a dinner party not long ago. One of the guests owns some kind of vintage clothing business, actually. Maybe you know her."

"Eve?" She stifled a grimace.

Helena must have noticed. "That's what I thought, too. She's a piece of work, that one. Beautiful, but — you know what I mean. I don't know why she's not in Hollywood."

Joanna nodded. "She'd have given Joan Crawford a run for her money."

The waitress deposited the Arnold Palmer and an ice-laden Old Fashioned on the table and left to tend to the white-haired men.

Helena turned to Joanna. "Now, what was it you wanted to talk about?"

Joanna took a breath. "Poppy, the auctioneer. And your diamonds."

"My diamonds?" Her hand went to the wrist where her tennis bracelet would have been.

"Yes." Joanna couldn't help but think a pearl bracelet might suit Helena better. Diamonds were so aging. "I'm not sure exactly how everything fits together, but I went to see Poppy in jail."

Helena studied her. "I heard she was arrested for selling stolen jewels. Do you think she has mine too?"

"No. She's not a thief. But the night Vivienne died — " Joanna stalled, then frowned. "I'm sorry for bringing it up, but the night she died she called Poppy."

Helena's jaw dropped. "Vivienne? What did she say?"

"Not much. A few things that didn't make a lot of sense, I guess. Something about voyeurs, maybe. Poppy couldn't make it out completely. Anyway, she called the police, but by then you and your husband had already come home and found her."

Helena continued to stare at Joanna.

"I'm sorry," Joanna repeated. "I didn't come here to upset you. There's more to the story."

Helena seemed to snap to the present. "No, no. I want to hear what happened. It's just that — it's just that every once in a while it hits me." She set down her glass. "Plus, the police didn't say anything about a call. But please go on."

"Well, to make a long story short, the diamonds that the police found were in one of Vivienne's lamps."

Helena wrinkled her brow. "Are you saying Vivienne stole my diamonds and hid them in the stuff she sent to auction?"

"I don't know why she'd do that. It doesn't make any sense, I admit. But I'm convinced Poppy had nothing to do with any of it." Joanna described the manifest and Travis getting fired for being at the auction house after hours. "I can't figure out how it all fits together, but as long as the police believe Poppy is guilty, we'll never know who really stole all those diamonds."

Helena sat back. Joanna picked up her Old Fashioned. Some of its ice had melted, and it tasted watery. She set it back on the sodden napkin.

"We need to figure out what Travis was trying to find and tell the police," Helena said.

"Exactly. The inventory sheet." Joanna warmed at Helena's use of "we." She wouldn't share the final detail, the part about the sting operation. After all, they might not find anything useful. Or the police might laugh at her. She'd wait and fill her in later if it all panned out.

"You have a legitimate reason to visit Poppy's," Joanna said. "I wondered, why I wanted to talk to you, well, would you be willing to go with me to the auction house tomorrow morning? I need you to distract the manager while I try to find the inventory sheet that goes with the manifest."

Helena held her glass mid-air. Her lips were parted, but she didn't say a thing. Then she nodded, first slowly, then faster. "Yes. Yes, I do want to know what really happened — for Gil's sake, too. He, I — " She paused. "I can help. Let's talk."

Chapter 13

Joanna pushed her way inside the dark auction house. "Ben?" she called out.

Helena entered next to her. "They're open, right?"

"Should be. It's almost nine."

The auction house was silent but for the splatter of rain on the windows and the distant rumble of commuter traffic. Victorian divans and Queen Anne dining room sets hulked in the warehouse's front room.

To the right, the shriek of a cuckoo clock set off an avalanche of chimes and bells from dozens of clocks as they struck the hour. The cacophony reverberated through her body, setting off a surge of adrenalin. She grabbed the door frame.

"Joanna?" Ben walked toward them.

She struggled to regain control of her breathing. "For God's sake. You should post a warning."

"Sorry. We're doing an auction of some guy's clock collection. I had to set them all for the appraiser. He'll be here soon."

"Hi, I'm Helena Schuyler North." Helena proffered a hand. "Vivienne North was my mother-in-law. She's been on my mind so much lately." She'd jumped right into her role.

Ben pushed his horn-rimmed glasses up the bridge of his nose. "I was so sorry to hear about her death."

"You must have a lot to do without Poppy to help," Joanna said.

"We have auctions lined up every weekend for the next month, and I've got to postpone them — at least until Poppy is free or until we can get a substitute auctioneer. There's a truck unloading for another one now, and I don't even know if we'll be able to pull it off."

Joanna had seen the Kay semi with its signature roadrunner logo pulled up to the loading dock. It had to be a nightmare for Ben to keep the business going, not knowing how long his boss would be out. People might cancel their auctions and take them elsewhere. He had his job to think of, too. If the auction house folded, he'd be out of work.

"That's what I'm here about," Helena said. "I'd like to talk about Vivienne's auction. See what we can do to take care of the people who bought things but haven't been able to take them home." Their signal.

"If you don't mind, I'd like to use the restroom," Joanna said.

"In the back by the loading bay."

The temperature dropped as Joanna passed through the door separating the work area from the heated front of the warehouse. She didn't have much time. Helena might be able to keep him talking for five or ten minutes, but probably not longer. Joanna glanced behind her to make sure they were out of sight.

Poppy's office was to the left, behind the counter where clients paid for their bids. Wood wainscoting framed the lower half of the office, and glass windows extended from waist height to the ceiling, allowing Poppy to keep an eye on things while she worked. Joanna tried the door handle and it opened. She whispered "yes" under her breath.

The inventories had to be here somewhere. A gooseneck desk lamp shone a pool of light on stacks of papers covering the desk.

Next to it was a coffee mug shaped like a margarita glass with "Cabo, Mexico" painted on its side. She slid open the deep bottom drawer of Poppy's desk. It was empty except for a jar of peanuts and a bag of potato chips with its top neatly folded.

After another glance to make sure Helena and Ben were still in the showroom, she tried one of the filing cabinets. Locked. Damn. Filing cabinet keys were too small to fit well on a keychain. She'd be willing to bet Poppy hid them somewhere. No room for a key above the door. She opened the top desk drawers and fished through pens and paperclips. No key there, either. She dipped her hand into the pencil holder. Her fingers touched a small, steel key. Success.

The office's overhead light switched on. Her heart stopped.

"What are you doing in here?" Ben leaned against the doorframe and folded his arms in front of his chest. Joanna had forgotten how tall he was.

She backed into the bookcases. "Where's Helena?"

"I asked you a question."

Her mind raced. "I wanted to see a list of the things I bought from the North lot. Poppy told me the inventory was in the filing cabinet," she lied. "I saw her in jail."

"So you just came in here and started looking around?"

Deep breath. Appear normal, she told herself. Calm. Why the hell hadn't Helena kept him away? Time for the back-up plan.

Joanna unclipped her purse and drew out a piece of a pronged jewelry setting. Ben wouldn't know it was costume, severed from an orphaned earring that morning and slipped into her purse just in case. "Look what I found outside the bathroom."

He leaned forward. She withdrew her hand before he could look too closely. "Evidence from the diamond thefts. Broken off of a stolen piece of jewelry. I'm bringing it to the police."

His face stiffened. "That's nothing. A piece of old metal. There's stuff like that all over the place here."

She clenched a fist to keep her hand from trembling. "I bet the thief left it behind when he pulled the diamonds from a setting. You know, so the jewelry couldn't be traced."

"You said 'he.' The police say it's Poppy."

Joanna mustered up a confident tone. "No way. She'll be out soon. Once the judge sets bail it shouldn't be long." She turned the broken jewelry setting in her palm. "Maybe this will help clear her."

Ben ran long fingers through his hair. "Give it to me. I'll take care of it." He reached for the setting.

She closed her fingers around it. "No. I'll deal with it." The real diamond thief had to be someone with access to both the warehouse and the office. Someone like Ben. A chill ran through her.

"Why? It was found on the auction house's premises."

"And I'm the one who found it. I'll give it to the police."

His glasses bizarrely magnified his eyes. They narrowed. "You don't trust me. You think I'm the thief, don't you?"

Ben's body filled the doorway. If she had to, she could grab the gooseneck lamp and swing it at him. She felt the cool wood of the bookcase behind her. They say women should fight with their legs. "It had to be someone here, right?"

"That's what I was thinking, too." He stepped forward and slumped into the chair across from the desk. Joanna's momentary panic faded. "Something's been a little off with Travis. When the police questioned me I didn't want to say anything. He's just a kid, you know?"

"Poppy told me something about you having to fire him." Was he trying to throw suspicion off himself?

"He was nosing around here after hours. Like you."

Where was Helena, anyway? She opened her mouth to reply but was interrupted by the creak of the door between the showroom and warehouse. "Anybody home?" a man's voice asked.

"Must be the appraiser." Ben heaved his body from the chair. The fluorescent overhead light emphasized the dark hollows under his eyes.

"I'll be right behind you," Joanna said.

"No. We're finished here. I'll lock up." Ben waited until she'd left Poppy's office. She glanced regretfully at the filing cabinet where the inventories were likely still locked away.

Helena, breathless, appeared from the showroom. "Joanna? Are you all right? I'm sorry. I got a call from Gil. I had to take it." Her skin was clammy, and she breathed shallowly. "He's at the hospital. Something is really wrong."

Chapter 14

That night, hours after the store closed, Joanna leaned over the tiki bar to tally receipts. The student had come back for the lemon chiffon prom dress, but otherwise the day's sales were pathetic. Joanna moved to her bills. The web designer agreed to take trade, but she faced the rent, a stack of dry cleaning invoices, and a shockingly large plumbing bill. Honestly, plumbers must earn more than plastic surgeons. She'd managed to put off the landlord until after the NAP auction, but he'd made it clear she wouldn't have a day longer. To make things worse, the first payment on her line of credit was coming due.

The store was dark but for a small pool of light from the Marie Antoinette-shaped lamp on the tiki bar. There was no way around it. Unless she got her hands on Vivienne's clothes, and fast, she couldn't make ends meet.

What was she going to do? Joanna shoved the bills to the side. She could ask Paul for a loan. He wasn't rich, but he said he had a few jobs in the offing. Warmth spread over her at the thought of him. Too bad he wasn't there right now, relaxing in the armchair by the dressing rooms. She glanced toward the chair at the darkened rear of the store, imagining his hands turning the page of a Raymond Chandler novel. But she wouldn't ask him for money. Especially when it originally came from Eve.

A faint sound, like a pebble hitting tile, tapped from behind her. The skin on Joanna's neck prickled. She rose from the stool and eased the bathroom door open. Night showed through the window to the alley. It must have been something out back—maybe a cat. She boosted the window open and glimpsed someone relieving himself behind the Dumpster down the block. She shut and locked the window and shook her head. Nerves.

She returned to the tiki bar and bundled the receipts to take home. To help pay bills she could get a roommate, but that thought galled. What if the roommate wanted to hang some mall crap in the living room or put in a microwave? Forget it. Of course, Paul could move in and share the mortgage. She shook her head. Not that it mattered, since by then her bills would be long past due.

A movement in the front window caught the corner of her eye. White skin and dark eyes, looking in. It was only there for a moment before ducking away. Adrenalin surged through her body. Calm down, Joanna willed herself. People pass by the window all the time. It's a busy street. Still, she couldn't shake the feeling that someone was watching her.

Nonsense, she thought. Everything that's been happening lately is getting to me, that's all. I'm going home. She piled the bills in her purse and clicked off the lamp.

The phone rang.

At this hour? As Joanna watched the phone, her uneasiness grew. The phone continued to ring three then four times, when the answering machine would pick it up. The machine clicked on to a dial tone. Joanna let out her breath. The caller probably just wanted to find out the store's hours and wasn't patient enough to wait through her message.

The phone rang again. The hairs on her arm stood up. This is ridiculous, she thought. Why are you afraid of the phone? She turned on the lamp again. At the third ring she grabbed the receiver. "Hello?"

"Hello, Joanna," a voice whispered harshly.

She sucked in her breath. "Who is this?"

"You're alone."

Her blood turned to ice. "No, I'm not. I have — have people here."

"I see you." The whisper's rasp removed any indication of whether the caller was a man or woman. "There's no one with you."

Her heart pounded. With the single light in the store, she'd be a clear target to anyone looking in. She glanced at the front window, but only the silhouettes of late night diners in the restaurant across the street moved. Too far away to hear her scream. Still clutching the phone, she sank to the floor behind the counter, out of view, and yanked the lamp's plug from the wall. "What do you want?" she asked.

"You can't hide from me, Joanna. I'll always find you. Stay out of business that doesn't concern you."

"What do you mean?" Her voice shook. Then, in a firmer tone, she said, "This is a hoax. Some kind of joke."

The raspy laughter was freakish. "Look in the dressing room. And don't say I didn't warn you." The phone call ended abruptly.

A cold sweat broke over Joanna's neck and forehead as she replaced the receiver. She sat still, hearing only the occasional car on the street. A minute passed, then two. I can't stay here forever, she thought. I have to get up, turn on a light. I have to go home.

Look in the dressing room, the voice had said.

Lights still off, Joanna felt around the tiki bar's lower shelf until she found a broken hat pin. As a weapon, it wasn't much, but it was all she had. Taking a deep breath, she crept from the protected area behind the counter and tiki bar. Cold Dupioni silk brushed her face as she passed a rack of dresses. Behind the zebra-striped chair, she paused again and listened. Silence. She leaned forward for a clear view of the front window. No one.

The curtains encircling both dressing rooms were closed. Who had been in the dressing rooms last? Apple closed shop today. She would have cleaned them both out before she left. They should be empty.

Shaking, Joanna stood and jerked open the curtains of the first dressing room. Nothing. All she saw were the small, velvet-topped bench and gold-framed mirror usually there. That left the other dressing room.

She glanced again at the darkened window, then focused on the dressing room's silk curtains. God, she wished someone were with her. She bit her lip and counted silently. One, two, three — she drew aside the curtain and instantly let it fall closed again. She clicked on the store's overhead lights then ripped aside the dressing room curtains. Hanging from a hook was a shredded silk nightgown, its top bunched like a head. It dangled from a tiny silken noose.

Joanna ran all the way home. Gasping and cursing her kitten-heeled pumps, she collapsed against her front door. Locked. Good. Inside, her house, lit by a single lamp on the fireplace mantel, was still. Pepper raised his head from the couch.

The police had been useless. They wouldn't even send a cop to the store to take a report. Once she'd reported nothing was stolen and no one hurt, the dispatcher had transferred her call to a sleepy sounding officer who replied "Uh huh" to everything she said and offered a case number. Probably doing a crossword puzzle the whole time they talked.

Remembering the caller's threat, her anxiety mounted. The voice — she couldn't tell if it was a man or woman — had warned her to mind her own business. The diamonds. It had to be about the diamonds. Or was it? The only thing she'd done was to see Travis and Ben. Maybe she'd struck closer to home than she'd thought.

"Damn it." She threw her purse on a chair. That caller would not have the last word. Destroying the nightgown, threatening her. Anger replaced fear.

First, she'd search the house to make sure she was alone. She grasped the fireplace poker, then took a trembling breath and began to sing at top volume while marching through the house. "Hello my honey, hello my baby, hello my ragtime gal." Pepper darted under the couch.

She paused at the bedroom door, then, poker raised, plunged in. It looked just as she'd left it that morning, down to the lilac-sprigged scarf she'd decided not to wear at the last minute and tossed on the bed cover.

Still singing, she moved on to the second bedroom, her office. "If you refuse me, honey you'll lose me, then you'll be left alone, so baby, telephone, and tell me I'm your own — you bastard." Nothing amiss here, either. Her voice was beginning to feel the strain as she made her way to the basement after checking out the kitchen and bathroom.

Everything looked in perfect order.

Upstairs again, she stopped singing and, emotionally exhausted, slumped against the door to the hall. She dropped the poker to the floor. What had she got herself into?

There was no way she was spending tonight at home. She shoved a few things into an overnight bag and called Paul.

"I'd like to come over, if you don't mind." The soundtrack from *The Good, the Bad, and the Ugly* played in the background.

"Of course not. You know that," Paul said. His voice was reassuring, if surprised. She'd be safe there. "Is something wrong? You sound funny."

"I was singing kind of loudly just now."

"Singing? What's going on?"

"Nothing. I just —"

"What's bothering you?"

The fear of the evening started to drain away, leaving her shaky. Paul had warned her not to get involved with the diamond thefts. If she told him, he'd make her promise to drop everything, and the sting operation — the chance to free Poppy — would be for nothing. She hesitated. She didn't want to hide anything from him, but...

"Tell me," he insisted. A little stubbornness had crept in.

Well, she could be stubborn, too. "Just a long day, I guess. I'll see you in a few minutes."

Joanna opened Paul's refrigerator as quietly as she could and reached for the milk. The refrigerator's light spilled into the dark kitchen. She hadn't dared turn on a lamp for fear of waking Paul, but the moon though the wood shop's high windows illuminated the room just enough for her to see to heat the milk and pour it into a mug.

It was well before dawn, and she couldn't sleep. Tonight, Paul's warmth in bed disconcerted more than comforted her. Not telling him was eating her alive. But if she told him, she'd have to admit that she'd already been working on Poppy's behalf, despite his warning, despite her promise. By not saying anything about trying to clear Poppy, she was lying to him. He'd be angry, for sure. If he found out about the call to the store — well, she ached at the thought of it.

Poppy was in jail with the very real possibility of staying there for years for something she didn't do. The police had no motivation to clear her. They thought they'd nabbed a key figure in a ring of diamond thieves. What was she supposed to do?

"Jo." Paul's voice above her was quiet, but clear.

She looked up to the sleeping loft, where his head and shoulders leaned over the bannister. Gemma's tail wagged twice between the rails from her blanket at the foot of the bed.

"I'm having a little trouble sleeping," Joanna said.

"Come back to bed. It's a lot easier to sleep that way."

She rinsed out her mug and climbed to the loft. The bed was still warm, and Paul pulled the quilt over them.

"What's wrong?" he asked once they'd settled. "I've had the feeling all night that something isn't quite right."

She tucked her chilled toes between his calves. He didn't flinch, and even pulled them closer to warm her. "I'm just — just uneasy. Money, you know." Poppy, her thoughts said. Gemma sighed from the foot of the bed as she rearranged herself on her blanket.

"We'll take care of the money problem together. Don't worry about it. I have a few jobs coming up."

"I'll be fine," she said. Could she risk telling him about her plans for Poppy? Yet, how could she not risk it? "It's just — " She drew a breath. "I have something to tell you." Her hands felt cold now, too. She clasped them and drew them under the covers.

"Yes?" Paul prompted.

Her throat clogged. Words wouldn't come.

A moment passed in silence. Finally, Paul said, "If something were wrong, you'd tell me, right?"

The exact words she'd used with Poppy. *If something were wrong, you'd tell me, right?* she'd asked. Poppy had looked so haunted. It wasn't right to abandon her. In a few days, everything would be sorted out. Paul would see. It would be all right.

She hoped.

"It's nothing. Nothing to bother you with. It'll be fine," she said. "Soon."

Chapter 15

Joanna tossed aside the Justice Center waiting room's copy of *American Police Beat*. Her thoughts bounced between her upcoming meeting with the detective in charge of Poppy's case, the terrifying phone call the night before, and Helena's panicked face when she said Gil was in the hospital.

She glanced at the wall clock. The NAP auction meeting was just an hour away. If she was going to convince the auction committee to let Poppy call the auction, she needed police support. If the detective assigned to her case ever showed up, that is.

"Finally," the receptionist said. "Alex, this lady has been waiting to see you for half an hour."

Joanna rose. The detective lifted one hand to shake hers. The other hand held a string bag bulging with produce. Bunches of chard and carrots burst from its opening.

"Alex Sedillo. How can I help you?"

"I'm here about Poppy Madewell," Joanna said.

"And?"

"She did not steal those diamonds. I may have proof." She slipped the manifest from her purse. Hopefully they'd consider her story even without the inventory to compare it to.

The detective hesitated.

"Ask Detective Crisp, in homicide. I know him. He'll vouch for me."

"Crisp, huh? I've been in touch with him about the North homicide."

"They're not— they're not the same case?"

"No. Not yet, at least. We'll see as things develop. Why? You know something?"

Joanna vigorously shook her head. "No." Definitely not.

"All right. Come with me." Alex waved his badge over a sensor by the door. His produce bag swung against his baggy pants—surely at least two sizes too big, despite his generous build. He led her to an office on the perimeter of the floor. "Have a seat." He gestured toward the chair across from his desk. Huffing from the exertion of crossing the office, he set the bag of produce on a chair pushed against the wall. "Farmers market today."

"Are the morels out yet?" Despite her eagerness to get to the manifest, Joanna couldn't help asking.

"Yep. Got some of those and some fava beans. I'll grill the favas and sauté the morels for a kick-butt bruschetta."

She unfolded the list she'd taken from Travis's apartment and smoothed it on his desk. "Have a look at this. There's something fishy about it."

"In a minute." He lowered himself slowly into the chair. "The chives are up now—I could chop a few tablespoons and sprinkle them on top." He lifted the receiver of his desk phone and asked someone to come by his office. Barely breaking stride, he picked up the food conversation again. "Here's hoping the favas are still tender, or I'll have to puree them, not that that's all that bad."

Joanna looked around the office for a clock. As it was, she was going to have to rush straight to the NAP meeting.

He pulled a plastic tub of protein powder from under his desk and scooped some into a tall carry-out cup. "Lap band surgery. God, I love food, but I got to keep it to very small portions, several times a day. This stuff helps." He shook the cup, his breath quickening again. "Lost almost fifty pounds, but I still got seventy-five to go."

Joanna jumped on the pause. "Poppy's sales records — "

A large woman with a mannish haircut appeared in the doorway. "You called?"

"Yes," Alex said. "Joanna Hayworth, this is Melinda, our forensic accountant. Joanna says she has something proving Madewell wasn't selling diamonds through the auction house."

"I'd like to see that." Melinda sounded skeptical.

Joanna tapped the manifest. "Here. This is the list of everything shipped as part of the Vivienne North lot. If I'm right, it's different from the inventory the auction house put together for the sale. For every lot that the auction house takes, they make an inventory with the owner. Each shipment that goes to the warehouse has a manifest listing its contents. When the truck's unloaded, they compare the manifest to the inventory to make sure they didn't miss anything."

"Manifests can be changed," Melinda said. "What's the date on that?"

Joanna passed it to the forensic accountant, who studied it a moment. She glanced up at Sedillo and waved the paper. "The missing manifest."

The detective set down his cup and grabbed the list. "Let me see."

Joanna paused. "There's just one problem."

"What?"

"I don't have the inventory. But you could easily get it from the auction house," she added quickly.

"No. We don't need to. Wait here." Melinda left the room.

"Where did you get this?" Sedillo asked.

Stolen from Travis's coffee table. Probably not what they'd call regular procedure. "From someone at the auction house."

"But we questioned everyone there, and no one knew where this was."

"Well," Joanna said. "It was someone who'd been fired. And he—he might not have wanted anyone to know he had it."

"If this is legitimate evidence, I'll need names and a statement," the detective said.

"Fine." Joanna knew that Travis would support anything that helped clear Poppy. He wasn't going to like this much, though.

The forensic accountant returned with a laptop. "From the auction house computer." She clicked expertly through digital files.

"What are those marks?" Alex pointed to the awkward check marks down the manifest.

"I think those were made by one of the warehouse hands who thought he'd screwed up. He was verifying the contents of the shipment."

"It doesn't look like he finished. See there? The checkmarks only go partway down the second page."

"He was fired," Joanna said. "He went back in the evening to finish up the reconciliation, and he was caught after business hours, against the rules."

A spreadsheet filled the laptop's screen. "North lot, May nineteenth." Melinda flattened the manifest on the table. "Same date, same lot. But the inventory doesn't match the manifest. It's subtle, but look." Joanna leaned forward for a better view. Melinda pointed to a line for box twelve. "The manifest lists 'glass,' but the inventory doesn't say anything about glass for that box."

"The same box the lamp with the diamonds was in?" Alex asked.
Melinda nodded.

Alex turned to Joanna. "You realize, if this manifest is legit, you've just given us evidence against your friend."

"All it proves is that someone at the auction house was receiving stolen diamonds. Not Poppy." She shook her head for emphasis. "Besides, I got a threatening call last night ordering me to lay off asking questions. It couldn't have been Poppy — she's in jail."

"Tell me what happened."

"I was at my shop — I have a vintage clothing store, Tallulah's Closet — and someone whispering so I couldn't recognize him warned me to leave other people's business alone. Then he said to look in the dressing room. I found a nightgown twisted like a hanged person."

"Did you report this to the police?"

"Sure. Not that it did me any good."

Sedillo was quiet.

"And the manifest and inventory. Poppy doesn't even deal with shipping. I got the manifest from the guy who'd been fired. It wasn't Poppy who fired him, it was her manager, Ben."

Alex and Melinda looked at each other again. At last, Alex spoke. "Where are you going with all this?"

"Someone at the auction house is selling stolen diamonds. Maybe Ben."

"Whoa. You're making some serious allegations."

"I saw him yesterday. I pretended I'd found a bit of a jewelry setting on the warehouse floor. He flipped out."

"And?" Alex asked.

"And I don't have solid proof, I know." She took a deep breath. "But I do have a plan for finding out. We could stage a — " She paused, realizing how ridiculous this sounded. "A sting operation."

Alex leaned back, his arms folded in front of his chest. "Uh huh."

"No, really. If Poppy were able to call at one more auction, the real diamond seller—"

"Assuming it's not Poppy, you mean," Melinda added.

"The real diamond seller would try it again, either to make up for the money he lost, or to completely implicate Poppy. All you have to do is be at the auction and wait until the sale goes down."

Alex shook his head. "No."

"Plus, you'd have complete control. You could inspect everything for sale at the auction ahead of time and even do background checks on the guest list," Joanna said.

"Guest list? Since when do auctions have guest lists?" Alex asked.

"The one I'm thinking of is a charity art auction for the Northwest AIDS Project. It's Saturday. Poppy was hired to be the auctioneer. Before she was arrested, that is."

The expressions on their faces brought home what a ludicrous idea a sting operation was. What were the police going to do? Swoop into one of the city's fanciest fundraisers and handcuff someone? Besides, a charity auction wasn't the kind of auction Poppy held in her warehouse where, presumably, the jewels were distributed. But she didn't have a lot of options. How else could she prove Poppy was innocent?

Alex's chair creaked as he leaned forward. A shelf of stomach rolled onto the edge of his desk. "Terrible idea. Police work is not the movies. We don't run sting operations just to see what happens. Too many ways things can go wrong."

"It's a solid chance to clear Poppy. You want to nail whoever did this, right?" Joanna leaned forward, too. "Besides, you'll sit at my table." She loaded her voice with urgency. "The food will be divine. Five chefs — three of them James Beard nominees — are putting together the menu. All spring specialties, locally sourced."

Alex sipped his protein shake. He frowned at the cup and pushed it away. "Saturday, huh?" A few seconds passed. Joanna heard a phone ring in a nearby office. "Normally I'd say no. But the judge set bail for Poppy this morning, and she'll be out by this afternoon anyway. It's against my better judgment, but I'm willing to think about it. Talk to Poppy and get back to me."

She let out her breath. Poppy shouldn't be the problem, Joanna thought. It's the NAP committee. What would they say to having a jailbird call the auction?

Joanna straightened and plastered a smile on her face. "I have some good news."

Clary and Lacey sat across from Joanna at the conference table. Jeffrey, the NAP special events coordinator, was near the head of the table. The group looked at her expectantly. Clary finally said, "Well?"

"Poppy is out on bail and can still do the auction." She kept a positive tone.

"No no no." Lacey shook her head. "No way we're letting her call the auction. She's hooked up with that diamond theft ring. Forget it."

"She's been accused of a crime, not convicted," Joanna said.

Jeffrey ignored her. "We have two days until the auction, not counting today. I've been calling around, and the closest available auctioneer I can find is in Kansas City. Give me the green light, and we'll fly him in."

Joanna grasped the edge of the table. "Please, hear me out. Poppy's the best person for the auction. She knows the audience—who can bid high, who will compete with whom. She'll raise the most money by far."

"But she's practically a felon. Who knows? Maybe she'll show up high or steal something," Lacey said. Her Pomeranian started barking at a high pitch. "Hush, Porsche. Mommy needs you to be quiet."

Jeffrey's head whipped from speaker to speaker.

"Calm down, Lacey," Clary said. "It's not like Poppy would pickpocket the guests. If anything, she'd be on her best behavior." He leaned back, crossing one leg over the other. "I like the idea."

Joanna shot him a bewildered glance. Well, well. Clary was full of surprises. "You wouldn't regret it. I'm certain."

"It's still a bad idea," Lacey said. "If anything goes wrong, not only will it screw up the evening, but no one will ever go to a NAP event again. Think about it. Half the people in that room had diamonds stolen from them or know somebody who did."

"But we'd sell out the remaining tables like that." Clary snapped his fingers. "Everyone would want to come out to see her." The group was quiet for a moment. Ticket sales for the dinner had been lagging. "A quick press release, and I guarantee people will be talking about the auction for months." He tapped a finger on the desk. "Yes. I like it."

Lacey shook her head and pulled her poodle closer. "If you really want to do it, fine. But I won't take any responsibility."

"Jeffrey, you're the only one here actually with NAP. What do you think?" Clary asked.

"Well," Jeffrey smiled uncertainly. "I can't really say—"

"Fine then. We'll do it," Clary said.

"Poindexter" indeed, Joanna thought. The man had some

take-charge in him.

"Problem solved. We already have a contract with Poppy, no?" Clary asked. Jeffrey nodded. "Then she's our auctioneer. It's settled."

Jeffrey sat back, apparently resigned to relinquishing control of the meeting to the Baronet.

"Great." Clary pushed his wire-rimmed glasses up the bridge of his nose and picked up the agenda. Not many people could make such stuffy glasses look more Cary Grant than Grandpa Walton, but he pulled it off. "Next up, dresses for the greeters. Joanna?"

Joanna leapt at the chance to move on. "Yes, I found some gorgeous late 1950s cocktail gowns, including two Traina-Norells and a Galanos."

Clary leaned forward at the conference table. He had rejected the coffee Jeffrey brought from NAP's break room. A paper demitasse of espresso from Spella Café, a small local roaster, sat at his elbow. "Let's see them. I talked to Eve, and if these don't work she said she's happy to lend us some of hers."

"Oh, I think you'll love them," Joanna said quickly.

"Did you bring pictures?" Lacey asked. As she talked, she dipped into the massive pale green handbag on the floor next to her and pulled out her buzzing phone. Instead of looking up for Joanna's reply, her fingers worked the phone's keyboard.

Joanna's smile froze. Damn. She'd forgotten to touch base with the Mother Superior, let alone bring photos. In fact, she hadn't even seen the dresses firsthand. She'd been so busy following up on Poppy, she hadn't stopped by the convent yet. If the nuns didn't come through, she had no idea where she'd scare up five "Hollywood Glamour" gowns in two days. "Do you have a laptop handy?"

Jeffrey pushed his laptop across the table.

"You'd better do it." Joanna looked at the computer. "I'm not so great with those things. Look up Sisters Vintage."

"Sisters Vintage? I thought your store was called something else. Louella's something or something like that," Lacey said.

"Tallulah's Closet. But I'm, well, as a special favor, I'm borrowing these dresses."

Jeffrey clicked past the Sisters Vintage opening screen and enlarged a photo of a black Galanos cocktail dress with a portrait collar.

"It says it's on hold." Lacey put her phone on the table.

Relief washed over Joanna. The Mother Superior had come through. "On hold for us."

"Nice styling," Clary said under his breath. Joanna filed that away to tell Sister Mary Alberta. "Where is this store? Somewhere in town?"

"It's internet-only," Joanna said. She didn't feel the need to go into the whole convent angle.

Jeffrey clicked to another dress, this one a vivid red satin. The model's tattoo snaked above the off-the-shoulder sleeves. "It looks like they're in some kind of church. Is that a crucifix?" He pointed at the screen.

Joanna stepped in. "The greeters will need to bring their own shoes, but I can provide jewelry. Apple and I will help with hair and getting them dressed."

The vintage dresses would stand out even among the guests' expensive evening clothes. The long, full skirts, the careful cut of an armhole and boning in a bodice were details even the fanciest boutiques in town couldn't provide these days. She'd have to remember to load her purse with business cards—if the committee okayed her selection. She glanced from face to face.

"I guess these will work." Clary picked up the agenda again. "Next up, food. Jeffrey, did you make sure we'll have enough gluten-free entrees?"

Chapter 16

Home at last. Joanna set her purse on the chaise longue and checked the blinking answering machine. Three messages. Paul kept warning her that one day she'd wear out her last answering machine tape and have to switch to voice mail, but until then she clung to her Clinton-era machines.

She pressed "play" and went to the kitchen. Pepper head-butted her calf as she lifted the container of kibble from the top of the refrigerator and poured some in his dish.

"Hey Jo." Paul. "Where have you been? I stopped by the store, but Apple said you'd asked her to work today. You've been kind of caught up in this whole Poppy thing, and I want to make sure you're all right."

That's sweet. She'd see him later tonight, anyway. She didn't plan to stay the night at her place alone until the auction was over and the threatening caller was in police custody.

The machine beeped again. "Babette, it's Ted Tyler," Apple said, using their code spy names from when they were children. Joanna laughed. They hadn't played Ted and Babs since fifth grade. "I'm stopping by after the shop closes to hear more about the covert operation. Over and out." She'd have to tell Apple about the threatening call when she stopped by, damn it. She'd put it off too long as it was.

The machine beeped again to deliver its third message. "Hi, it's

Helena." Joanna stared at the answering machine as if she'd hear more clearly that way. "I'm sorry about yesterday. I know I let you down. It's just that I was so worried about Gil. He — he — anyway, he's fine now. He'd had a panic attack, that's all. I guess I overreacted." She laughed weakly. "No cause for alarm. I'll see you at the NAP auction."

Joanna pressed "rewind." She put her hands on her hips and looked at the portrait of Aunt Vanderburgh. "Strange, huh? What do you think, Auntie V? Something going on between Helena and her husband?"

The portrait stared in its usual disapproval. Something strange is always going on, it seemed to say.

"Just a quick one, then. I'm due at Paul's for dinner." Joanna pulled a jar of honey from the cupboard and set it next to the lemon and bottle of gin on the kitchen table. "What are the proportions?"

Apple perched on the kitchen's stepping stool, which with its seat flipped down made a chair. In her hands was Ted Saucer's *Bottoms Up* cocktail manual from the early 1950s. "Naughty illustrations." She held up the book to show a pin-up girl naked but for black stockings, seen through an upturned champagne saucer.

"Booze and dames." Joanna rolled a lemon on a cutting board to loosen up its juice. "I put the reference librarians to work tracking it down once I heard the Bee's Knees was Vivienne's favorite cocktail."

"I hope you tell those librarians how much you appreciate them. For Goddess's sake, Jo. Everyone else knows how to use a search engine."

"Don't worry. Last week I dropped off a Spode teapot for the break room. Bee's Knees please."

"Let's see. Juice of one-quarter lemon, one teaspoon honey, half a glass of gin. Dissolve honey in lemon juice, add gin and ice. Shake well and serve in cocktail glass. Says it's courtesy of the Hotel Ritz in Paris."

Joanna cut the lemon and squeezed half into a cocktail shaker. "Helena, Vivienne's daughter-in-law, said Vivienne first had them in Paris before World War Two. She had one every night, including the night she died." She opened the jar of honey and dipped a spoon into it, letting the amber ribbon twist into the cocktail shaker with the lemon juice. "Here. You mix this up while I get ice."

Apple set the book on the counter and took the shaker and a wooden spoon Joanna handed her. When Apple was finished, Joanna filled the shaker with ice then used one of the cocktail glasses to measure gin. She wrapped the shaker in a cotton dishcloth and shook. The dishtowel stuck to the shaker's icy wall as she unwrapped it. She poured frothy pale yellow liquid into each glass and handed one to Apple.

"Cheers."

"Not bad. Kind of like grown-up lemonade," Apple said. Considering she stuck to tea and rarely even drank wine, the Bee's Knees was a hit.

They took their drinks to the living room. It wasn't dark enough to merit turning on a lamp, but Joanna lit a verveine candle on the fireplace mantel and settled on the couch. She pulled up her feet and covered them with a mohair throw. Pepper jumped up and began kneading his paws on the edge of the blanket. Apple took the deco club chair closest to the fireplace.

"Is that Paul's shirt?" Apple pointed at a pile of plaid wool Pepper had turned into a nest.

"Uh huh. I'll bring it to him tonight." Paul hadn't brought up her sudden insistence on seeing him after the threatening phone call at the store, but he'd seemed occupied as he watched her unpack a few things. He'd handed her a hanger for her Chinese silk dressing gown and pushed aside his scratchy wool robe to make room for it. She hadn't said a word about the sting operation.

"Hmm." Apple squinted her eyes slightly, like she did when she was getting her "intuitions." "So, fill me in, starting with the visit to the auction house."

"It was kind of a bust, really, but it all worked out in the end." She told Apple about Ben catching her in Poppy's office before she'd got to the inventories, and about the visit to Detective Sedillo. "The worse part was getting caught." She shuddered at the memory of Ben clicking on the overhead light as she was reaching for the filing cabinet and his anger when she showed him the jewelry setting. "Helena was supposed to keep him busy, but she got a phone call saying her husband was in the hospital."

Apple's glass, drained, sat on the coffee table on a stack of old New Yorkers. Joanna still nursed hers. These Bee's Knees could be deadly for an inexperienced drinker.

"Is Gil all right?"

Joanna's hand stopped mid-pet. Pepper looked up. "Helena left me a message this afternoon. Might have been a panic attack. Why? You sound like you know him."

"He's a painter. I see him at life drawing." Apple and some other artists gathered at one of the neighborhood studios to paint from a model a few times a month. They all chipped in to pay the model's fees.

"Seems like he could afford his own model, if he wanted."

"I think he likes to hang out with us bohemian types." She gave a short laugh. "The first time he came he had a really expensive easel. The next time he showed up with something beat up, paint all over it. He must have bought it off craigslist." Apple gestured to her empty glass. "I'm tempted to ask for another of these, but I'm not sure I'd be able to stand up after I drank it."

"Practice, dear Apple. It's all in the pacing." A half inch of Bee's Knees remained in Joanna's glass. "Helena adores him, but I get the sense she worries about him, too."

Apple leaned forward. "There is one thing. You know the big painting Gil did, *Pacific Five?* It won the gold medal in the biennial this year?"

"Sure." The painting Helena had mentioned at her house. "That's the one that's in the NAP auction."

"Something's not right about it. It isn't like his other work. *Pacific Five* is this big post-modernist piece, but I've only seen him working on impressionistic nudes." Apple lay back.

"So?" That hardly qualified as meaty gossip. "You've seen him at life drawing. Of course it's going to be nudes. Maybe he does other stuff at home."

Apple shook her head. "No, it's not a natural progression. Besides, Gil's work is all right, but not great. Barely good enough to get into the biennial, let alone take home a prize."

"What are you telling me? Someone else painted *Pacific Five?*"

"I don't want to go that far, but — "

"Stop it." Joanna picked up Apple's glass and waved it. "You want another one of these?"

"Hmm." She tilted her cocktail glass and watched the little bit left swirl up one side and down. "Yes, please." Apple followed her to the kitchen and took her place on the stepping stool. "Hand me the shaker. I'll stir again."

"Gil comes from a wealthy family. I'm sure the trustees at the art museum made sure his painting got a second look." She rinsed out Apple's glass and cut a new lemon twist. "Better let me carry that in for you."

Apple plopped herself into the deco chair again, narrowly missing Pepper, who'd found the warm spot left by her rump. "One of the guys who goes to life drawing, Tranh, has a weird bond with Gil. I sense it." She took a long sip of her new cocktail. "Something is a little off."

"You're not making a lot of sense. What do you mean?"

"Nothing." Apple waved her hand dismissively. "Forget I said anything about it. God, these are good."

"You're tipsy." She folded her arms. "How were things at the store today?"

"Slow. I wish I could say they were better."

She couldn't put it off any longer. She had to tell Apple about the caller. It wasn't fair to leave her in the store alone, not knowing someone could be watching her. "Last night —" She tossed back the rest of her cocktail. "Last night I was at the shop trying to figure out the bills and got a threatening phone call."

"What?"

"Someone told me I should leave other people's business alone. Then he told me to look in the dressing room, and I found one of the store's nighties mangled."

"Yesterday? But I emptied the dressing rooms when I closed up."

"I know. I can't figure it out. They —" She put her glass on the side table. "They twisted the nightgown and tied it with a ribbon to the hook so it looked like a hanged person."

Apple stared, mouth agape. "But how did they get in?"

"I don't know. The door, the window — everything looked normal."

Apple leaned back, surprise still showing on her face. "I don't like this."

"I filed a police report. Just be careful. Maybe it was some kind of joke."

Apple tilted her head. "It's no joke. I knew something was wrong. I'm glad Paul is looking after you."

"He doesn't know. I don't want to get him worked up."

"For crying out loud. Why don't you tell him? By this time with Gavin, I think we were married. Maybe not legally, but spiritually for sure."

She had heard the story many times, about how Apple had started dreaming of him two weeks before they met, then how they were both in the same aisle of a bookstore, locked eyes, and that was that. Meet cute, pagan style. Joanna had given them an Eastlake nightstand as a wedding present. Poppy had helped her find it. Poppy. She was not fencing diamonds, and the sooner she was proven innocent the better. Just a few more days, she repeated to herself. It had nearly become a mantra.

A moment of silence passed.

"Jo, are you listening? Your energy is all over the place tonight. What's going on?"

She wrenched her attention back to Apple. "I was thinking about Poppy. I promised Paul I'd leave things with her alone, but — "

"But you haven't." Another moment passed. Apple yawned.

"A few nights ago Paul even mentioned something about moving in together."

"What's wrong with that? You're happy, right?"

"Yes." She was. It still surprised her how he listened to her. Sometimes she'd be chopping vegetables and telling a story about an estate sale she'd been to, and she'd look up to find him smiling.

"And there's nothing wrong in other — uh — departments?"

"No, not at all." She looked down at her empty glass.

"Then what's the deal?"

"Like I said, I promised him I wouldn't get involved with Poppy's case."

"What did he think you'd do?" She paused. "Could this have to do with his sister's death?"

"I don't know. This feels different. You know that way he has with always joking about things?"

Apple nodded.

"He's serious about this. I don't know what it is. He seems more edgy about it. And I promised him," she repeated. "But I can't do it." Joanna's gaze shifted between Apple and Aunt Vanderburgh, both disapproving, but Apple markedly more relaxed. Almost sleepy.

"So talk to him about it," Apple said. "Say you have to look into Poppy's situation, that you owe it to her. Don't lie to him." She paused but when Joanna didn't respond, Apple yawned again and lay her head back. "Never mind. You better watch out, or you're going to mess this up for good."

God, Apple was pushy. But she had a point. She glanced at Apple's empty glass, the lemon zest already beginning to tighten and die. Hiding her involvement with Poppy probably wasn't the smartest way to move forward with Paul. But if she told him, he'd be furious. After all, she'd promised him to stay out of it. She could end up blowing the whole relationship apart. Yet there was no way she'd give up on

Poppy now. It wasn't fair that he'd expect it of her. Just two more days until the auction, then it would be over. In the meantime, she hated hiding it from Paul, but what was the alternative?

"Oh Apple," she said quietly. "What should I do?"

Slow, even breathing came from the club chair. Apple was asleep.

Chapter 17

The Mother Superior leaned back on her pillows, a spring breeze rustling the nodding orchid on her night stand. She breathed in and relaxed into a what was surely a rare smile. Joanna moved to the window. Paul, on a ladder outside, stuck a penknife into a first floor window frame.

"What is he doing now?" the Mother Superior asked.

"Checking for dry rot is my guess."

"Thank you, dear, for arranging for your gentleman friend to take stock of the convent." Her smiled dimmed a watt. "He's not standing in the flower beds, is he?"

Joanna laughed. "No. He's careful about things like that." She turned again to the window. Paul moved the ladder near the kitchen door. He scaled it confidently, one hand on the ladder, the other reaching into his back pocket for a screwdriver. He saw her in the upper window and waved. Joanna waved back, then looked at the Mother Superior. "Do you ever go into the garden?"

"Not often. It's easier if I'm carried, and the sisters can't do it." She paused. "Well, Mary Alberta probably could. I can walk a little with a cane."

"Would you like to sit in the garden now? Between Paul and me, we could carry you downstairs easily, I'd think. It's a little cool, but it looks like there's a spot in the sun back there."

"Oh, I couldn't impose," the Mother Superior said, but she was already sitting a little straighter. "However, the south veranda is quite warm."

"I'll go find one of the sisters to get you a coat and see if Paul can come up."

A few minutes later Joanna returned with Paul. She noticed the Mother Superior had combed her hair and sat with her hands crossed coyly in front of her, her crucifix dangling above them.

"Mary Frances is gathering some blankets," Joanna said.

Paul approached the bed, and the Mother Superior lifted back the blankets and held up her arms. Was that a flirtatious smile? "I'll just pick you up, if that's all right," he said.

"Yes. Mind the orchid, please."

The Mother's body was thin as a child's. "Where to?" he asked.

"South veranda."

The Mother directed them toward the back door. To the side of the house a cement patio lay under a portico of wooden beams with a wisteria vine beginning to unfurl its blossoms on the peeling paint. Three chairs, freshly cleaned and painted the sky blue of the sisters' habits, surrounded a glass-topped table.

"Right there, please." The Mother Superior gestured to the chair with the best view of the garden and the sloping lawn to the street. Paul set her on her feet, while still holding her at the waist. She felt for the chair's arms and sat down. "Thank you, sister," she said to Mary Carmen who had appeared with a folded plaid blanket. She tucked it around the Mother's shoulders and arms. "Tell Mary Edwina we're ready for lunch. Out here, like we discussed earlier."

Joanna and Paul traded glances. The Mother had obviously planned this in advance. A neighbor pushing a stroller with a pug tied to its frame passed on the sidewalk and looked up as if this were the first time she'd seen anyone outside the convent.

"You will stay for lunch, won't you?" The Mother said this more as a statement than a question. "Mary Edwina is an exceptional cook, if you like Hungarian food, that is. Goulash is her specialty. It's not fancy," she said to Paul and placed her withered hand on his, "But we old women do the best we can. And Mary Edwina has made some pots de crème for us, as well. I do know men enjoy sweets."

"Pot de crème—I'm not sure exactly what that is," Paul said.

"It's a very nice chocolate pudding," the Mother said.

"Sounds good." He smiled.

Joanna had never known Paul to be much for dessert, but she might need to dig out Julia Child for a good chocolate mousse recipe. A small woman, her habit covered by a stained apron and her hands in bright oven mitts, hoisted an enameled stock pot to the table and set it on a trivet.

"Not there," the Mother said sharply. "In the center. That's better."

Coming behind the cook, Mary Carmen brought plates and silverware wrapped in large cotton napkins. Joanna unrolled one in her lap. The butter-soft napkins clearly had been washed and tumbled dry hundreds of times.

"Thank you, sisters," the Mother said as they left. "Just a moment while we thank the Lord." She held her crucifix between her hands, closed her eyes, and said, "Bless this my Lord, and these thy guests, who are about to receive thy bounty—"

Paul reached under the table, put his hand on Joanna's knee, and squeezed. She smiled and grasped his wrist.

"From Christ, our Lord. Amen. Please, everyone, eat. Paul, I do appreciate your coming out to look at the house. How does it look?" Her tone sweetened remarkably when she talked to him.

"I haven't had the chance to check out the inside yet, but you're right, you need a new roof. You're on your third layer, too, so it will need to be completely torn off and rebuilt." He tore a piece of bread off the baguette delivered with the salad.

Steam escaped from the goulash as Joanna dipped the serving spoon and scooped some onto the Mother's plate.

"Thank you, that's plenty." Then to Paul, "How much do you think it would cost to replace the roof?"

"I specialize in finish work, things like trim and cabinets, so I can't say for sure, but I'd guess at least ten thousand dollars, probably more."

The Mother crossed herself and muttered a few words.

"There's something else, too." He glanced at Joanna before returning his gaze to the mother. "The convent isn't very secure. It would take less than five minutes to break in and make off with anything you have that's valuable."

"We're just a bunch of old women here. We don't have anything anyone would want. Well, maybe Mary Alberta's computer, but that's it."

"You never know."

After lunch, Paul went to inspect the inside of the house. "Thank you again, son, for all your work. God bless." Once he turned the corner, the Mother's smile faded and her voice snapped to all business. "Joanna. You remember our deal? You have something to report about Vivienne?"

"Yes. I've been doing some following up, but —"

"I understand the auctioneer is in jail for possessing stolen diamonds. Is that true?"

Joanna remembered Poppy in the bleak visitor's room. "She's not a criminal. I've known her a long time." This morning she'd followed up on her meeting with the police to square arrangements for the NAP auction, but she couldn't tell that to the Mother — not until it was over.

"Of course you'd think so. Have they linked the thefts to Vivienne's death?"

"The police are handling them as separate cases." It was a turn of events for which she was grateful. Having Poppy accused of fencing diamonds was bad enough. Joanna briefly relayed her theory that someone in Poppy's auction house was responsible. "But there's something I need to tell you."

The Mother sat, hands in lap, with an eyebrow raised.

"This will have to be my last report about Vivienne." Paul might rather she were finished with both cases, but at least she could walk away from Vivienne's.

"It's not over yet, child. I'm expecting more from you."

Joanna pushed her plate away. "The police are following up on her murder, and it's not safe — and may be counterproductive — for me to get involved."

The Mother's expression hardened. She probably wasn't used to being disobeyed. "What risk can it be? You ask a few questions here and there."

"Two nights ago I was at my store alone, and I got a threatening call." She described the mangled nightdress. "And that was simply because I'm trying to help Poppy. Imagine if a murderer knew I was getting involved."

The Mother took a moment to digest this. "So, you're still helping your friend, but you won't ask around about Vivienne," she said finally.

"I'm sorry. But that's how it needs to be. I'll give you the homicide detective's phone number, and you can call him yourself." Crisp would love that.

The Mother stared at her, and Joanna looked away. When she ventured a glance across the table again, the Mother wore a faint smile. "Of course, you'll report back to me. If you're investigating for your friend, you'll also be investigating for Vivienne. They may be linked after all. We don't know for sure."

"The police don't think so. I need to help Poppy. She might end up in prison otherwise. But Vivienne—" She was going to say that "it was too late now" but bit off the words. "I'm sorry, Mother, but I can't. I told you."

"We'll see." The Mother nodded, the smile still playing on her lips. "I haven't forgotten, dear, that you need our dresses."

A momentary panic settled over Joanna. She wouldn't withhold them, would she?

The Mother tilted back her head. "Mary Frances," she yelled. "Vivienne's dresses."

Joanna let out her breath.

The Mother shook her head. "Poor Vivienne. She was blessed in so many ways, but the things she wanted, really, were simple. Grandchildren, for example. Of course, there'd be no question of a bequest if she'd had grandchildren, but it would have made her happy."

"Too bad Helena doesn't want children."

The Mother looked up. "You mean Helena isn't able to have children. She loves them."

Mary Frances appeared with five garment bags. She draped them over a chair. "Thank you, sister," Mother said.

Helena had been adamant she didn't want kids, but it wasn't worth arguing with a nun about. "I'm sorry Vivienne was disappointed."

"We'll be hearing from you again, child," the Mother said with finality. "Vivienne's business has not yet been settled."

Both heads turned as Paul strode across the veranda. He placed a hand on Joanna's shoulder. "The inside of the house needs cosmetic work, but the plumbing and electrical systems are solid. Did you have the convent rewired?"

"Mary Alberta did a little work last Christmas when a lamp shorted."

"It was good work. Up to code, even."

Mary Alberta again. Was there anything she couldn't do? The Mother shivered. "Are you cold?" Joanna asked. "I could fetch another blanket."

"No, child. I'm just thinking about the ten thousand dollars. It doesn't seem like much money, yet it might as well be a million. We don't have a lot of hope unless we're paid for the auction of Vivienne's things." She looked to the garden bordering the street, where the retaining wall crumbled. A condensed version of the stations of the cross ran through its small space.

"I can't help with the roof, but I'd be happy to fix the dry rot on the east side of the house. Maybe this weekend?" Paul offered.

The Mother raised her eyes to the heavens. "Blessed Father." Then, to Paul, "That would be wonderful."

Joanna rose. "Lunch was delicious. Thank you. I'll return the dresses within a week."

"And you'll come back and tell me about the auction?"

"Of course. About the auction." But not about Vivienne, she added silently as she heaped the garment bags over her arms.

The Mother Superior fussed with her blanket. Paul scooped her out of her chair and carried her inside. "I feel like we're in a scene in one of Joanna's old movies." He pulled at the edge of the Mother's habit — something Joanna would never dare — and the Mother giggled.

He returned a few minutes later. He'd shaved for the sisters, and his smooth face showed a strong jaw. How did she get so lucky to find him? Warmth washed over her.

"Ready to go?" he asked.

"Can we stop at your house?"

He smiled, revealing the gap between his front teeth. "You have something you need to do?"

"Yes." She touched his shoulder and whispered, "Green light."

He broke into a broad grin, and he took the dresses from her arms. "Let's go."

Chapter 18

"I dread it. I know I have to do it, but I don't want to. I wish I'd never signed that contract." Poppy turned from the window in her office and plopped into the chair behind her desk. A pile of mail slid sideways from her inbox, and she absently re-stacked it. The ordeal of being in jail had taken its toll. Her cheeks were thin, and shadows smudged her eyes.

"It's the best way to show you're innocent. All you have to do is get up there and do your job. The job you've won awards for. The job you love," Joanna said. From Poppy's office, she saw Ben lead a photographer to a wall of paintings in the warehouse. Probably getting ready for the next auction.

"Everyone will be looking at me," Poppy said.

"And seeing how sure and confident you are. You'll show them you're the same person, not a criminal. Sure, they'll be curious, but after a few drinks they'll forget all about it."

"Some of the people in that room had their jewelry stolen. You really think they'll be happy to see me?"

"And they all have fat insurance checks to show for it. Besides, you didn't do it. Plus, you know how much you love auctioneering."

Poppy didn't reply at first. She fidgeted with a pen, then looked out toward the warehouse. "I know. Thank you for your encouragement.

I just—I have a bad feeling about it, that's all."

Joanna chose her words carefully. Detective Sedillo had warned her not to tell Poppy about the sting. Poppy had to respond naturally to whatever came up. Still, if Joanna could comfort her just the tiniest bit... "I've been thinking about the charges. The police must have good evidence—"

"I didn't do it!"

"—Not against you, but against the auction house. You're not the only person who works here. There are the guys in the warehouse, the spotters, and even Ben." She ached to tell Poppy about the chance that she'd have her named cleared, but Sedillo's warning had been stern.

Like faraway lightning, the photographer's flash pulsed twice in the dim warehouse.

"The police talked to everyone, I'm sure," Poppy said.

"But if one of them were involved, he might want to cast the blame on you."

Poppy leaned forward. "What are you getting at?"

"Assume the police are right." How close could she get to hinting at the sting operation?

"But they're not."

"I know you're innocent, but Poppy, hear me out. Let's assume someone really is using the auction house to sell stolen diamonds. That person would get the jewels somewhere, then hide them in things auctioned off, then ship them out. Or, the items are arriving with the diamonds already hidden, and someone here knows that."

"My lawyer told me about what the police found when they compared the inventories and manifests."

Since Joanna's visit to the police, officers had taken a year's worth of inventories from Poppy's office. "Exactly. Someone changed the manifests after the shipments came in. Who has access to your computer besides you?"

"Ben," Poppy said. They looked at each other. "You don't think—?" Poppy began. The flash pulsed again, a rat-a-tat of light through the office windows.

Joanna lowered her voice. "Who else could it be? Plus, he's the only other one with a key to your office. And, he was the one who fired Travis. I think Travis has a crush on you, by the way."

"You talked to Travis?"

"I had to. I had to make sure there was some evidence to move forward before I talked to the police and—"

"You talked to the police, too?" Poppy pushed her chair back from the desk and looked at Joanna in shock. "Why didn't you tell me?"

She'd gone too far. "I haven't had the chance until now." Joanna kept her voice low in an attempt to calm Poppy. "It's just that I know you're innocent." She drew a breath. "Remember, you asked me to help."

"I know." Poppy shook her head and gazed out the office window. "If you're right, why would he use the auction house at all? If Ben—or someone else—were selling stolen diamonds, why not just deliver them?"

"I'm not sure. Maybe he's only the middle man and isn't supposed to know the identity of the people doing the selling." Joanna drew back. "There's one other thing I can't figure out, either."

"What?"

"How all this ties in with Vivienne's murder. If it does."

The animation left Poppy's face. If they could just make it through the NAP auction, people would see she was the same person they knew and trusted.

Flash, flash went the photographer's light. Joanna turned so her back was to the window. "Oh Poppy. Don't worry. First things first — let's get through the auction."

The phone rang, a trilling old-fashioned ring. "Someone else can get it," Poppy said.

"It's going to turn out all right. I know it." Joanna turned to the sound of a sharp rapping on the window of Poppy's office.

It was Ben. Joanna looked away. "Phone for you," he said to Poppy. "The police. They're releasing the North estate."

Paul slid one of the trunks from the bed of his pickup. "Do you have the end?"

"Yes," Joanna said. Her voice strained from effort of holding the clothes-laden trunk, but her body thrummed with excitement.

"Here, push it back in. I'll go get the dolly."

She was impatient to get at the clothes again, touch their fabric and see if they were as impressive as she'd remembered, but Paul was right. The trunk was too heavy. A moment later he emerged from Tallulah's Closet rolling a hand truck. With two pulls, he eased the trunk onto the hand truck and wheeled it into the store.

Joanna took a rag from the bathroom and mopped off the trunk's damp surface. The trunk stood on its end like a compact wardrobe. She fidgeted with the latch, then opened it, and the fragrance of cedar and faint perfume reached her nose. Fracas. It must have been Vivienne's signature scent. Satisfaction — and relief — nearly stole her breath. Paul left to get the other two trunks.

She pulled an afternoon dress from the first trunk. "Oh Paul. Look at this," she said when he returned. The dress was light gray wool with satin piping at the sleeves, waist, and neck.

"It looks kind of plain, really."

"Deceptively simple." She flipped the dress around and put a hand under the skirt. "Check out the shaping. Six darts on the back alone. And see the sleeves? These tucks mold them so they're perfectly smooth when your arm is at its most natural position, which isn't straight like you'd think, but slightly bent." She looked up at Paul. "Mainbocher. One of the Duchess of Windsor's favorites. And the tailoring is immaculate. You can be sure this dress fit Vivienne in a way it would fit no one else. Its matching jacket," she said as she reached into the trunk. She ran her fingers over barely perceptible pinholes where Vivienne must have habitually worn a brooch. "Just gorgeous."

"I love seeing you like this. It's like you can see the lives lived in the clothing. Amazing."

"Sometimes it feels that way." She looked at him and smiled, but returned at once to the wardrobe. "Look! A Scaasi evening dress. It's so heavy." She unfolded a blanket over the bench in the middle of the store and slid the dress onto it. The thick, peacock-blue fabric was folded with dove-gray silk into a sleeveless, floor-length gown with a small tie at the chest. "Here's its coat. These lines are practically Japanese." The back of the coat dropped straight from folds at the top of the shoulder into a short train. "So, so beautiful. From the Meier and Frank Crest Room, the tag says. She bought it here in town."

"There's a note on the hanger. Worn at the opening of the Hilton Hotel, January 1960," he read.

"Scaasi's 1959 collection. I might even have a picture of this dress in a book. Amazing." Joanna sighed with happiness. A truly beautiful article of clothing squeezed her heart. If she were lucky, the sensation came along once a month. Now the heart-squeezing dizzied her. Sipping a Martini while sitting in a nineteenth-century apartment overlooking the Eiffel Tower wouldn't produce as satisfying a high. "I almost don't believe I really have them. I think somehow I thought these clothes were gone for good, that I'd never get them."

The store was dark but for the standing lamp she'd clicked on, illuminating the trunk and bathing the room in sepia tones. Paul examined the trunk the clothes were in. "This isn't bad, either. It's tricked out as a wardrobe. Even has its own little drawers."

"You can have it when I'm done. I don't care," she said, distracted by the clothing.

Vivienne's life hung in the trunk, from her days as a Dior house model to the dresses she must have bought on trips to Europe or New York in the 1950s to the designer ready-to-wear she was able to get in Portland. She probably had a favorite sales woman at the Crest Room who called her when especially beautiful dresses arrived. Vivienne would have been a good customer. Joanna remembered Meier & Frank's lattice-roofed dining room at the top of the store, now gone. Maybe Vivienne had lunch there from time to time. She would have tucked her gloves in her purse, shopping bags at her feet, while a waiter presented her a scoop of chicken salad in a silver cup of crushed ice.

"Maybe you should go home," Joanna said. "I could be here for hours. I just want to look at everything, see what I really bought."

"Will the clothes be safe here?"

"I'll put them in the basement storage in the morning — it'll take a while to get everything downstairs. They should be all right overnight." Gazing at the trunks, an almost tearful joy surfaced. "I hate to sell them, but I'll need to unload a few pieces right away so I can start paying back the loan." She ran a hand over the trunk. "The Dior suit really should go to a museum."

Paul nodded. "Money. It always seems to come back to that, doesn't it? I know once summer starts there will be plenty of work, but until then at least I have one good job, and you know I'll help you out."

Joanna looked up just as Paul turned toward the front window. His face reflected off the plate glass. "What job is that?" she asked, suspecting the answer. Her jaw tensed.

Paul turned squarely toward her. "Eve's showroom. You remember."

The bliss over Vivienne's wardrobe melted. A cold anxiety took its place. "Do you have to?" She shouldn't have asked. She was too emotional already. God knew what would come out of her mouth.

"I do, Jo. I need the money. This is a good job. We already talked about it. Besides, I'm not sure exactly what you're worrying about."

"I see." She pulled open one of the trunk's drawers and withdrew a satin evening bag. She unclipped it. Inside were a torn ticket stub and a handkerchief. A mixture of disappointment and apprehension surged. "You didn't have to take that job. Once these dresses start selling I'll have plenty of money for both of us. Really. I'll have so much more time after the auction, when Poppy—" She stopped short.

"When Poppy what?" Paul's knuckles whitened where he clutched the edge of the trunk. It wasn't often he was so serious. "I thought she was in jail."

"She's out on bail." Joanna turned toward the trunk and kept her hands busy.

"You mentioned the auction and Poppy. What's going on that you haven't told me?"

"I just don't trust Eve," Joanna said. "You know how she's tried to stab me in the back every chance she's had."

"Stop changing the subject. This isn't about Eve. Joanna" — he put a finger under her chin — "look at me."

She pulled her head away and slid onto the bench. "Stop it. What do you expect me to do — let Poppy rot in prison for something she never did?"

Paul stood. "I don't believe it. You promised me you'd leave this alone."

"You don't understand. I —"

"What's happening at the auction, anyway?" A look of comprehension crossed his face. "No. A sting operation. You did it, didn't you? You took up the idea of a sting operation —"

"The police are involved. It's not me —"

"Joanna." The force of his words took her breath away. "I'm giving you a choice. Right now. Leave Poppy to the police, or that's it."

An ultimatum. The words hung in the air. The room was unnaturally quiet.

"You're joking." He had to be. They'd come so far since the summer before. They'd built up so much. He'd never put her in this kind of position.

"No. I'm not."

"Paul. You can't do this to me. You can't force me to make this choice." Didn't he get it? Her friend was in trouble, and she was in a position to help.

"You just made it." He felt his pocket for his keys.

"Poppy's in trouble. She could go to jail for years for a crime she didn't do. What am I supposed to do? Let it be? That's not right."

He shook his head. "Risking your own life for hers is pure stupidity. You don't know what could happen. Trust me."

"Who says I'm risking my life?" He didn't even know about the phone call, the nightgown in the dressing room. Maybe he had a point. But she'd come this far, and there was no turning back. Not now. "Don't go."

"I can't be with you if you're going to take these kind of risks. And break promises." He stopped, looked at the ground, then turned to the door. "I'm leaving." The door shut firmly behind him.

She knew that determined tone. Joanna shoved her hand under her thigh to stop its trembling. He wouldn't change his mind. Or would he? Sure, he was stubborn, but this concern seemed out of line. Uncharacteristic. Maybe he'd come back and say it was all a mistake. She'd apologize then, they'd talk it out. He'd understand why she did what she did.

The door to Dot's Café opened, and three men arguing about a new band spilled on to the street. Their voices faded as they passed down the block. A car door slammed in the distance. Joanna, surrounded by piles of silk and Italian wool, sat down and cried.

Paul did not return.

Chapter 19

The receptionist at the Justice Center buzzed a dull-eyed Joanna through and pointed her toward a conference room along the back wall. Even though it was Saturday, people clicked at keyboards in the central pool of cubicles. Not surprising, she supposed. It wasn't as if crime kept office hours.

Four of the chairs in the conference room were already filled. Detective Sedillo heaved himself out of his chair and held out his hand. "Nice to see you, Joanna. Cup of coffee?"

She nodded. She'd barely slept. It had given her plenty of time to replay the scene with Paul in her head and wonder how she could have handled it differently. She'd had hours to tally her regrets, and it looked like she might have a lot longer. He hadn't returned her calls. She held her breath to hold back the tears that threatened to rise.

She took in the half-empty mugs around the conference room table, then blinked at the morning sun streaming over the Willamette River.

"Oh, I wouldn't serve you what they give us in the break room," Sedillo said, perhaps assuming her silence had to do with the quality of the coffee. "I've got a thermos in my office. Private blend from a garage roaster in my neighborhood. Let me get you some."

"Thank you. I'd love a cup."

"I'll get it," said one of the other officers as he leapt up.

"Thanks, Lee." Sedillo's chair creaked in protest as he lowered himself. "Have a seat. This here's Tommy Lewis — " A small, tidy man with hooded eyes nodded. " — And that was Lee Macon getting you the coffee. We'll be the primary team for tonight's operation. At the end of the table is Martin Greenberg, FBI."

The FBI was involved with this? Greenberg rose and clenched Joanna's palm in a bruising grip. "Pleasure," he said just as Lee returned with her coffee and a glass canister of off-yellow powder.

"We only have instant creamer, I'm afraid."

"That's fine." She stirred the powder into her cup. Given her lack of appetite, non-dairy creamer might be the only solid food she had all day.

Sedillo tapped the table with his pen. "First on the agenda is the auction's layout." He clicked the projector attached to his laptop. "Lee, close the blinds, will you?" A floor plan filled the screen. Sedillo waved a laser pointer at the largest room, on the far right. Tiny circles indicating tables filled it. A long rectangle extended from the inner wall. "The whole deal takes place in a warehouse. Right here is where the dinner and auction will be. Fifty tables give or take. This" — the laser pointer hovered over the long rectangle— "is the stage where the auctioneer will be. Her spotters will be on each side of the stage. Over here" — now the pointer moved to the smaller rooms on the left of the diagram— "is the green room, with a door to the main dining area, there next to the stage, and a sort of prep area just below the green room."

"The green room, where I'll be dressing the hostesses," Joanna said.

The policemen around the conference table fidgeted. Lee's head was pointed at the screen, but his eyes had a faraway cast. Tommy played with his phone and stifled a yawn. Only the guy from the

FBI looked alert. First he watched Detective Sedillo, then Joanna. She might not be at the top of her game this morning, but that was no excuse for the others to be so lax.

"Correct. As you see, the loading dock goes straight into the prep area, and from there you enter the green room." He moved his pointer to the far right of the diagram. "There are three entrances to the dining room. The door to the green room I just showed you, the main entrance to Couch street, and the side door where the catering tents are set up."

Joanna looked around the table. Why wasn't anyone paying attention?

"If there are any last minute instructions before dinner is served, I'll send Tommy or Lee to the green room. We'll keep it low key, though. They'll simply ask, 'Did you order the vegan meal?' and that will be your cue to follow them to somewhere you can talk."

"I see," Joanna said. "Where will you guys be?"

The policemen all looked up, but Sedillo spoke. "I was just getting to that. I'll be at your table as your guest." The laser pointer drifted to a table at the edge of the dining room. "Tommy and Lee will be outfitted as caterers. Some of the service staff will have earpieces and radios, so the boys won't look out of place."

"Hmm. You know what Ben looks like, right?"

Greenberg cut in. "Sedillo sent out photos. We've already searched the art for the auction. Didn't find anything. We'll keep one man on the auctioneer and another on the spotters. Sedillo will handle, uh, general surveillance."

Something was off. This was the big briefing before the auction, yet the police were clearly somewhere else mentally. She glanced at the now-empty coffee cups. "Did you guys already talk through this, without me?"

Sedillo and Greenberg exchanged glances. "We went over the schedule for the night, that's all. Stuff you already know. You know, time guests arrive, when dinner starts — all that."

"You did talk about it. You've already met. All this" — she waved her hands over the table — "is show. For me. Why?"

Detective Sedillo leaned forward, fanning the papers in front of him. The chart on top looked like a guest list, and a yellow streak highlighted one name she couldn't quite make out. "Listen. You have an important role. We'll need you to keep tabs on Poppy. Tommy will always know where she is, but as she moves around — the ladies room, green room — we'll need you to keep track. Don't do anything that will draw too much attention to yourself. Got it?"

If Tommy was already in charge of Poppy, why did they need her involved? It sounded like make-work. "There's something you're not telling me."

"I told you this was a mistake," the FBI agent said.

"There's one critical thing we need you to know," Sedillo added. "The auctioneer — Poppy — can't get wind of what's happening tonight. If she has any idea, the operation's kaput."

"But she's innocent. That's what this is all about," Joanna protested.

Greenberg ignored her outburst. "If Poppy knows, she could betray the operation just by looking at someone too long or second-guessing herself. Her performance tonight must be completely natural." He locked glances with Joanna. "Promise me you haven't told her about it already."

"No. I got Detective Sedillo's warning. I haven't said anything." Not to Poppy, anyway, she thought, remembering her discussion with Apple.

"What?" Sedillo said.

"Well, I did tell my friend about it."

A chorus of moans circled the table. "Your boyfriend, I bet?" Lee said.

Right in the heart, like all the songs say. Right now Paul was probably taking Gemma the Beast on her morning walk and reflecting on how he was sorry he'd ever known her. "No." She looked at her coffee cup. He knew there was some kind of sting, but he didn't know the details. "My friend, Apple. She'll be at the auction, too. She's discreet."

Greenberg rose. "Get the friend's name and we'll run her through the database. We're done here." He grabbed his coffee mug and moved toward the door. "And you," he said, pointing at Joanna, "Keep your mouth shut, understand?"

Chapter 20

"This one is perfect for Bekah. We'll put it with the rhinestone chandelier earrings — she seems to like her bling." Apple pulled a flowered dress with a double-tiered skirt — one full, and the other, longer skirt designed to hug the legs — from the portable clothing rack in the green room. With a box of shoes and jewelry, the rack took up most of the green room. "Jo, did you even hear me? Hop to it. We need to get the greeters dressed."

For once, Joanna was grateful for Apple's bossiness. Armed with a list of measurements and coloring of the greeters, they'd spent most of the afternoon together assembling the clothes for the auction, along with matching accessories. She'd had little time to give in to the heartache that threatened to lay her out. Now, just before the NAP auction, most of the trucks had unloaded and left, and only the bustle of the catering staff in the adjoining dining room and occasional microphone checks disturbed their work.

"I don't know where the detective is. He should have been here by now."

"Let him do his job, and you'll do yours. Take this to Bekah," Apple said.

Joanna obeyed, handing the dress through some sheets they'd jury-rigged as a dressing area. She lowered her voice when she returned to Apple. "If he doesn't show up, the whole thing will be a bust." Not only would Poppy still be in a mess, but she would have iced things with Paul for nothing. The knot in her throat thickened. Maybe she should have listened to him. Too late now.

"Knock it off. Guests will be here any minute, and we don't even have everyone dressed. He'll either be here or he won't."

Footsteps approached the door. Detective Sedillo?

Poppy breezed into the green room. "Hello Joanna, Apple. Gawd. This place reminds me of when I did livestock auctions," she said, looking at the raw walls and exposed beams. A heater in the corner made little progress against the spring evening's chill.

"The committee wanted a creative" — Joanna made quote marks with her fingers— "venue for the auction this year, instead of the convention center. Somebody knew somebody who had an empty warehouse, and voilà."

Poppy barely paid attention to her words. She wore a scarlet Lili Ann dinner suit with an elaborate rhinestone necklace filling its open shawl collar. Her stilettos, modern, clicked across the concrete floor as she approached Joanna. "Are you ready for tonight?" Then, a second later, "You don't look so good."

"Oh, it's nothing. I didn't sleep very well. You know, stress about the event. How are you?" Joanna hardly needed to ask. From Poppy's focused, fueled expression, she was in top form.

"I feel great. Oh Jo, it's so good to be working again. You were right—this is the right thing to do."

Jeffrey, the events coordinator, popped his head behind the green room's curtain. "Poppy? Do you have a minute to go over the seating chart with me? We added two tables with real potential."

"Where did you put the Stilsons? They're usually big art buyers." Still discussing bidding strategy, she followed him out.

Joanna moved closer to Apple so the greeters wouldn't hear. "The two detectives I met are dressed like caterers. One of them was supposed to keep an eye on Poppy, but I haven't seen him, either. Sedillo's coming black tie."

"If they're around, they aren't likely to be obvious about it, are they?" Apple handed the last dress to a greeter and turned to Joanna. "We're finished here. Let's go to the dining room."

"I'll meet you there. I want to look around a little, make sure I'm not missing them."

Instead of following Apple through the doorway connecting the green room with the dining room, she passed into the adjoining room where the art for the oral auction posed on easels and leaned against walls, waiting to be paraded through the dining room when Poppy called the auction. The detectives might be there, inspecting the art for hidden diamonds.

A volunteer, undoubtedly posted to guard the art, slumped on his stool, but otherwise the room was quiet. "Can I help you?" he said.

"I'm just—just looking for a friend."

"No one here but me."

As he spoke, a man entered from the door connecting with the dining room. At first, Joanna noticed his tuxedo—Sedillo?—before realizing the man was much too tall, and slender, to be the detective. But on second glance, she did know him. She knew him from his resemblance to his mother. It was Gil, Helena's husband.

"Here to look at the art?" Joanna said, closing the distance between them. "I'm Joanna Hayworth. You must be Gil North."

Gil looked momentarily flustered. He pushed back a lock of hair that had flopped free of its Brylcreemed set. "Yes. I was looking for the restroom."

"I think they're on the other side, near the catering tent."

Gil showed no inclination to leave, yet he seemed unsettled. He buried his hands in his pockets and scanned the paintings, his gaze settling on a sculpture woven of glass rods. "Very interesting," he said. "I'm not familiar with this artist's work." At last he seemed to grow more comfortable. "What a fascinating juxtaposition of strength and delicacy."

A shadow passed by the doorway. Joanna turned. Whoever it was, he was gone now. She needed to get into the dining room. She was supposed to be keeping an eye on Poppy. At least maybe the other detectives had shown up, if she could recognize them in catering attire.

"I'm looking forward to seeing your painting, Mr. North. I understand it's the centerpiece of the auction." She smiled, preparing to leave, but stopped when she saw Gil's head turn again and settle on a large abstract painting. "Is that it? *Pacific Five?*" Only a few lights illuminated the warehouse room, just enough to make out undulations of color.

Gil's breath quickened. He lifted a handkerchief from his jacket's inside pocket and patted his forehead. He stumbled as he turned away from the painting.

"Are you all right? Why don't we go into the dining room and sit down."

"Yes. Fine. I'm fine," he said. "I just need some water."

"Let me help you." Helena had said he'd already had one panic attack. Maybe he was on the verge of another.

"You want me to get someone?" The volunteer was at their side.

"No," Gil said, his voice suddenly firm. "I said I'm fine." He strode from the room.

Joanna hurried to the dining room after him, but he was quickly absorbed into the chattering crowd beginning to fill the room. Keeping with the Hollywood Glamour theme, a red carpet led up the center of the massive central room, and canisters threw a moving pattern of mini-spotlights on the warehouse's ceiling. Stems of moth orchids, a scarlet runner, and a silver bucket with a cooling magnum of champagne decorated each table. A miniature Oscar statue held down donation envelopes. Music from Academy Award-nominated movies competed with the clinking from the caterer's tent. Right now it was the theme to *Gone With the Wind*. The room was already beginning to warm from the heat of the guests.

Joanna scanned the crowd for Sedillo, then realized it would be useless to try to pick him out in the sea of gowns and tuxedos. She found her table toward the back and sat down. A column partially obscured her view of the stage. Still, she knew she and Apple were lucky to get even part of a table at the auction. Clary had been right — it had sold out quickly once news got out that Poppy would be the auctioneer.

On the plate next to hers was a name card for Paul. Her heart dropped. She turned the card away so it wouldn't taunt her. The detective could sit there — if he ever showed up.

Lacey appeared at her side, waving a white marabou stole at someone a table away. Porsche's head poked out, his little black nose sniffing the air. "No rain tonight, lucky us," she shouted above the rising chatter of the crowd.

"No kidding, it being Rose Festival and all," the guest shouted back.

Joanna practically mouthed the words "Rose Festival" along with her. Someone should make it into a drinking game.

Lacey glanced at Poppy then leaned toward Joanna. "Poppy looks all right so far."

From the stage where she was adjusting her microphone, Poppy threw back her head and laughed. Joanna smiled. "She's happy. She'll do a bang-up job tonight. Thanks for giving her a chance."

"You're lucky. If things don't go well, I'll make sure everyone knows you're responsible." She flung the stole over one shoulder and clicked toward her table, Porsche's furry rump sticking out from under her arm. A caterer approached her, but Lacey waved him away. "The dog stays. Service animal."

Apple was nowhere in sight. Joanna waved at Summer Seasons, a popular drag queen, but more importantly to Joanna, an expert seamstress she relied on for repairs. Summer, in full sequin-bedecked drag, was chatting with one of the Von Trapp Family Singers. Only in Portland.

Before long, sparkly evening bags dangled from chair backs. Waiters fanned through the dining room, setting salads at each place, hoping to lure guests back to their tables. No Sedillo yet. Had he changed his mind and decided it wasn't worth the effort to send anyone?

She scanned the room again. There was Gil, seated next to Helena at a table next to the stage. Clary, wearing a crisp tuxedo, sat with them. His hand draped casually over the back of Helena's chair. Candlelight gleamed off the tux's satin trim and caught the edge of his glasses.

Apple slid into the chair next to Joanna. "I saw Tranh," Apple said.

"What?"

"Remember? The artist I told you about from life drawing? He's the waiter over there. Looks like he's going to say hi to Gil."

A thin Asian man with a shaved head approached Gil with a tray of hors d'oeuvres. The two men were too far away for Joanna to hear, but Tranh's expression was placid, while Gil's eyes shot around the room. Gil placed a hand on Tranh's shoulder, and Tranh moved on with his tray.

Behind Gil, Helena engaged Clary, her eyes fixed fully on him. She turned away briefly and saw Joanna, but when Joanna smiled and waved, Helena returned her smile before turning to Clary. If all went well, at the end of the evening she'd tell her their efforts at the auction house had paid off.

Still no sign of the detective.

"Can I borrow your phone?" Joanna asked Apple.

"You've already left him a bunch of messages. Let it be. Besides, you should get your own phone," she said.

Joanna winced. "No. Not Paul. I want to call Detective Sedillo. See where he is." Damn him. He wouldn't lead her on and then let the whole plan drop, would he? The lights dimmed twice, signaling the guests to be seated.

A hand rested on her shoulder. Detective Sedillo.

"Thank God you showed up," she said. "I thought you'd blown me off."

"Sorry I'm late — you know how hard it is to find a good bou-tonniere in this town?" He sat and spread a linen napkin over the knife-sharp pleats in his tuxedo pants. The fragrance of the detec-tive's gardenia mingled with the scent of dinner drifting from the caterers' entrance.

Joanna leaned closer. "Where are Lee and Tommy? I haven't seen them anywhere."

The detective ignored Joanna's question. "Where's Poppy?" the detective asked. "You're supposed to be watching her."

"She's near the stage. Didn't you come earlier? You know, prepare?"

"Don't worry about it," Sedillo said. "What's for dinner?" Despite his question, the detective's gaze was fixed on the other side of the stage where Poppy, the emcee at her side, pointed here and there in the room, then back to a piece of paper in her hand. Ben and a tall African American man, Poppy's spotters tonight, joined her. They both wore black pants and starched white dress shirts with red bow ties. Of course. Poppy would have coordinated their outfits with hers.

"That one's Ben, her office manager. I'm surprised to see him. He doesn't usually work as a spotter. I don't know the taller guy to his left. If our theory's right—and I think it is—Ben's the one to watch," Joanna said.

"Mmhmm," the detective said as he picked up the menu card at his place. "Don't worry. We talked about all this, remember? Do you think there's cilantro in the Bollywood saumon en croûte? Can't abide the stuff. Julia Child felt the same way, you know."

"You heard what I said about the spotters, right?"

"I heard." He turned over a bit of lettuce on his salad. "Nice. Whole herbs here. A leaf of tarragon." He transferred the tarragon from fork to mouth. "Much better than cilantro."

"Do you even care about Poppy?" Joanna said in frustration. So far it looked like he was only here for the free dinner.

The detective pulled a folded spreadsheet from his jacket's inside pocket. A column of names ran down its long side. Sedillo's finger stopped next to one. "Do you know him?"

Daniel S. Kay. "The trucking guy? I see his name plastered on semis all over. Why?"

"He's at table eight."

"And?"

The detective didn't answer. He slid the list back into his pocket. Most of the guests were seated now. Volunteers hoisted the paintings to be auctioned into the room and placed them on easels along the wall. The music quieted as the emcee rose from her stool at the back of the stage.

Sedillo raised his hand at a passing waiter. "Is there cilantro in the salmon course?"

Come on. Was the detective here to work or eat? Maybe the plan would turn out to be a bust. And what was this about the trucker?

Sedillo held his hand over his wine glass when the waiter passed. "Just water for me tonight."

She hoped this was a good sign.

Chapter 21

A flourish from a five-piece brass ensemble signaled that the program was about to start. The crowd quieted as the emcee took the microphone. "Welcome to Northwest AIDS Project's twenty-sixth annual art auction. With your help, we can prevent new HIV infections and care for people already living with HIV and AIDS. All you have to do is enjoy dinner and take home work from some of the Pacific Northwest's most revered artists."

The emcee, an anchorperson on a local television station, was smaller than she looked on TV. Her starched, frosted hair, however, was larger. Between her hair and sequined mini dress, she resembled an aging refugee from Josie and the Pussycats. Joanna had seen her earlier that evening smoking a cigarette on the loading dock and trading salty words with a security guy. If Joanna had the chance, she'd give her a business card for Tallulah's Closet. In stock now was a size two Angel Sanchez jersey disco dress that was just her style.

From Joanna's seat, she had a straight shot past a table of already-tipsy real estate agents to Helena, Gil, and Clary nearer the stage. She craned her head a bit to get a better view of the guests at that table and made out an attorney who was rumored to be planning a run for City Council, and a smaller, blond woman she didn't recognize. As the woman turned her head, Joanna's stomach dropped. It was Eve. She didn't seem to have noticed Joanna. Eve laughed, and a spray of sparkling fringe from her earrings caught the light. The waiter pouring wine turned his head toward her, and Clary had to touch his arm to draw his attention away from Eve's brilliant smile and back to his empty glass.

Joanna calmed her breathing. Maybe Paul had called her at home and left a message. It would only take a minute to try the pay phone down the street again, to try to explain. The detective had things under control here.

Apple followed Joanna's gaze to the table where Eve sat. She leaned toward Joanna. "Don't even think of calling him again." She tapped the salad plate. "Eat."

The detective, loading up his fork, took Apple's advice to heart, but halfway to his mouth he lowered the fork and emptied it but for a strand of watercress. Finally, he pushed the salad plate away and rose from the table. "I'll be back," he said and lumbered toward the exit.

A handful of black-clad volunteers wearing white gloves stood at the edge of the room in a line next to the easels holding art to be auctioned. One of the volunteers nodded and lifted a painting. Ben was stationed on the other side of the central stage. Only the back of his head showed.

"They're starting, and Sedillo just left," Joanna whispered to Apple.

A waiter slid plates of salmon with roasted cauliflower and potatoes in front of them. "This should bring him back," Apple said.

As the volunteer wove through the dining room holding the painting, the emcee gave a short description of the artist who painted it. "A postmodern masterpiece by one of the Northwest's most esteemed artists," she finished.

Poppy strode to the center of the stage, microphone in hand. As always, Joanna marveled at the presence she commanded. The air around her practically crackled with energy. "Do I have five thousand dollars? Five thousand?" She gestured to a waved bid card. Her words came rapid fire. "Six thousand? A work of art your neighbors will envy. Seven thousand? Mr. Bronson, seven thousand. Seven fifty? Seven thousand five hundred dollars? Sold for seven thousand dollars to Mr. Bronson, bidder number one-thirteen. Congratulations, sir."

A woman holding an abstract sculpture ascended the stage. Joanna scanned the dining room. The detective was still gone. Ben was now in view and seemed to search the crowd, too. Their eyes met for a second. Joanna quickly looked away.

The next painting up was Gil North's. He seemed deliberately not to notice. Two men held *Pacific Five* between them and hovered at the edge of the room until they were summoned to mount the stage. Tranh, Apple and Gil's painting friend, a bus tray held flat in front of him, stood, transfixed, a stone's throw from the painting. Although Apple said he and Gil were close, Gil had his back toward him. Gil turned away from his own painting, too. Curious. It was the rare artist who skipped the chance to gaze at his own work.

"Next, we are honored to present *Pacific Five* by Gil North," the emcee said. Applause rippled through the dining room. "Mr. North donated the painting to the auction before it earned its gold medal. Now is your chance to it take home."

The emcee called Gil to the stage. He rose reluctantly and blinked into the audience.

"Gil North, people." The emcee's sequined dress sparkled in the baby spot light. More applause and a few hoots filled the room. "Tell us about this amazing painting."

From near the caterer's entrance, Tranh stared. He waved away a waiter who tried to draw him toward the kitchen.

"There he is," Joanna whispered to Apple. The detective lurked on the other side of the room, his black tux blending in with the pipe and drape, except for the pinpoint glow of his gardenia.

Gil fidgeted. "I don't really have much to say."

"Reluctant artist." The emcee tossed her bleached waves. "What does this painting mean to you?"

"To me, it's about, well…" a few seconds passed as the painting absorbed him. "It's about the twin sides of freedom. The exhilaration and the responsibility, the choices and the limits." His voice picked up intensity. "The act of painting itself embodies these conflicting but complementary forces. It's choice against limitless options."

He's not an artist so much, Joanna thought, as a thinker about art. A critic, maybe, or a professor. She searched the room again for the detective, but he was gone.

The emcee released Gil to return to his table, where Helena rose and kissed his cheek. Poppy again took center stage. Gil settled next to his wife.

"Do I have five thousand for *Pacific Five*. Bidder seventy-three. Seven-fifty? A masterful work of art, biennial gold medal winner. Thank you, sir. Ten thousand dollars. Do I have ten thousand?" Poppy's words came fast. The spotters moved through the crowd gesturing toward bidders, the white cuffs of their shirts flashing as they stretched their arms.

Helena raised her hand. She was bidding on her own husband's painting. Joanna traded glances with Apple.

"Thank you, Ms. North." A murmur rose from the crowd. "Ms. North at ten thousand dollars. Do I have twelve-fifty, twelve-fifty?"

The detective reappeared near a pillar a few tables down from

Joanna's. His mouth moved and eyes narrowed. He had a radio in his ear. What was going on? He nodded toward someone across the room, and Joanna followed his line of vision to Tommy, in plain black pants and a black button-up shirt. He could have passed for one of the waiters but for his lack of an apron. Tommy nodded in return and his hand moved inside his blazer.

What happened next took only seconds. *Pacific Five* bobbed and fell forward, and the art handlers scrambled to catch it. The crowd gasped. Apple grabbed Joanna's arm. Ben appeared to stoop to the ground for a second, but he was too far away for Joanna to see more than the top of his head disappear. Guests at the table near Ben leapt to their feet. Tommy yanked a pair of handcuffs from his blazer.

"Ben?" Poppy's chatter stopped. Her voice echoed through the warehouse as the room quieted. Even the table of real estate agents halted their alcohol-fueled gabbing. "What's going on?"

Lee joined Tommy now. Ben made an anguished sound as one of them cuffed his wrists. The policeman's lips moved, probably to the Miranda warning. Ben's mouth gaped.

Quick steps nearer Joanna drew her attention away from Ben. Moving with surprising agility, Sedillo grabbed Daniel Kay, the trucking magnate, by the shoulder and pulled his arms behind his back, yanking him to a standing position.

"What the hell is this?" Kay yelled and kicked backward. The table rocked, and red stains spread from fallen wine glasses. The Oscar statuette toppled into a crème brûlée.

"What's happening?" Apple asked. "This isn't what was supposed to happen."

"Everyone stay calm," Sedillo shouted. "Stay in your seats." Tommy and Lee led Ben and the trucking magnate, handcuffed, from the room.

"I don't know," Joanna said. The half-drunk coffee, the bored expressions in that meeting at the police station — this is what they discussed before she arrived. The houselights flashed on, revealing extension cords duct-taped to the concrete floor and highlighting the cheap texture of the table cloths. "I think Sedillo was looking to nail Kay the whole time."

Ben and Daniel Kay. Not Poppy. Despite the commotion around them, Joanna felt joyful, almost giddy with relief. Their plan had worked — somehow. Whatever it was that had transpired, one thing seemed clear: Poppy would not be going back to jail.

Poppy's microphone swung at her side as she stared at the audience. She approached the emcee and whispered in her ear, then descended the stairs.

The detective reappeared next to Joanna and settled in his chair. "The uniforms are taking care of the rest." She had to lean forward to hear him over the mayhem. Sedillo picked up his fork and stabbed a cherry tomato.

"You were after Kay all along, weren't you?" Joanna asked.

Sedillo, his mouth full of salmon, nodded and swallowed. "Uh huh. Once we saw the guest list, we put two and two together."

"That's when you decided to go ahead with the sting."

"Yep. Kay wouldn't pass up the chance to make sure any link between him and the diamonds was severed completely, so he hid gems in the frame of that last painting just before the dinner began. He wanted to foist the blame completely on the auction house. Lee has it all on tape. We've been after him for better than a year."

"But what about Ben?"

"He had no idea — probably still doesn't — who sent the diamonds to the auction house. All he knows is they showed up, and his job was to take them out of their settings and polish off serial numbers, then hide them back in the item they showed up in. Kay had a ring of jewel thieves up and down the coast selling to him."

"So, Poppy is free now, right?"

"We'll have a few loose ends to tie up, but this pretty much clinches it."

The emcee struggled to regain control of the frantic crowd. Clary and Jeffrey argued next to the stage. Jeffrey, his wireless headset bobbing, waved his hands helplessly. Clary spun and walked away, disappearing behind the stage. The brass ensemble stumbled into the theme to *Dr. Zhivago*. Eve coolly sipped wine and examined the Oscar statuette in front of her.

The emcee's microphone squealed. "For chrissakes, everyone shut up!"

The lights dimmed again, but it did little to calm the crowd. The detective sighed and put down his fork. "Follow me."

Joanna trailed Sedillo to the side of the stage, where Jeffrey dispatched one of the caterers to open more champagne in the hopes of quieting the crowd.

The detective stuck out his hand. "Alex Sedillo, Portland P.D. Joanna here will fill you in." He patted Joanna on the shoulder and wandered back toward the table. Jeffrey raised his eyebrows.

"The police caught Donald Kay hiding stolen diamonds in a painting. He'd been moving the diamonds through Poppy's auction house, but she didn't know anything about it. Poppy's completely innocent. Let's make an announcement."

"You." Lacey pushed Jeffrey aside and punched a finger into Joanna's chest. "You ruined this night. I told you we shouldn't have let Poppy come back."

Jeffrey stepped between Lacey and Joanna. "Mr. Kay? But we're hoping on a big gift from him during the paddle raise."

"Yeah, well that's clearly not going to happen now," Joanna said.

Jeffrey hesitated and pulled at his bow tie. "I don't know."

"The party is destroyed, and it's all the fault of that auctioneer," Lacey said.

"Lacey, I think I saw Porsche squatting under table six," Joanna lied.

"Porsche!" Lacey disappeared into the crowd.

Joanna turned to Jeffrey. "Look. People want to know what's going on. We can't just leave them hanging like this. Take charge."

"I can't make this decision myself. I have to ask Clary. Where is he?"

That figures. Joanna squelched her irritation. "I don't know—he was here a second ago. Let me go see if I can find him."

The crowd, drawn to the tables by the pop of champagne corks, was quieting. Joanna glanced toward the table where Clary should be sitting. Helena slid into her chair and checked her lipstick in the reflection off a knife. Clary's chair was empty. Eve locked eyes with Joanna and smiled the classic "teeth together, lips apart."

Damn. It looked as if there would be no way to avoid this. Joanna took a deep breath and approached the table. "Hello, Eve. So nice to see you here." She adjusted her smile. "Where's Clary?"

"He went to the little boy's room." Her silky voice smoothed over the noise like butter on warm brioche. "Where's Paul? I don't see him."

Joanna's face burned. Did Eve know about their fight and was playing with her? She wouldn't put it past her. Joanna forced a laugh. "Not dealing with this mess, that's for sure."

"I would have thought he'd want to be here with you, see what you did with the greeter's dresses. Besides, he's been working pretty hard at my place." Her lips parted slightly. "The man needs a break."

Joanna's blood pressure mounted. "He sure does. I don't know how he puts up with everything he does at work — especially lately." Joanna started to care less about finding Clary than about finding Poppy. Kind, compassionate Poppy. The anti-Eve.

Helena cleared her throat. She seemed to size up the situation at once. "Eve, you have lipstick on your teeth." Eve grabbed her evening bag and pulled out a compact. Meanwhile, Helena leaned closer to Joanna. "What's going on? The police took Donald Kay away."

Eve, examining her flawless, un-lipsticked teeth, opened her mouth to say something, but a hand on Joanna's shoulder drew her attention away. Clary. "Jeffrey told me what happened," he said. "Poppy seems to have disappeared. Go find her and tell her we're getting started again. I'll make an announcement."

Yes, Poppy. At the very least they needed a celebratory glass of bubbly when the night was over. "I'll be back in a minute," Joanna said to Helena.

First Clary, now Poppy. Apparently she was going to spend the rest of the evening rounding up people. She scanned the room. A few tables over, Apple pulled Joanna's dessert to her place and cracked the crème brûlée's top with her spoon. The detective's seat was empty. No Poppy in the dining room.

She might have gone back to the green room to freshen up. Joanna glanced toward the door connecting the green room to the main part of the warehouse. No way she was going that direction — Eve's table was too close. She'd get to the green room through the loading dock.

Joanna pushed through the crowd, then slipped out the side door into the cool night air. A few volunteers stood in the alley smoking cigarettes, their feet crunching the gravel as they moved to let her pass. Gripping the cold handrail, she climbed the cement stairs to the warehouse.

A naked bulb lit the back room. "Poppy?" Joanna called. Muffled speech, probably Clary making the announcement about the arrests, filtered through the concrete walls. Cheers and applause greeted his words. Joanna's heels clicked as she crossed the cement floor to the green room at the back of the warehouse. It was almost unnervingly calm here compared to the chaos next door. "Poppy?" Her voice echoed.

No reply.

Huh. Maybe Poppy had returned to the dining room or the police had asked her to go downtown to answer a few questions. She rubbed her bare shoulders against the chill. Well, since she was here, she might as well grab her wrap. Joanna parted the curtains cordoning off the green room and fumbled for the cord to the shop lamp clamped to the curtain rod. The darkened silhouettes of wardrobe bags draped a rack.

She clicked the light's switch. The shop fixture's brilliant light blinded Joanna for a second. As she blinked away the white orbs, she dropped her purse and backed against the curtain, sending it crashing it down. There, dangling from a beam, was Poppy.

Chapter 22

Joanna ran blindly through the warehouse and to the loading dock. She grasped the railing. "Call the police," she gasped. "The police. The green room."

One of the smokers tossed his cigarette into the gravel and hurried into the dining room. Joanna breathed hard and fast but couldn't get enough air. "Sit down," she heard. Another voice said, "She's going to pass out. Make her breathe into this."

Joanna slumped to the concrete pad. A paper bag that smelled of take-out burrito clamped over her mouth. She pulled the bag away. "Get her—" She wanted to tell them to get Poppy down, take her down. The bag clamped to her mouth again, and again she swatted it away. "I have to—" She tried to suck in air, but her lungs were so tight. She had to tell them. She had to get Poppy down.

Someone pushed her back on the concrete and fastened the bag over her mouth with callused fingers. Another hand cradled her head. "Shut up and breathe."

The next few minutes seemed to stretch forever. Joanna's vision faded, and voices drifted far away as her consciousness waned. Eventually, struggling for oxygen, her lungs loosened and drew deeply.

The hand lifted the bag from her mouth. "That's better," a deep voice said.

"Let me talk to her." Detective Sedillo. His bulky form knelt on the loading dock. The scent of his gardenia pierced the settling cigarette smoke.

"Did you get her down?" Joanna's breathing was still uneven, but she wasn't going to faint now.

"She's down." The words sounded final.

"And?" It's not too late, she prayed. Whatever happened, they'd get past it, they'd celebrate yet.

"I'm sorry."

No, she thought. Please. No. "Sorry?" she whispered.

Sedillo shifted knees. "The medical examiner will say for sure, but it looks like suicide."

"It was my fault." Joanna told Apple. She kicked her heels off on her living room floor and fell into the couch. "Poppy didn't want to do the auction, but I convinced her. I keep thinking of her, the rope. One of her shoes had fallen—" She'd pushed away the image of Poppy's body, but that shoe haunted her. One black calf stiletto on its side.

"I know, I know," Apple said gently. She put her handbag on Joanna's dining room table. "I'm going to make some tea. It's practically morning, anyway."

"Go ahead. I'm getting out of this dress."

In the bedroom, Joanna stripped off her gown and pulled on a plaid Beacon bathrobe, leaving a pile of black rayon and rhinestones on the bed. She shivered. "Let's make a fire. It's cold in here. I don't see myself going to sleep any time soon." Maybe never, with the way she felt.

Soon, Apple and Joanna sat on cushions in front of the fire with mugs of dark tea. Pepper padded in from the bedroom and stretched on the tile hearth, his black fur soaking up the heat.

Apple searched Joanna's face. "Do you really think she killed herself?"

"No." Sure, Poppy had hesitated to work again, to be in public in front of so many people, but she'd seemed so vibrant and happy at the auction. "She couldn't have. Besides, the sting worked. She knew she wouldn't go back to jail. There's no way."

"I don't think so, either. Her energy was so good."

Joanna's breathing quickened.

"Inhale. A long one. There." Apple came over to the couch and sat down.

"I should have never convinced her to work the auction. She didn't want to, you know. She said she had a bad feeling about it." Joanna had tried to make things better and failed. Colossally. Had she listened to Poppy—and Paul—Poppy might still be alive.

"You didn't hang her, Jo. If someone was bent on killing her, he would have done it whether she was at the auction or not. It's just that the hullaballoo of arresting Ben gave the murderer good cover. Poppy seemed happy at the auction, not like she was there against her will."

"Then at the station." Fluorescent lights, raised voices, the clatter of the keyboard. "I told Sedillo everything I could think of. They brought in Detective Crisp from homicide, and he worked me over, too." She shifted her hips. The fire's warmth was beginning to reach her.

"Let's talk about something else. You need to relax." The fire popped and a cinder flew into the chain curtain. Pepper started, then settled again to warm his other side.

"I'm fine, thanks. I just need a while to process everything."

Apple returned to her chair. Her eyes shifted to the answering machine.

Paul. Joanna knew the machine's light shone steady — she'd checked it as soon as they entered. "No, he didn't call."

Apple jumped on this new topic of conversation. "Where did you leave things with him?"

Joanna sighed and leaned back. "This is not relaxing chat, by the way. But the answer to your question is 'nowhere.' He told me I had to choose between him and Poppy, and when I wouldn't do it he walked out. Now he won't return my calls."

"I don't know why you promised not to get involved in the first place. Why didn't you explain it to him?"

"I couldn't. I know it sounds stupid now, but I was afraid he'd break up with me. I figured I could pull everything off without telling him. It didn't seem like such a big deal at the time. Besides, why should he be telling me what to do?"

"Look how well that worked. I'm not saying he doesn't have issues, but you could have talked it over earlier."

"Right." Joanna stared at the fire.

"Jo?"

"I keep thinking about Poppy. I had a hand in this — this trouble — and now there's nothing I can do to make it better."

"You need to put your mind somewhere else for a few days. Take it easy." Pepper jumped into Apple's lap. "Focus on Paul. Explain things to him. That, at least, you can do something about."

Joanna showed no signs of hearing Apple. Her gaze remained fixed on the fire. "I never could figure out how Vivienne's death tied into the diamonds, either."

"Diamonds were found in Vivienne's things. That's the most obvious connection."

"Might have been coincidence. Maybe the police only found them because they were looking. Diamonds could have been hidden in other lots. Who knows? But maybe somehow Vivienne found out what was going on, so she was poisoned." She pulled a piece of split alder from the basket next to the fireplace and opened the screen. When the new log caught fire, she returned to the couch.

"If Poppy's death wasn't suicide, then whoever killed Poppy had to be at the event," Apple said.

The adrenaline that had kept Joanna up all night was starting to ebb. She rubbed her eyes. "That limits the suspects to about five hundred people."

Apple settled a hand on Pepper's back. "Or worse. The back of the warehouse—the area we set up in—was open all night. Once the event started, it was empty. The caterers were all on the opposite side. Anyone could have gone in there."

Joanna picked up her mug of tea. The Sunday newspaper thunked at her front door. Pepper lifted his head. What an awful, awful day.

"Don't go there, Jo." Apple set her tea cup on the coffee table. "I need to get home. Gavin's waiting, but I don't want to leave you alone." She dumped Pepper off her lap and pushed open a velvet curtain. An apricot sunrise streaked the sky. Across the street, a bundled woman walked a Bernese Mountain dog. "People are already up." She turned to Joanna. "Will you be all right?"

Joanna rose and hugged Apple. "I'm fine. Thanks for seeing me home."

She locked the door behind Apple and turned toward the living room. The fire was dying. Paul's work shirt still draped across the couch's arm. Where the hell was he, anyway? Didn't he know she needed him? She touched his shirt, then pulled it over her and settled on the couch to sleep, willing away the image of Poppy's dangling body.

Chapter 23

When Joanna awoke, the fire was dead and the midday sun streamed through the front window. Pepper had made himself at home sleeping on her stomach. She lifted him off, then swung her legs to the floor. She stretched her back. The couch was no Posturepedic, that was for sure.

She brought a cup of coffee to the bathroom and drew a bath. Last night's mascara caked around her eyes. Normally a bath equalized her moods, but today all the soap in the world wouldn't wash away her sadness—and foreboding.

She reached for a towel. What was Paul doing today? He usually started his workday early, but this was Sunday. He might be at the convent, or—Joanna let the thought pass quickly—at Eve's. Maybe Eve called him after the auction to fill him in on the diamond bust and Poppy's death. But he might be at home, too, reading the Sunday paper with Gemma at his feet.

If this were a normal Sunday, they'd be together. They'd make waffles or omelets or walk up to the bakery for pastries. He'd let her talk about Poppy, and his presence alone would be a comfort. Not today.

Tallulah's Closet wasn't due to open yet, but she could go in early and sort through Vivienne's clothes. Three trunks full needed sizing and tagging. Joanna let that idea rest in her brain. Nothing. Not the tiniest hint of excitement. When gazing at vintage Dior couture didn't rouse her, something was truly wrong. Not that she should be surprised.

"Aunt Vanderburgh," Joanna asked the pastel of a tight-lipped woman on the living room wall, "What should I do?"

Auntie V stared reproachfully.

"Okay, you win." Apple was right—maybe she couldn't do anything about Poppy, but she could at least find out where she stood with Paul, try to explain. She pulled her "pinochle dress," a 1950s housedress with a blue and gray print of alternating queen of hearts and jack of spades, from her closet and took a thick wool cardigan from a hook inside the door. With both hands she pulled her hair into a pony tail—no time, or need, to get fancy. She dabbed some vintage Femme perfume between her breasts for luck.

Paul clearly wasn't going to respond to her calls. If he wouldn't come to her, she'd go to him.

Paul's shop windows were dark. Joanna knocked on the door anyway and heard the dog bark. "Hush, Gemma," Joanna said through the door, and Gemma the Beast gave a short, happy yip, nails scrambling on the cement floor. Joanna had bought some muffins for Paul as a peace offering. Their fragrance wafted from their bag.

She cupped her hands around her eyes to peer through the door's window. Two unfinished drawers sat on Paul's workbench, but he didn't appear to be home. Gemma scratched at the door again and ran in a tight circle. Joanna paused. He hadn't asked for his key back. If they were broken up, she had no right to be there. But everything had happened so suddenly. It couldn't be over yet. They still needed to talk. "Oh, all right," she said to Gemma and let herself in.

The dog whined and licked her hand. Joanna pulled a jar from on top of the refrigerator and gave her a dog biscuit. Gemma took it to the corner of the workshop, near her bed, to eat.

Joanna stood in the center of the shop, immobile. Now that she was in, she knew she shouldn't be there. A few days ago, he would have welcomed her dropping by and leaving a note. Not now. Besides, she'd broken his trust already. She'd better leave before he returned.

Had she had left footprints in the sawdust? No, the path from the front door to the kitchen had been swept clean. A faint clattering pierced the silence, and Joanna jumped before realizing it must have come from the cleaning crew in the kitchen of the restaurant next door.

"Bye, Gemma," Joanna said, bending to give her a last stroke between the ears, when a small piece of ivory bond paper on the floor caught her attention. She leaned forward. Eve's name and phone number were written in a woman's loose script. Her heart tightened. Of course he'd need Eve's phone number, she thought. He was doing work for her. He had to be able to get in touch with her to work.

Or something else.

She struggled to slow her breath. Turn and walk away, she told herself, but stopped short. Cradled in tissue paper next to some small-tipped hand tools on the workbench was a box no bigger than her palm. She crept closer to examine it. Dozens of dovetails fastened its edges. Finely honed strips of wood — pink, pale yellow, the honey tones of pine — were sanded to a satin finish. An ornate letter "J" was inlaid across its lid. This box was — had been — for her. She knew it would have taken Paul countless evenings to make it, to hone its edges seamless. She lifted its lid. Empty.

Ashamed, she turned toward the door. Her stupid reluctance to talk had ruined everything. It couldn't be too late, though, could it? If she could just see Paul again and explain how she'd had to try to help Poppy. They could make it work. She'd tell him so — if he ever talked to her again, that is.

She took a last glance around the shop and strode the few steps to the door.

The rumble of an engine cutting out disturbed the silence. Gemma raised her head. Paul? Joanna stood motionless, holding her breath. A car door slammed shut, jarring her. Her purse tumbled off her arm to the floor, spilling its contents. A second later she heard two voices — neither of them Paul's — cross the alley. She let out her breath.

Before Joanna could stop her, the dog had ripped through the bakery bag and made short work of one of the muffins. A shrunken blueberry stuck to her lip.

Joanna knelt to pick up lipsticks and crumpled receipts and stuff them back in her purse. God, she was exhausted. This was ridiculous. She had to forget about Paul for the moment, leave him alone. But what next? She couldn't just go home. She'd climb the walls. She had to do something.

The Mother Superior. Yes, that's what she'd do. She'd go tell the Mother Superior about the auction as she'd promised. Plus she needed to talk to Mary Alberta about Tallulah's Closet's website. First she'd stop by the store, then go to the convent. Maybe by then she'd have the energy to inventory and tag some of Vivienne's clothing.

The light filtering through the windows on the garage door dimmed as the sun moved behind clouds. Time to get out of here now, before anything else happened. The dog jumped into an armchair licking her lips then her paw. Standing at the door looking back at the shop, Joanna couldn't see any trace she'd been there.

She closed the door. It locked behind her.

Chapter 24

"I'd wondered if you'd come in today." Apple set down the pen she was using to write price tags.

Joanna tossed her purse behind the tiki bar and absently picked up a price tag. "You'll be spotted in this lovely leopard cardigan," she read. "That line never gets old. Did you get to bed once you got home?"

"Surprisingly, yes. Gavin's the one who suffered. He stayed up waiting for me, then couldn't get to sleep. I hope he went back to bed after I left. What about you?"

"I conked out on the couch. I kept thinking about Poppy, though."

They were both quiet a moment, Joanna staring at her hands, and Apple looking out the window.

"She's passed over," Apple said. "She's in a better place now."

It could have sounded trite, but Apple's words comforted Joanna. She reached out and touched Apple's shoulder in thanks. Apple grabbed her hand and squeezed it.

"I thought about Paul, too. All this with Poppy drives home, well..." Joanna started. "I went to see him this morning, but he wasn't home." She leaned on the tiki bar. "I messed it up for good with him." She looked up, hopeful Apple might have another take on the situation. "Or maybe not?"

Apple averted her eyes and busied herself with a display of scarves.

"I don't know. You can give it a try."

Joanna sat on the red velvet bench at the center of the store. "Poppy, Paul — it's too much. I feel like I'm losing it. I want to do something, but I can't. And — " She bit her lip. "I'm turning into a crazy stalker. I've got to pull it together."

Apple hurried to the bench and took Joanna by the shoulders. "Jo, honey, it's all right."

She leaned her head against Apple's sturdy shoulder. "Thanks for being my friend." Her eyes started to tear up.

"As your friend," Apple said, "I suggest you hustle to the bathroom. Here comes the Baronet up the street, and it looks like he's headed to the store."

Clary? Head bent, Joanna rushed to the tiny bathroom at the rear of the store, just beyond the tiki bar. She closed the flimsy door and ran water on a paper towel.

"...Joanna?" She heard Clary say.

"She's running errands now. I can tell her you stopped by," Apple said. "How did the auction do, I mean, given everything — "

"Fine, fine. I don't know." Clary sounded a little confused.

"And Poppy. I can't believe it. We were at the police station nearly all night."

"A tragedy. We're donating a portion of the auction's proceeds to the Cat Adoption Team, one of Poppy's charities. Feeble, I know, but it's the least we can do."

There was a pause. "Was there something in particular you wanted from Joanna? Maybe something I can help you with?"

Joanna willed her breathing to calm and leaned against the bathroom door to hear more clearly.

"I wanted to buy a gift, for a woman." Confidence returned to

Clary's voice.

Joanna raised an eyebrow.

"Great, tell me about her. We have an amazing selection of costume jewelry right now."

"She's a woman with very fine taste, you know what I mean? I'd like to buy her something rare, not ostentatious, but something other people wouldn't have. That's why I was thinking vintage."

Who was Clary buying for? He wasn't at the auction with a date. Of course, as the committee chair he was working that night.

"How about a minaudière? We have a 1980s Judith Leiber shaped like a peony."

A pause. Joanna leaned closer to the door. "Nice, but too flashy. Do you have something more subtle, something high quality but that doesn't draw attention to itself? The kind of thing Joanna would like."

Clary's voice faded. Apple must be leading him to another part of the store. Joanna dabbed her eyes with the paper towel again and examined her face in the mirror. The bathroom window let in the scant light from the alley. The skin under her eyes had darkened.

"That would be perfect," she heard Clary say. "It's not priced, though."

"We just got it in. It's Hermès, a classic pattern. These are almost impossible to find, especially in such great condition. Look how the hem is rolled and hand stitched, not even crushed after all these years." God, Apple was good. "We're pricing it at three hundred dollars." Joanna gasped. She would have put the scarf at one twenty-five and been open to bargaining.

"Sold. Do you have a box?" Clary asked.

Apple deserved a raise.

"Uh, Joanna...is she still seeing that construction worker?"

"You mean Paul?" Apple asked.

Joanna wrinkled her nose. Construction worker, right. Artisan was more like it, the snob. But why did Clary care about her personal life? It couldn't be that — no. No, he wouldn't be interested in her, would he? If so, he certainly wouldn't be buying gifts for her at her own shop. That Joanna had ever even found him attractive mystified her. He probably didn't know a drill press from a band saw. What's the use of having a boyfriend if you're the one who always has to fix the toilet?

"Yeah, whatever his name is. I didn't see him at the auction."

"He had something to take care of," Apple said. "Here's the scarf. I'm sure she'll love it. Thanks again."

After a minute, Apple opened the bathroom door. "The coast is clear."

"Nice work with the scarf. I wonder who it's for?"

Apple put away Clary's credit card receipt. "Maybe Helena. I saw them at the auction. They looked — intimate."

"Ha. That was Vivienne's scarf." The scarf would suit Helena. Clary had good taste. "They can't be having an affair, though. She's wild about her husband."

"I got the sense there was something between them."

"I don't believe it," Joanna said.

Apple shrugged. "Stranger things have happened."

Chapter 25

Joanna pulled Old Blue up the horseshoe-shaped driveway at the side of the convent near the kitchen door. The Toyota's engine shuddered off with a wheeze. Drizzle misted the air, but the garden trellis, choked with clematis, kept Joanna dry as she popped the trunk and began to unload the dresses she had borrowed for the auction.

Curiously, no one came out to help. Light shone from the kitchen, but none of the sisters appeared at the window. Joanna laid the dresses back in the trunk and walked around the side of the house. So that's where everyone was. A ladder leaned against the siding, and standing near its top was Paul, putty knife in hand. Her heart seized. Of course. He'd promised to come back and repair the dry rot this weekend. Clustered at the bottom of the ladder were a handful of Marys watching with various levels of adoration. Mary Alberta, hand on hip, stood at the edge.

Paul glanced down and nodded at Joanna but continued working. Her face burned. She cleared her throat. "Mary Alberta, I brought back Vivienne's dresses. They're in my trunk. And I was hoping to talk to you about maybe doing some design work for my website."

Mary Alberta, who seemed more interested in the spectacle than in watching Paul sand a window frame, followed Joanna to the car. "Praise the Lord, we just got a check for what we earned from

Vivienne's estate. Mary Frances is doing all the figuring, but we're getting a new roof, a furnace, and maybe even a flat screen TV. Mary Carmen hates to go to the bars to watch her hockey matches."

Joanna's glance stole back to Paul.

"You'd think they'd have something better to do than stand around and gape at someone working. Honestly." Mary Alberta nudged Joanna back to the car. "Although he's your boyfriend and all."

"Uh huh," Joanna said and unlocked the trunk again.

"Trouble?"

"Let's not talk about that." She looked at Mary Alberta. "Please."

"As you like. I'll help you with those." Mary Alberta slung the dresses over a beefy arm and led the way into kitchen. "Let's put them in Mary Estelle's old room, upstairs."

They mounted the stairs and entered a small bedroom at the front of the convent. Even on the opposite side of the house from where Paul worked Joanna was acutely aware of his presence.

Faded wallpaper festooned with roses lined the bedroom's walls. Two rolling wardrobe racks sat to one side, and a desk with Mary Alberta's laptop filled the niche between the painted chimney of the fireplace and the outside wall.

"It's nice to be able to use this room since Mary Estelle died." Mary Alberta hung up the dresses in their wardrobe bags. She paused a moment and looked out the window. "I miss her. But I feel like she's helping me as I work. And I've kept up her subscription to *Vogue*." She pushed open the closet to reveal stacks of fashion magazines, including some from the early 1950s, squashed on the bottom.

Joanna recognized a little of the heartache she herself felt. "You're doing good work. The website you made was brilliant. I'm hoping you're willing to work on mine. Now that I have Vivienne's dresses,

I really need to ramp it up." Yes, and sell at least two of them before the end of the month so she could make her loan payment. "The web designer I hired just didn't get it."

Mary Alberta's thoughtful look disappeared. "Come downstairs and let's talk about concept. I'm thinking we could go with a hyper-sophisticated, stark layout similar to Irving Penn's late 1940s, early 1950s fashion work. If you know anyone skinny enough to model for it, that is." She unplugged the laptop and started down the hall. "Alternatively, I see an elegant, slightly Dada interface with visual references to Luis Buñuel."

Luis Buñuel? The TV would be showing more than hockey games, Joanna noted.

Downstairs, white streaked the edges of the a few of living room's windowpanes. Mary Alberta, seeing her glance, said, "Paul replaced the bottom pane and fixed some dry rot." She put her hands on her hips. "Did he cheat on you?"

Joanna's jaw dropped. "No, nothing like that."

"I didn't think so. Doesn't seem the type, but you never know."

Mary Alberta plugged the laptop in an outlet near the coffee table. Images of Vivienne's dresses sprang to life.

"Such lovely dresses," Joanna said. "Did Vivienne know the Mother Superior a long time?"

"A while. I think they went back some years but hadn't seen each other until recently. They ran into each other at the hospital, of all places. Mother doesn't leave the convent much, and usually the doctor'll come here, but that time he wanted her for X-rays."

Joanna shifted to avoid a spring in the sofa that poked at her rump. "When was that?"

"About a year ago, give or take, I'd guess. So, maybe you were cheating on Paul? Looking around a little?"

"Mary Alberta. Absolutely not. I told you I didn't want to talk about it."

"Well, you're asking a lot of questions, and we're supposed to be talking business," she pointed out. Something interrupted Mary Alberta's line of sight. She bolted to her feet. "I'm going upstairs for a minute."

Joanna turned to see what had distracted her. Paul came into the room, almost brushing shoulders with the sister as she hurried down the hall.

"How are you? I heard about Poppy. I'm sorry." He kept his distance.

Breath quickening, she stood. "I'm fine." What a stupid thing to say. She was not fine. "I mean —" Her voice broke. "Did you get my phone messages?"

He nodded. "Yes. Sorry I didn't get back to you right away." He glanced out the window. "I needed to take some time to think."

This did not sound good.

"I'm too worried about you. You promised me you'd stay out of Poppy's business, but you didn't."

"But I —" She faltered.

He shook his head and looked away from Joanna. "You broke your promise. And look what happened."

A lump hardened in Joanna's throat. "I know. But what choice did I have?"

He took a deep breath. "I'm sorry about Poppy. You two were friends. I know how awful you must feel. But there's nothing more to say. I'm afraid this would be just the beginning for you."

"Look, I made a mistake in not telling you, okay? You can trust me."

He shook his head and looked away. "I care about you. I do. But we need to take a break. Take some time apart and think about things."

The corny old songs were right, the pain really does burn in the heart. In this case the pain seemed to occupy her whole chest cavity. She sank to the couch and leaned back. Of course, "a break" is what he said. Just a break. Maybe he'd realize he missed her and they could work things out. Or—her heart twisted again—he'd be happier without her.

"Do you understand?" he asked.

She pulled her cardigan tighter. "No," she said in a small voice. "But I'm not sure that matters." So that was it. They locked eyes for a moment before he turned away.

The hall door opened and the Mother's wheelchair ground across the floor. With a push, the Mother heaved her chair over the molding dividing the living room's worn carpet from the wood in the hall. "That Paul is a lovely man. Thank you, Joanna, for bringing him to us. Truly a blessing."

Mary Alberta appeared behind her. She drew a finger across her neck and shook her head. "She doesn't want to talk about it, Mother. They're taking a break. And she's asking a lot of questions. Probably thinks we might have killed the auctioneer who handled Vivienne's things."

The Mother smiled benignly. "Of course she does. Hysterical, probably, from romantic problems."

"It's not like that. You were listening, weren't you?" Joanna shot a glowering look at Mary Alberta.

"Child," the Mother said, "I know you told me you wouldn't follow up on Vivienne's death — "

"That doesn't matter anymore," Joanna said, her voice dull. "The person who killed Vivienne might have killed Poppy, too. I'm convinced it wasn't suicide. I want to find the murderer." She had nothing to lose now.

Without turning her head, the Mother shouted, "Mary Frances, make some tea. The good tea. Enough for two." She rolled her wheelchair further into the room. "Then sit down and put that romantic nonsense out of your head for a minute. We have a lot to talk about."

Joanna obeyed, lowering herself onto the sofa.

"I've been getting a very bad feeling about Vivienne's situation," the Mother Superior said. She cranked her wheelchair a few inches closer. "Our money's been released, and I should be relieved. Something is wrong." She leaned back. "I'm overdue for a report. Talk to me. I need some insight."

Joanna remembered Apple's observation that the Mother "was psychic, too." Apple was pagan, and Joanna had spent hours hearing her chat about spells or ponder the meaning of a dream. But a nun? It was hard to imagine the Pope being keen on clairvoyance. "What do you mean about a 'very bad feeling'?"

"Your friend, the one named after a fruit. She gets it."

"Apple." Joanna sat, hands in lap, and waited for an explanation. Warm tea would feel good. The waning adrenaline from her talk with Paul added to her exhaustion left her hands cold and shaky.

"Maybe you think it's strange I get these feelings. It's not. I'm an old woman, Joanna, and I grew up in New Orleans. We learned to pay attention to these things."

Mary Frances returned with a tray — its silver worn in patches — a teapot, and cups. "I brought out the good teapot since you're using the good tea. I hope that's all right."

"It's quite all right, thank you." Mary Frances's wimple fluttered as she left the room. "Would you pour this for me?" the Mother asked.

Joanna lifted the teapot. Bone china. The tea's amber shadow shone through painted lilies on the teapot's thin wall. The tea was fragrant with vanilla and fruit.

The mother breathed its perfume and the muscles in her face relaxed. "Marco Polo. One of my favorite blends. A former donné sends us a tin every Christmas."

"But what about the church? What does it think about these feelings you get?"

The Mother swatted air with her free hand. "Pshaw. God gives us gifts. Look at the Bible, it's full of visions." She set the cup in its saucer. "My mother, for instance. She could cure just about anything with one of her special herbal mixtures. I, on the other hand, have the gift of knowing things — some things — before they happen. Oh, it's not like I get a full picture of whatever it is," she added hurriedly. "I just get a feeling, a snatch of sound. An image."

"But maybe it's all the subconscious. You notice someone's discomfort or sense a sort of change in the weather, and that's where these psychic flashes come from."

"Maybe." She reached for her cup again. "You have a gift, too, you know."

"Me?" This ought to be good. Joanna was as practical as they came. Her greatest gift was putting together an outfit around a plaid 1940s suit jacket.

"You notice things. You didn't think I saw you watching the tea through the porcelain pot?"

Joanna laughed, a little relieved. "Who doesn't?"

"A lot of people don't. Tell me, what's on the table next to my bed upstairs?"

"What?"

"Tell me."

"All right." Joanna turned her head to the right and let her gaze soften. A picture of the Mother's nightstand assembled itself in her brain. "A green orchid with ruffled petals tinged in carmine red. In a pink cache pot."

"A lot of people would have noticed that, although perhaps not the exact colors. What else?"

"A Spode saucer in the primrose pattern with a chip on one side and what looked like pink macaron crumbs on it; a pale blue folded handkerchief, cotton; a pair of red clear plastic reading glasses. And you're missing one of the two knobs on the drawer." Joanna hesitated. "One more thing."

"Yes?"

"A paperback copy of a Mickey Spillane mystery with what looked like a prayer card stuck in as a bookmark. *My Gun is Quick,*" she finished.

The Mother sniffed. "Jesus is always in our minds, but perhaps not always in our reading material. But you see what I mean. You pay attention, daughter. You see things, feel them, smell them. Vivienne had that gift, too." Her voice quieted. "You'd be surprised how rare that is."

"That's not so rare."

The Mother held up a hand, palm out in a "stop" gesture. "It is. But that's not all. You make things come to you."

Joanna had raised her teacup partway to her lips, but she lowered it. It clinked in the saucer. "Make things come to me? I don't understand."

"You think about things, and they come to you. If you want something, you will manifest it."

Joanna remembered Paul and shook her head.

"No, it doesn't work with people. But how often have you thought you needed something — say, dresses for the charity auction — and you found them?"

"That was simply following up." Her face burned. How did the Mother know she was thinking of Paul?

"As you say, dear. I bet if you put your mind to finding, say, a copy of *My Gun is Quick* it would come your way without effort."

Ridiculous. Sure, she was often lucky at thrift stores and estate sales, but that was plain old perseverance. That's how life was. You buy an orange car and suddenly you see orange cars everywhere. You realize the store needs more shoes, you find a few pairs of vintage shoes at Goodwill.

"Another cup of tea, please," the Mother Superior said. "And I'm ready for your report on the charity auction."

"All right." Joanna reached for the teapot. "It was an awful night." She told the Mother about the sting operation, ending with finding Poppy in the green room, dead. As she talked, she rose and paced the room. The Mother nodded every few seconds. "It couldn't be suicide," Joanna concluded. "I'm convinced."

The Mother's hands clenched then released the wheels on her chair. The veins on her hands corded blue beneath her white skin.

"I feel horrible — responsible," Joanna added.

"You couldn't know what would happen, child."

"No, but if I hadn't suggested Poppy work the auction she wouldn't have been killed." She'd wanted to clear Poppy's name. Paul had warned her against it. But what good was proving her innocent of selling diamonds if she was dead? "I've been wracking my brain trying to figure out what I can do that the police can't."

"Sit down." the Mother patted the sofa. "All that pacing makes me nervous. Now, I have something to share that might help."

Joanna's head shot up. "I'm listening."

"I said it might help. I don't know. A few weeks ago, maybe three, Vivienne" — the Mother made the sign of the cross— "came with us to Oaks Amusement Park. We're working with a group that serves foster children, and that day we took the children for the morning session. We do that sometimes. They can go on the rides, and there's a story hour with cookies and milk. I didn't think I'd go, but Vivienne convinced me it would be good to get out of the house. She brought Helena to help with the wheelchair."

"Yes." Joanna settled on the sofa. Her full attention was on the Mother.

"During story hour — it's charming, they have one of the state dairy princesses read a story— Helena and Vivienne went for a walk to see the rest of the park. Neither of them had been there before. They couldn't have been gone five minutes when Vivienne came back alone. She said Helena had run off. Vivienne was distracted the rest of the morning."

Joanna leaned forward. "I don't suppose you know what happened between Vivienne and Helena?"

"No. No, I don't. Vivienne kept saying, 'I knew something wasn't right. I knew it.' But she never explained. Perhaps that's a clue." She emphasized the word "clue." "Anything else unusual you've noted? Something you might have overlooked?"

"No. I've gone over it in my head a hundred times. I thought we'd catch the real diamond thief at the NAP auction and clear Poppy's name. Then from there the police could figure out who killed Vivienne. Separately."

"Think harder, dear. What else? Use your gift." The Mother's tone became more insistent. "What else is strange about anyone involved in the case? Anything. Anything might point us in the right direction." She rapped the table. "We need to think about things the police missed."

In another world, the Mother would have made a good police detective. "Well, a friend of Helena's, Clary, bought an expensive gift for a woman. Apple thinks it might be for Helena."

"Interesting. Interesting. Of course, you'll visit Helena and follow up on that. See if you sense any untoward relationship. Some people will do almost anything to hide an affair. What else?" The mother's arthritic knuckles were knobs around the teacup's handle.

Joanna concentrated. "It probably doesn't mean anything, but Vivienne's son, Gil, painted something that won a prize in the art biennial, but he seems bizarrely disconnected from it, almost like he's ashamed. Plus, Apple says something is going on between him and another artist, Tranh."

"You'll visit this gentleman, too, of course. I'll expect to hear back right away." She set her cup on the coffee table. "When is Poppy's funeral? You'll go to that and look for clues. It's the plan."

The plan. Yes, a plan. The Mother was right. Joanna had been successful at rooting out the diamond sales. She could surely dig up more information about Poppy's death — and so perhaps Vivienne's, assuming that they were linked — that the police might miss.

"I expect regular reports. And don't dilly dally about it. In fact, you still have time today."

Joanna paused, lost in thought.

The Mother stared at her. "You have work to do, dear." She leaned her head back and yelled. "Mary Frances? Clear Joanna's things. She's leaving. The Lord helps those who help themselves, and we don't have time to spare."

Joanna tossed back the last of her cooling tea before Mary Frances wrenched the cup from her hand.

"Too bad you spoiled your chances with Paul, or he could have helped you," the Mother said.

That did it. She rose and slid her purse's strap over her shoulder. "You're right, I have to go."

Satisfied smile on her face, the Mother wheeled her chair from the room.

Mary Alberta met Joanna in the hall. "I'll work up some design concepts, then Mary Frances and I will get back to you with a proposal."

Joanna looked up, surprised. Oh yes, Tallulah's Closet's website. "Thanks."

The sister opened the door to damp, cool air. "So about Paul. Did he go about leaving the toilet seat up and watching sports? Is that why you broke up?"

"Give it up, Mary Alberta."

$\mathcal{C}$hapter 26

Joanna placed the grocery bag on the kitchen counter. From its depths she lifted a bag of clams, thick slices of applewood smoked bacon wrapped by the butcher, a red bell pepper, and a bottle of Pinot Noir. Despite the Mother's insistence she track down "clues" immediately, she was going to stay in this evening and revive her pre-Paul tradition of Hors d'Oeuvres Sunday. She'd make clams casino for dinner.

There were a lot of things she used to do before she met Paul, and she missed them. For one thing, music. Joanna went to the stereo and slid Wagner's *Tristan und Isolde* from her stack of record albums. Paul wasn't a big fan of opera, but sometimes she craved it. The record dropped to the turntable, and the strings of the overture filled the living room.

She returned to the kitchen and dumped the clams into a strainer. She opened the wine and poured a glass and lifted it to her nose. Pinot Noir's mossy perfume beat the fragrance of any other wine she knew. Tonight would be a good night. Maybe it wasn't so bad that she and Paul were taking a break, she told herself. She began methodically opening the clams and setting each bite of meat in its half shell on a baking dish. Paul would never consent to a meal of clams casino and nothing else. It wouldn't be enough for him.

Of course, if she added one more appetizer—say, stuffed mush-rooms—he might go for it. He might even think it was fun. Or not. She'd never asked him. He used to love it when she made something new for him, and he'd become expert in tasting the difference between marjoram and oregano, or morels and chanterelles.

While Birgit Nielsson lamented Tristan's love, Joanna layered a square of red bell pepper and bacon over each clam, then sprinkled chopped parsley and butter in the baking dish. She poured in a little vermouth and slid the dish into the oven. While the clams baked, it was time for step two of her old Sunday night ritual: her bath.

She brought the glass of wine to the bathroom and turned on the taps. World War Two-era houses didn't normally have clawfoot bathtubs, but Joanna had found a tub used as a planter, then had it refinished and its feet plated with nickel. It took three men an hour peppered with sailorly exclamations to shoehorn the tub into her tiny bathroom, but it paid itself back every time she slipped into its white porcelain.

Joanna fixed a chopstick through her hair to keep it out of the water and stepped into the tub. Ahh, the warm water. She set her wineglass on the toilet tank, which she'd draped with a towel. One of the beauties of having a small bathroom was that the toilet tank doubled as a tub-side table.

The record player dropped the next LP and its arm settled into the groove. Yearning filled the singers' voices. Joanna sighed. Maybe this opera wasn't such a good choice after all.

Last night at this time she was sitting down with Apple at the auction. Poppy was still alive. The Mother Superior told her she had the gift of noticing and remembering things. Joanna closed her eyes and replayed the part of the evening after Ben and Donald Kaye were arrested, before Poppy was killed. What happened?

She saw Poppy standing on the stage, holding the microphone. Poppy whispered something to the emcee, then stepped down the back of the stage to the door connecting to the green room. What was going on in the dining room? Chaos, that's what. The house lights went on and Joanna's attention had been drawn back to Detective Sedillo at her table. Then they decided to make an announcement about the arrests, then Joanna went to find Poppy. Poppy, her head flopped like a rag doll's. She took a big gulp of wine and choked a bit. All told, Poppy had been out of the room not more than fifteen minutes before Joanna found her.

During that time, someone had seen Poppy leave and followed her. Who was it? Clary had been gone from his table when Joanna looked for him. Eve was still there. Helena came back from some-where— the restroom?— and sat down just as Joanna approached the table. Wait, Gil had been gone, too. They arrived at the table at the same time. Had Gil come from the direction of the kitchen, or was he with Helena? She couldn't tell. He had definitely been upset by Helena's bidding on his painting.

In the bedroom, Joanna had laid out one of her best dressing gowns— a ruched-silk lavender gown from the 1930s with a small train and lucite buttons. She planned to do it up right tonight. Wrapped in a towel, Joanna looked at the dressing gown, now with Pepper's black body curled up on it. Maybe she'd go with comfort instead. She reached for the thick Beacon robe hanging on the edge of the door and stepped into shearling-lined slippers instead of her fur-tipped satin slides.

She pulled the clams casino from the oven, topped off her wine, and prepared for step three of her Sunday night ritual: an old movie.

Tonight it would be *My Man Godfrey*. Sure, she'd already seen it a dozen times, but with every viewing she noticed an interesting cut to a gown's sleeve or a chic table lamp in the background she hadn't seen before.

After turning off the stereo, she made a fire, then settled onto the couch with her food and drew the mohair throw over her knees. Paul seemed to like film noir, but he wasn't keen on pre-code screwball comedies. At least, she didn't think he was. Although he did seem to enjoy it when she brought over *Ball of Fire*. He'd loved the scene where the gangsters were dumped in the garbage truck.

And another thing—if this were a typical Sunday night with him, they'd be at his house. Whenever they stayed the night together, it was at his house. Paul's dog couldn't be alone for a whole evening and night without someone to let her out. Of course, Paul did mention once or twice that they could bring Gemma to Joanna's and see how she did with Pepper. Gemma wasn't known to chase cats, and Pepper had briefly lived with Curly, a dog Joanna watched until his dead owner's relatives adopted him.

But, come on. Joanna's gaze took in the vase of tuberoses on the mantel, the delicate chaise longue under the front window, the velvet curtains drawn against the night.

"Is there really a place for a man here?" she asked Aunt Vanderburgh.

The portrait's gaze was unflinching.

"Oh really? Just because I liked hanging out at his wood shop doesn't mean he'd be able to stand all this girliness."

Joanna could have sworn the portrait's lip tightened. With false bravado, she crossed her arms in front of her chest, ignoring the ache within. "Well, it's too late to find out now."

In the movie, Carole Lombard pushed her way into the hotel

lobby thronged with socialites playing a scavenger hunt. Lombard had arrived with William Powell, a Depression-era "forgotten man," the scavenger hunt's top prize. Lombard's bias-cut evening gown shimmered as she pulled Powell to the counter to claim her points.

The contestants packed around her holding all sorts of scavenged items—fish bowls, a chair, animals. Joanna laughed. "Look at the goat," she said without thinking and turned to where Paul would be sitting. No one was there.

Chapter 27

"Bring food," Apple had said when she set down the phone after arranging Joanna's visit to Tranh's studio. "He's a little guy, but a big eater. Kind of fits that old cliche of starving artist. I wish I could go with you."

"One of us has to watch the store. I'll be fine."

Joanna struggled to balance the hot pan of lasagna in one hand while she locked the car with the other. A drizzle tapped against the lasagna's foil cover. The woman behind the counter at the Italian deli had sealed it well, saying the inevitable, "It always rains during Rose Festival, you know. I'd better put an extra sheet of foil on this." Getting information from Tranh would be trickier than from Helena, especially since Joanna wasn't quite sure what she wanted to know. It was probably a dead end, anyway, but she had to try.

As instructed, she descended the stairs to the basement entrance of one of the grander houses in Ladd's Addition, an old neighborhood shaded by towering elm trees. Bleeding hearts brushed her shoulders as she knocked on the door.

The trim Asian man Joanna had seen at the NAP auction answered. "Joanna?" His eyes darted to the pan, then to her face. "Come in."

The scent of turpentine lingered in the cool air. Small windows did little to brighten the studio, but round lamps on stands cast pools of white light on a large canvas against a concrete wall. Another freshly stretched canvas leaned against the opposite wall.

"Thank you for making time to show me your paintings. I brought lasagna. Apple said you liked it." She held out the pan.

"Oh, noodle cake. That's what my family calls it. Let's put it over here." On the dimmest side of the room was a small counter and sink. Tranh laid a fresh dishtowel over the counter and set the lasagna on it. He clicked on a desk lamp. "I detest fluorescent lights. Until I have a studio with bigger windows, this will have to do. A piece for you, too?" His voice carried only a trace of an accent.

"Thank you."

He carried plates of lasagna to two stools facing the painting he was working on and handed one to Joanna before sitting down. Paint smeared his sweatshirt and white painter's pants, but his tennis shoes were pristine red. "Where did you see my work? I haven't been in a lot of shows," he said between bites.

Here came the tricky part. "Apple told me about it. She thought I'd like it."

"Have a look around. I'm working on one of the nudes right now." Tranh had already finished his lasagna and got up to load his plate with more. Apple was right. For such a little guy, he could sure put it away.

On an easel leaned a painting of a nude woman resting in a chair. Her hands clasped the chair's arms. Tranh had been detailing her face. Her body was only an outline in green-blue paint on gesso. It was nice, but no different than lots of student work she'd seen.

Get him talking about Gil, Joanna thought. "Was this a model from the life paintings Apple goes to, also?"

Tranh's fork dug into the new slab of lasagna. "Uh huh."

"What a great idea you guys had, chipping in on a model. Are there a lot of you?"

"Me, Apple, a few others."

He wasn't making this easy. "I seem to remember Apple mentioning Gil North painted with you sometimes, too."

"Uh huh." His fork hovered mid-air. He looked at Joanna. "There are some more nudes over there, against the wall. Don't miss those."

Joanna arranged three of the smaller canvases next to each other, but she barely saw the flesh-toned paint. "You'd think Gil could afford his own model."

He set his fork and empty plate under his stool. "I guess he likes to hang out with other artists sometimes."

Her back to Tranh, she absently pulled a few other nudes from the stack and stepped back as if she were looking at them, but her brain churned. How to get Tranh to open up about Gil? The swirling colors of his painting against Helena's fireplace were still vivid. "*Pacific Five* sure is gorgeous," she said almost without thinking.

"Thank you." Tranh's voice had softened.

Eyes wide, Joanna turned to face him.

"I know Gil would want me to thank you," he added quickly.

He knew something. Apple said Tranh and Gil had an "odd" relationship. Joanna struggled to remember her exact words. Could Tranh have had a hand in painting *Pacific Five?* If so, he'd be working off of larger canvases than the nudes.

"What's on that big canvas, over there?" Joanna wandered toward a dark edge of the studio. The smell of oil was stronger. The canvas was propped, painted side in, against the wall. She tipped the painting back to glance at its face.

"No, that's not for sale." Tranh leapt off his stool. "I was just working on it — it's not ready."

She ignored him and pulled it from the wall. Joanna stared at Tranh's painting in progress. It was astonishingly similar to Gil's painting. They were both large canvases with stretches that looked post modernist in their swathes of color, but tiny, precise images of objects — people, suitcases, cooking utensils — peeked from behind the waves.

Tranh's hands dropped to his side. Gingerly, Joanna pulled the painting around, face out. Tranh lifted it and carried it into the light. He turned his head defiantly toward her.

"You — " Joanna started, then stopped. "Are you copying Gil's work, or — ?"

"Not copying." He picked up his palate, a rectangular piece of acrylic covered in splotches of mixed paint. He selected a fine-tipped paintbrush and mixed two circles of paint from his palette to create a third.

"Tranh, what do you call this painting?"

"*Pacific Five.*" His eyes were defiant. The electric heater in the corner of the room kicked on with a whirring sound. "I'm always painting *Pacific Five.*"

"So you did paint it — Gil's painting." Apple was right. This put a whole new light on the situation. Gil took credit for someone else's work. Tranh knew more than he was letting on. He had to.

At first he didn't respond. As he painted, his hand covered a small part of the canvas, the brush moving in a space no larger than a nickel. Surely he'd heard her.

"Yes," Tranh said, finally. He put down his paintbrush and sat on the stool again. "My family — there are five of us — came here from Laos. Our ocean crossing was a real sea change. A cliche, but true. Here, we were the same people, but also had the chance to be someone new. I think of us as the *Pacific Five*."

"Are you saying Gil won a prize for your painting?"

Another long minute passed before Tranh spoke. "Surprised me, too."

"That seems kind of mild. I mean, he claimed your work as his own and even submitted it to the art competition."

"Gil is searching for his own sea change. He didn't want to be some rich guy owning a vegetable cannery." He got up for his third helping of lasagna.

He was oddly philosophical for an artist whose work had been co-opted by someone else, then entered in the art biennial for a prize. "You don't resent it? You aren't mad that he's going around telling people he painted your work?"

"Nah." His back was toward her. She couldn't see his expression.

Really? He didn't mind that someone else stole credit for his art? "But if it got out that Gil didn't paint *Pacific Five,* his reputation would be trashed. Word would spread like wildfire." She imagined the scandal, the shushed tables at restaurants when Gil entered, the art dealers' doors slammed in his face.

"In a way, he did me a favor," Tranh said. "This town is rough on artists. Once you get a name, you're golden. But until then, it's a struggle. What gallery is going to even look at the work of a Laotian refugee, unless it's something ethnic? With Gil's name on it, the panel at the art museum would be sure to consider it."

"But that's just it. Gil's name is on it, not yours."

"It will all come out eventually. I'll be on top. Who knows? I might even benefit more if it turns into a scandal."

Joanna's mind turned. "How did Gil come to have your painting, anyway?"

Tranh set his plate down for the third time and pushed it under his stool with a foot. "In life drawing, I work on detail, the little bits here and there on this canvas." He waved a paintbrush at a delicately portrayed fly, almost hidden in a gray swath of paint. "Gil wanted to see my work, so we came back here. He's an all right painter, but one thing I'll say for him is that he has an amazing eye. The guy could teach art history or something."

Joanna set her lasagna plate in the sink as Tranh talked. She returned to the stool and the relative warmth of the studio lights.

"So," Tranh said, "he fell in love with one of my first *Pacific Fives*. Couldn't stop talking about it. I ended up selling it to him. After that, the best I can figure is someone saw it at his house, and he claimed he'd painted it. Then it showed up in the biennial." His expression was almost studiously calm.

Joanna was sitting on the edge of her stool. Her mind ran through the gamut of possibilities. He might have wanted to prove something to Vivienne. Surely he didn't set out to steal credit for the painting. "He had to know you'd find out."

"Of course. He felt guilty, too, I could tell. I saw him at a wedding where I was working, and he seemed horrified. He tried to give me money, just like that, straight from his wallet. Then an anonymous money order for a thousand dollars—exactly the prize amount in the biennial—came in the mail."

Joanna took in the cement floor and raw wall of the basement. "I bet that money came in handy."

"I'm doing all right. I donated it to a refugee organization."

"But all those hours working for the catering company—"

"My family's business. They live upstairs. We own the house."

Joanna's face warmed with embarrassment. She had fallen into the same trap the people Tranh was talking about did, assuming because he was an immigrant he wasn't successful.

"That's quite a story. But you're not bitter? Or angry?"

Tranh drifted to the canvas again and picked up his paintbrush. "At first, yes. Maybe just a little." He suddenly spun toward her. "And why shouldn't I be?"

"I get it." Joanna clutched the edge of the stool.

Tranh sighed. He turned again to the canvas. "The night of the biennial I drove over to Gil's to talk to him, but he'd already left."

"The night Vivienne was poisoned."

"From her cocktail. I know."

Joanna tilted her head. The police hadn't released information about the Bee's Knees. "How did you know she was poisoned from her drink?"

Tranh squinted at his painting. He refused to look at Joanna. "I don't know. From the news, I guess." He set down the paintbrush and grabbed his napkin. He absently twisted it in his fingers.

"It wasn't in the news, Tranh."

"Maybe Gil told me. Anyway, I talked it over with my family, and in the end I understand why Gil did what he did, and I made peace with it. It will all work out in the end. People make assumptions all the time about each other. It's just that some of us are braver than others about showing who we really are."

Joanna remained silent. Tranh looked at her and shrugged. He picked up the paintbrush again, dipped it into a hay-tinted smear of paint, then paused, brush in the air. Worry passed over his face. "You're not here to buy a painting, are you? Why are you asking all these questions? Are you from the museum? Or" —he carefully set down the paintbrush— "the police?"

"No, no." Joanna slipped off the stool. Maybe he had been the person drinking the second cocktail at the North's. Helena had said the cocktail was in a tumbler. Not a Bee's Knees. "You're right that I'm not here to buy a painting, though. Remember the auctioneer Saturday night? Poppy?"

He grimaced. "Of course. The hanging."

"She was a good friend." The funeral was tomorrow morning. Her heart tugged. "So much — weirdness surrounded her, what with the diamond theft charges and Vivienne North's death. I heard you were friends with Gil and wondered if you knew something the police don't." There was more he wasn't telling her. She was sure.

"Except for the NAP auction, I haven't seen Gil since his mother died. I never met the auctioneer at all."

Didn't he just say Gil might have told him about Vivienne's cocktail? She settled back on the stool. He was lying to her. Why? "Tranh, does anyone else know you painted *Pacific Five?*"

His back was to her as he returned to work on the canvas. "No. I haven't told anyone. And you won't either, will you?" He stared at her. "After all, it's really none of your business."

She didn't reply.

"Anyway," Tranh continued, "I almost think Gil would be relieved if the truth came out. Who knows? Besides, now that the biennial and the art auction are over, people will forget about the painting."

And he won't have it rubbed in his face. She leaned forward. "You are upset about it, aren't you?"

"No," he said. "I'm fine. Really." On the canvas behind him, painted with the detail of a Flemish master, was a noose with a frayed end.

⁎⁎⁎

Helena slipped off her gauntlet-like beekeeper's gloves. "I was sorting through some things and found one of Vivienne's dresses. I thought you might like it." A netted hat lay on the floor next to her.

"I'm glad you thought of me," Joanna said. She didn't even need to make up an excuse to pry about Helena and Clary, thanks to Helena's message waiting when she returned to Tallulah's Closet. Joanna suspected Helena knew nothing about *Pacific Five's* real creator, and she wouldn't tell her, either. Tranh was right. It wasn't any of her business. As long as it didn't have anything to do with Poppy or Vivienne's deaths. Then, all bets were off.

"Can you believe this warm weather?" Helena asked. "Glorious. The garden is exploding. I'm sure it will be raining tomorrow, though. After all—"

"—It always rains during Rose Festival," they said at the same time.

Helena laughed. "I get so tired of hearing that. Anyway, I thought I'd take advantage of the lull to check on the bees. Hive mites. The colony died out." The words clearly had led to a new line of thought. Her expression darkened. "I was—shocked to hear about the auctioneer. What a horrible night."

"I still can't get over it." Good thing she hadn't told Helena about the sting operation ahead of time. They'd both be miserable.

"I'm sorry. It's terrible to lose a friend." Helena's voice was gentle. "There's been so much loss lately."

"Yes." A sudden urge to cry overcame her. She drew a long breath and let it out slowly. Joanna wasn't the only one feeling loss. This big house must feel so quiet without Vivienne. Helena's mood seemed to slip along with Joanna's. Joanna glanced toward the den, the den where Tranh may have shared a drink with Vivienne and revealed Gil's secret. And then—what? Demanded money? Threatened him?

Pacific Five leaned against the unlit fireplace. "Your husband's painting — I didn't get to see it up close at the auction. It's so striking."

The painting's colors drew her closer. She was no expert on contemporary art, but she understood how the painting mesmerized with its broad, rolling shapes punctuated with tiny, precisely rendered objects. A perfect monkey wrench, not more than an inch long, was painted near the canvas's edge as if it were resting on a cushion of blue waves.

"Gil wasn't very happy I brought it home." Helena was next to her. "I'm not sure why. It won him a prize. I thought for sure he'd want to keep it."

"It's beautiful," Joanna said, still entranced by the painting. "Maybe he was reluctant because, well, because of Poppy and all. Or his mother's death might have set him off kilter. It happens."

Helena nodded. "Friends have been really supportive. You know who's been particularly helpful — to me, at least?" Helena started tentatively, but her words picked up speed. "Clary. He's been such a godsend." She looked as earnest as a teenager.

"I noticed he was at your table at the NAP art auction." Joanna was alert now.

"He was so sweet to invite me. He knows how much Gil has been preoccupied with his painting. Then with Vivienne's death." Helena tucked a strand of hair behind an ear. "Although Vivienne…"

"Yes?" Joanna encouraged.

"Vivienne — well, Vivienne never approved of Clary. She never thought he was good enough."

Joanna moved to the den's white sofa. "I'm surprised. He's so generous, too," she added, thinking of the Hermès scarf.

Helena lowered herself next to Joanna. "Maybe it was her European background, but she was downright mean about Clary. He used to make her so mad that she'd slip into French. She thought he only wanted to know us because of our standing. She called him a poseur."

Maybe he was — a bit. But surely Clary's love of history and romance for another time inspired the "baronet" business. He wasn't looking to conquer Portland's social hierarchy. At least, she didn't think so. "But he's a good guy. Look at all the work he did for the auction."

"I know. Vivienne and I had a big fight about him the night she died." Her eyes dropped. "Oh, Joanna, I feel so bad."

"But I thought Vivienne was more forgiving — you know, more spiritual than that."

"You mean the convent? She could be a total snob. Sure, she'd been a fashion model and everything, but her background wasn't as high and mighty as she led people to believe. She was from some village in central France with more sheep than people. Her father was a tanner."

Joanna had always imagined Vivienne cradled in Paris nightlife. Apparently, you never knew where people really came from. "I'm sorry," she murmured. "You can't blame yourself for her death."

Helena hesitated. "I haven't told anyone about this, because I didn't think it mattered. But with Poppy's death — "

"Where was Gil?"

Helena's gaze had traveled the room, from liquor cabinet to fireplace to bookshelves, as she spoke. Now she fastened it on Joanna. "The night Vivienne died, Gil was upstairs getting ready for the biennial's award ceremony. Vivienne stayed in. She said she wasn't feeling well."

"You told the police about the fight, right? Or didn't you?"

"No, I didn't even tell Gil. What good would it have done? I figured, well, I figured I'd stop seeing Clary." She crossed and uncrossed her legs. "Not that I was seeing Clary that way. I mean, we're just friends." She looked at Joanna to make sure she understood.

"If Gil found out, got the wrong idea—"

Helena dismissed the idea with a wave of the hand. "Gil wouldn't care. Maybe it would have made a difference if he did." Her voice wavered. "Anyway, I called Clary from my room that night before I went out. I—" She cut her sentence short.

Joanna sat up straight. "You don't think—" Clary? Kill Vivienne? "Did your husband hear you make that call?"

"I don't know. Maybe. I don't know what to think. Honestly."

"You've got to tell the police."

"Joanna, I can't. I don't have any proof. Besides, I don't want to get anyone in trouble."

This was not right. "You can't shelter Clary—or your husband. It's best to come clean."

"Gil didn't do anything," she said emphatically. "And Clary doesn't deserve to be raked over the coals by the police. If anything happened—and I'm not saying it did," Helena added quickly, "Vivienne's death had to have been an accident."

Poisoning? Not likely an accident. "What about the other cocktail glass? Plus, the police said someone was hanging around."

Helena shrugged that off, too. "It's a public street. And I'm not saying someone wasn't here—maybe even Clary. But that doesn't make him a killer."

She was hiding something. Joanna was sure of it. "Do you know if the police have any theories yet?"

"No. Gil has talked to Detective Crisp. It doesn't sound like he has any solid leads."

"This morning I saw the Mother Superior at the convent Vivienne was involved with," Joanna said. Helena leaned in. "The Mother said Vivienne acted strange after your visit to Oaks Park. I wonder," Why not be straightforward? "Could she have seen you and Clary together?"

"Oaks Park?" Her voice was urgent. "Did she tell anyone else?"

"I don't know," Joanna said. "I doubt it."

"No. Not Clary." Helena clenched her hands. She seemed to be making a decision. "Okay. Yes. Yes, she saw me and Clary. He had something he needed to tell me. In person. I didn't think he'd actually come to Oaks Park. And, yes, Vivienne saw us. Please don't tell anyone, though. I know, I just know, he didn't have anything to do with Vivienne's death. He couldn't have. You won't tell anyone, will you?" She grabbed Joanna's hands.

"What was so important that he tracked you down at an amusement park?"

Helena lowered her eyes.

"What's going on with you two?" Before today, Joanna would have sworn Helena was deeply in love with her husband.

"Nothing. I told you."

"If the police asked me, I'd have to tell them. Remember, Poppy was killed, too." Joanna looked at her hands, still in Helena's tight clasp.

Helena released them and wound her own hands in her lap. "But, the auctioneer — didn't she hang herself?"

"No," Joanna whispered. "She couldn't have done it. Couldn't have." She now regretted sitting down in the den, the room where Vivienne died. The day outside, once so crisp and clear, started to cloud over. The den's beeswax and lemon started to feel oppressive.

"Do you really think Clary had anything to do with Vivienne's death?" Helena began to twist the hem of her blouse. "I mean, I don't understand it. He killed Poppy, too?"

"It's hard to imagine Clary a killer," Joanna said. He was strong enough, though, to carry out Poppy's murder, and he bought a gift for a woman very like Helena. He was clever enough to figure out how to poison Vivienne's drink while sipping a glass of scotch next to her. Her stomach turned at the thought. Were the Hapsburgs poisoners?

"Helena, someone is a murderer. And it might be someone you never suspected."

"I know," she whispered.

They sat in silence for a moment.

Helena sighed. "Let's go get Vivienne's dress. It's up in my bedroom." Helena's voice sounded calmer. They climbed the stairs to the second floor, passing a bedroom with its door ajar, allowing a glimpse of a leather easy chair and plaid bedspread. A man's room. Helena's room was at the end of the hall, the opposite end from the entrance to Vivienne's suite above the garage. A French regency bedroom spread over white carpet. It looked like a little girl's vision of a princess's bedchamber. The nightstand was bare except for a ruffle-shaded lamp and a book on herb gardening. A long, blue dress hung from the closet door.

"Is this the dress?" Joanna asked, disappointed. The dress looked expensive, sure, but only a few years old. Not the kind of thing she'd sell at Tallulah's Closet.

"No, I'm wearing that to the Rose Festival gala tomorrow. Vivienne's dress is here."

She strode to the closet and placed one hand on the hanger of a dress, then backed up and sat on the bed. "I really don't want Clary to get in trouble. Just because Gil..."

"What?" Then, more quietly, "Helena?"

"I made such a big mistake. Oh, Joanna. Sometimes it hurts even to breathe."

Concern coursed through Joanna's body. "It's going to be okay. These things work themselves out. Are you sure you won't go to the police?"

"I don't know," she said. She slumped on the bed and stared toward the corner of the room.

The chimes of the doorbell broke the silence. Helena sighed and stood. "Here's Vivienne's dress. I hope you can sell it." She lifted the hanger from her closet, and a full rayon skirt swished from out of the earth-toned blouses.

"That looks great. What can I pay you for it?" Joanna took the dress, barely looking at it. Helena had mentioned a "big mistake." What could it be?

"Nothing. Oh, if you gave some of the money to the convent, that would be great. I know Vivienne would've appreciated it." She led Joanna from the bedroom and hurried down the steps to the front hall. She opened the door to two men in overalls. Behind them, a rusted pickup truck ticked as its engine cooled.

"Ms. — uh — North? This says you got some beehives to take away?"

"Yes, around back. I'll open the side gate."

Joanna draped the dress over her arm. "I'd better be going."

Helena turned to her and lowered her voice. "Thank you for coming over and for listening to my — troubles. I'm sorry I kind of lost it for a minute. I need some time away. I'm trying to talk Gil into a week at our place on the coast. Wait." She spun toward the kitchen. "Why don't you take a jar of honey? You like to cook, right?" Without waiting for her response, Helena disappeared into the kitchen and returned with a small mason jar of amber liquid. "Gil and I put these up."

The honey was cloudy, nearly opaque. "It looks like it's started to crystallize."

"Oh, that's extra pollen. It's good for you, especially if you have hay fever. An old folk remedy."

"Thank you." Joanna slipped the jar into her bag.

"It's the least I can do. You've been so kind to listen to me."

In the car, Joanna laid the dress, a peach-toned, mid-1950s day dress, on the seat next to her. Funny, Vivienne wouldn't have looked good in peach at all.

Chapter 28

Joanna hung the Dior Bar suit on the rack behind the counter at Tallulah's Closet. Although the design dated from 1947, it was the 1955 photo of model Renée taken on the banks of the Seine that elevated the suit to icon. Say "New Look," and fashion lovers flash to Renée's black-gloved pose, one hand palm up, the other pointing gracefully at the cobblestones, an alley of bare plane trees stretching into the distance behind her.

The suit was a worthy distraction, but nothing kept the knotty question of Vivienne's and Poppy's deaths far from her mind. Vivienne didn't trust Clary. Clary wanted Helena, and Gil might be on to it. Gil lied about his painting. Tranh resented Gil winning a medal for his work. Vivienne had refused to leave her money to her family. What was going on?

She turned up the volume of Marty Robbins's "Gunfighter Ballads and Trail Songs." Just for a moment she might look at the Dior and ignore the thought of Poppy's funeral the next morning. While she contemplated the jacket's padded hips and nipped waist she could tune it all out. And Paul. She wouldn't think of Paul at all. No. She wouldn't.

"Really?" A voice rang from behind her.

Joanna dropped the Dior's black jersey and spun around.

"Cowboy songs? For real?" Eve asked.

Irritated, Joanna turned down the volume. The woman would have to show up now. "Eve. What a surprise."

"I need a date night dress — " Eve dropped her purse on the counter. "Oh my God. That's the Dior Bar, isn't it? Is it real?"

Joanna nudged the collar open, revealing the rectangular silk label reading "Printemps - Eté 1947." "Numbered and everything. Only fifteen sold to private clients. This one was Vivienne North's."

Silently they stared at the suit. "Looks like it's in good shape," Eve said.

"Isn't it amazing to see it in real life? You can touch it, if you'd like. The ridges on the Shantung jacket almost feel like grosgrain ribbon."

Eve reverently touched the jacket, then the skirt's soft wool. "Wow."

"It was meant to be a day suit. I bet Vivienne didn't wear it much once she got to Oregon." She boosted a canvas dressmaker's dummy from behind the counter. "I'm going to take a few photos and see if I can interest a curator in it."

"My God. It's definitely museum-worthy. I know someone at the Brooklyn Museum who might be interested. I'll give you her number."

Joanna studied Eve. Maybe she really did love vintage clothing. It was hard to tell with all the trendy boutique items she wore. And she was being suspiciously nice right now. Other than that remark about Marty Robbins, that is. It would kill Joanna to send one of her dresses home with Eve, but right now she needed the sale. The rent was taken care of, thanks to the Scaasi and a local collector, but the plumber was still waiting.

"Thanks. And thanks, too, for coming by for a dress. You didn't have anything in stock?"

"No. I want to surprise a man with a new dress. He's seen everything I have at the store. I want something sexy. What do you have in a two?"

"Are you thinking black, or do you want to go with color?" What poor schlub was she seeing now?

"If you have something in a romantic color, that would be good. No busy patterns, though."

"The color cocktail dresses are here." Joanna walked to a rack on the opposite wall and pulled a rose-pink satin dress with a swagged back that dipped low. "This color would look fabulous on you." And it would, damn it.

Eve shook her head. "The front's too uptight. I want something that shows a little cleavage. So far we've had some heavy flirtation, but nothing serious. This might be the night, you know what I mean?"

Sure, she knew. And if Eve put her mind to it, no man would be able to resist. Joanna held up a red lurex dress from the forties. "How about this? Definitely figure hugging."

"He won't like it. Too cheap looking."

Cheap? Sure, if Rita Hayworth at the Mambo Room was "cheap." "Wait. I have a Peggy Hunt with a chiffon yolk and sleeves. It's a great combination of revealing and concealing. Should be your size. It's black, though."

"Let me see it." Eve grabbed the hanger from Joanna and passed one hand over the bodice, pausing to run a finger over the crystals woven into the chiffon. "Perfect. I'll try it on." She carried the dress to the dressing room and closed the curtain.

Joanna slid the Marty Robbins record back into its sleeve and flipped through the LPs until she found the one she wanted. The harmonies of the Andrew Sisters soon filled the air.

"You must really miss not having Paul around," Eve said from behind the curtain.

Joanna dropped the stereo's cover with a bang. What did she know?

"I'm not sure what you mean."

"You know. He's always at my studio. Late, sometimes. It seems like every time I turn around, there he is." She emerged from the dressing room and posed, hand on hip, in front of the mirror. She turned to check out her profile. "Of course, not that I'm complaining. The man is easy on the eyes."

Joanna's stomach dropped. No. It couldn't be. Eve couldn't have the gall to march into her store to buy a dress to wear for Paul. Or would she? "This man you're seeing, the one for the dress, is he—is he anyone I know?" She held her breath and willed Eve to say no.

Eve's smile widened. "You don't know? That's funny, I thought you would." She turned toward the dressing room. "I guess I won't say then."

Joanna's heart beat so fast she could barely hear above the rush in her ears.

Eve pulled the curtain shut, then opened it again and stuck out her head. "You can write up a receipt for the dress. I'm taking it."

To pay her bills, Joanna had to get at least a few of Vivienne's things displayed on the floor at Tallulah's Closet. Besides, why go home? She'd only beat herself up over Paul. And Poppy. The funeral was the next day. An aching emptiness seemed to have taken over where her vital organs should have been.

She sighed. First step, inventory and tag some items. She'd start with jewelry. She flipped the "open" sign to "closed" and turned off all of the store lights except a gooseneck lamp over the glass-topped jewelry counter.

She spread out a tumble of rhinestones, gold chains, and pastel beads. She'd been so taken by Vivienne's dresses that she'd hardly paid attention to the accessories. But the trunk's drawers surrendered several parures, at least a dozen pairs of earrings, and more bracelets, brooches, and necklaces than she could count at a glance. Shreds of yellowed tissue showed that at one point they'd been individually wrapped, but over the years they'd worked themselves loose and would require patience and tweezers to untangle.

That was fine. The events of the past week, culminating with Eve's visit that afternoon — could she really be seeing Paul? — rattled her. Sorting through the jewelry would be a distraction. She pulled Joni Mitchell's *Court and Spark* from the shelf and and set it on the turntable. She lowered the hi fi's needle. A faint crackle gave way to guitar and Mitchell's sinuous voice.

An hour passed as Joanna filled her notepad with a list of Vivienne's jewelry. Night fell. She worked free a Miriam Haskell brooch mounted on Russian gold with seed pearls encircling square-cut crystals. She tilted it under the lamp, and it threw a rainbow of light against the ceiling. She'd be willing to bet its matching earrings languished somewhere in the tangle. She put the brooch to the side and set to releasing a necklace of black baroque pearls.

The necklace was stuck on something. She eased her fingers into a knot of beads and shook loose a gold locket the size of a quarter. Etched on the outside was "A Maman." She pried it open with her fingernail. Inside was a photo of a curly-headed boy barely old enough for kindergarten. The boy's serious eyes gave him away. Gil.

She set the locket next to the brooch to give to Helena. Helena seemed so nervous about her husband lately. Maybe the locket would bring back better times.

As Joanna turned to put on a new record, the phone rang. Memories of the call she'd received before the auction flashed back. But that had been about the diamonds. That was all over now. She hesitated, then picked up the phone.

"Joanna," a harsh whisper said. "I warned you."

She inhaled sharply. "Who is this?"

"I'm watching you. Working all alone. That jewelry must be quite interesting."

The bathroom door was shut, so no one could be looking in at her through the back window. She swallowed hard. That left the front. She squinted at the front window, but the intensity of the light from the gooseneck lamp blocked her vision. Heart hammering, she clicked it off, plunging the store in darkness. There was no way the stranger was getting the better of her this time.

The voice laughed, setting the hair on her neck on end. "That doesn't help."

Her eyes slowly adjusted to the dark. Thanks to the streetlights, she could see out better than anyone could see in. All she needed was a glimpse of the caller, to identify him or her. She dropped behind the tiki bar. Her hands shook as she loosened the cord coiled behind the phone.

"What do you want?" Joanna asked.

"I told you to leave other people's business alone. You didn't listen."

Keep the caller talking. "About the diamonds?" Staying low, she moved from behind the tiki bar to the shelter of the red velvet bench.

"Don't be coy, Joanna. About the killings, of course."

Her breath caught in her throat. He'd said "killings." Plural. "What do you want from me?" The last time, she'd retreated from the caller. Not this time. No. She crept to the far wall, trailing the phone's cord behind her and pressed herself into a rack of black cocktail dresses. A feathered pillbox hat dropped from the shelf above. She gripped the phone, terrified the caller would see the movement.

"What are you doing?" the voice asked.

"Nothing." Her breath was coming too quickly.

"Don't make either of us sorry." A pause. "I need you to do one simple thing, or no guarantees."

"What?" The word came out almost a whisper.

"Tell the police you saw Helena Schuyler North leaving the auctioneer's body. Tell them. You were the one who found it."

"But I didn't see anyone."

"Tell them, or you're next."

Only a few feet of phone cord remained, and the door was still a body's length away. The blood pounded in her ears. Staying low, she stretched as close as she could to the windowed door. All she wanted was a look. With Dot's so close, the caller couldn't do anything too rash.

A shadowy figure moved in the entrance Tallulah's Closet shared with Dot's. If she could just get a little closer...

"All right." Joanna's voice trembled. "I'll tell them. Whatever you want."

Nearly blind with fear, Joanna dropped the phone and sprang to her feet to yank open the door. Before her hand reached the knob, the door exploded. It was the last thing she remembered.

Chapter 29

The floor was cold under Joanna's back. She opened her eyes to people streaming out of Dot's. A siren wailed in the distance. The store's overhead lights clicked on.

A bearded man in a plaid shirt stepped through the door's window frame, his boots crunching on glass. "I don't know what happened, but you're damned lucky that was safety glass," he said.

The window lay around Joanna in rounded pieces, some still in sheets, some as small as baguette-cut rhinestones. It was coming back now. The caller. She boosted herself onto her elbows, and her head spun. She lay down again.

"Can you help me up?" she said when the room's spin slowed. The bearded man lifted her to her feet.

She'd been so close to seeing the caller. She rubbed the back of her head. She must have smacked it hard on the platform. All she could remember was a medium-sized figure. Not too tall, but not too short, either. Average build. Not a very useful description.

"I think someone shot at the door. Did you see anyone?"

"No," the bearded man said. "You okay? You don't look so steady."

"I'd better sit down." Joanna parked herself on the red velvet bench. Nausea rose in her gut. What had just happened? The phone squawked from being off the hook. The bearded man's friend, another bearded man, but bald, put the receiver in its cradle.

Slamming car doors announced the police's arrival. Detective Foster Crisp reached through the door frame and unbolted the door. After a glance at Joanna, he told the uniformed policeman behind him to call a medic. "Ms. Hayworth. What happened?"

Crisp hadn't changed much from the year before when her friend Marnie had died. Same long face and jutting ears, same bolo tie and cowboy boots. Joanna had once made the mistake of thinking he was just another bureaucrat waiting for retirement—a mistake she wouldn't make again.

She told Crisp about the caller, then pointed toward the door. "He—or she—must have shot at me."

"You were just on the other side of the door?"

She nodded.

"Then he was a lousy shot."

Two paramedics arrived, and Crisp told her he'd return in a moment. One medic, who looked barely out of training, felt her head while the other, a gray-haired woman, asked questions.

"Any cuts or abrasions?" the woman asked.

Miraculously, no. Thank God for the safety glass. "My elbow is a little banged up." She must have broken the fall with her arm.

Joanna winced when the younger medic touched the back of her head. He tipped up her face and looked in her eyes. "Dilated," he said. "Stand up."

The floor felt unsteady under her feet. "Whoa."

"How many fingers am I holding up?" the woman asked. "Any nausea?"

"Two and, yes, but just a little." The younger medic slipped a blood pressure cuff over one arm.

The caller demanded she tell the police that she'd seen Helena leave Poppy's body. Someone was setting her up. Who would want to destroy Helena — or the North family? Someone afraid the police were too close to the truth, maybe. As the cuff swelled over her arm, she looked around the store. The front door was a goner, but the dresses looked to be all right.

"Blood pressure's a little low." The younger man clipped shut his kit. "Slight concussion."

And whoever the caller was, it was someone involved with both deaths, Vivienne's and Poppy's.

"Ma'am, pay attention." The older medic pulled Joanna's face toward her with a finger. "You may feel out of sorts, drowsy, over the next few days. Maybe even a little depressed, but that should go away after a week or so. Are you listening?"

She nodded.

"No sudden movements, either. I wouldn't drive for the next few days if you can help it. Is there someone at home to keep an eye on you?"

Paul. "No."

"Then you'll need to stay at a friend's and call your doctor in the morning."

"Thank you. I'll see what I can do." Apple was out for the evening, but she'd think of something.

Detective Crisp passed the medics as they left. "No one saw the shooter outside. An evidence crew should be here in a few minutes." Crisp glanced out the door, then back in the store. "This was your second threatening call, wasn't it?"

"Yes. I reported the first one, but I didn't think anyone took notice."

"Show me where you were when the phone rang. Let's walk through this."

Joanna rose slowly. The room wobbled as if she were standing on the deck of a boat.

"Easy there," Crisp said and grabbed her arm.

"I'm okay." She picked up the phone and took it back to the tiki bar. "I was here, sorting jewelry." She clicked on the gooseneck lamp. "The store was dark except for this lamp."

Crisp walked to the front of the store, his cowboy boots tapping on the linoleum, crunching on the odd shard of glass. He turned off the overhead lights and looked first through the plate glass window fronting Tallulah's Closet, then through the door. He flipped the lights back on when he returned.

"What happened next?"

"The phone rang." Joanna glanced at the phone now piled on its cord. "It was the same caller as before, the same whisper." Her neck prickled. "I had to see who it was. I knew the caller could see me, so I turned off this light" —she patted the lamp— "and crawled toward the door. I almost saw him, too."

"What did the caller want?"

"To threaten me. To warn me not to try to find Poppy's murderer." She stared at Crisp. "She was murdered, wasn't she? It wasn't suicide at all."

Crisp took a step closer. "You're right. The autopsy showed she'd been strangled, then hung."

Bile rose in Joanna's throat. She knew it had been true, but hearing the words still shocked.

"You've been nosing around in her death?" Crisp asked.

She remained silent.

"Never mind. We'll come back to that in a minute. Tell me again what the caller wanted."

"I did. He threatened me." Should she tell him the caller wanted her to lie? What if the caller found out? He'd killed twice and shot at her. Was it worth the risk? Crisp watched her intently. She touched the tender crown of her skull.

"You're not telling me something," Crisp said.

Poppy was already dead. She wasn't letting Helena get killed, too. "He — the caller wanted me to lie to you."

Crisp nodded. "About what?"

"To say that I saw Helena Schuyler North leaving the green room when I found Poppy's body." She spoke quietly, as if the caller might somehow hear.

Crisp relaxed back, still nodding. "Got it."

"It's not the truth, though. I didn't see anyone. She couldn't have done it," Joanna said quickly. She glanced anxiously toward the front window. A few patrons of Dot's stood on the sidewalk watching the police work.

Crisp marked her distress. "They can't hear us out there. We're fine. As far as the caller knows, you're telling me exactly what he wants you to." He put his hands flat on the counter and leaned forward. "As far as Ms. North goes — "

"Yes?"

"You couldn't have seen her in the green room. Impossible. We have witnesses that place her at her table when you found the body."

Then Crisp must have considered Helena a suspect at some point. Joanna absently reached for a brooch from the pile of jewelry and turned it in her hand. Its loose fastener pricked her finger. She dropped it on the counter. "What about her husband, Gil?"

"We've interviewed everyone. Which brings me to my next point. Why is the caller concerned about you? What have you been up to?"

A man in overalls strode toward Crisp. "Crime scene investigator is here."

Blue-green glass littered the front third of the store, and the front door gaped open. A man set a camera on a tripod.

Crisp turned to Joanna. "You were saying?"

"It's true that I've talked to a couple of people, just to see what they might know. Poppy was a good friend, and I feel responsible for her death. She never would have been at that auction if not for me."

"Who have you talked to?"

"Helena, of course. An artist, Tranh, who knows Helena's husband, Gil. That's all."

"And this artist. Why him?"

Oh God. If she told Crisp Tranh painted *3,* she could ruin the Norths. "It's probably nothing, but you might want to talk to him, too."

"You haven't answered my question."

The man wouldn't let it go. Maybe she could sidestep the issue. "He might have been hanging around the North house the night of Vivienne's death." There. Let the detective figure out the bit about *Pacific Five* on his own.

"Is that all?"

She nodded but wouldn't meet his eyes.

"You're sure?"

"Uh huh." She needed to sit down. The room was starting to sway a bit.

Crisp stood still, his gaze, unfocused, through the front window. He didn't speak, but showed no signs of leaving. The crowd on the sidewalk had dissipated, probably to return to their pool games and half-drunk beers at Dot's.

Finally the detective straightened and turned toward her. "Someone wanted you to tell me a lie he knew could be proved false. You were being set up. He chose not to kill you this time." They locked eyes. "Be careful, Joanna."

Chapter 30

"It's no trouble." Sister Mary Alberta fluffed a pillow and set it on a twin bed. She wore a flannel nightgown sprigged with flowers, and her hair, free of its wimple, escaped from a wiry gray braid. "You'll sleep here. In my room. That way I can keep an eye on your symptoms."

"Thank you so much. I really appreciate it." Joanna set her train case on a quilt at the foot of the bed.

"You'll be safe here. The important thing is that you stay hydrated and get some rest."

"Joanna?" The Mother Superior called from down the hall.

Mary Alberta nodded. "Better go see what she wants."

The hall was a bustle of activity, with nuns going up and down the stairs. Three nuns waited with toothbrushes outside the bathroom. They all wore identical long flannel nightgowns. The Lanz factory must have been busy that year.

"Sit here." Mother pointed to the pink armchair near her bed. "Are you comfortable?"

"Yes, thank you. Mary Alberta is taking good care of me."

"She was a nurse in the Navy, you know. Served in Vietnam."

Settled in the armchair, Joanna was low enough to appreciate what the Mother Superior saw from bed. The orchids on her night-stand gave off a sweet, humid fragrance. A silvered tea cup, probably

Limoges, sat next to them. Behind the cup was a small, black and white photo in a celluloid frame. It hadn't been there before.

"Is that you?"

"You can pick it up if you like."

The photo showed two girls, probably in their teens, in school uniforms. They stood in a cobblestoned courtyard. One girl was tall and angular and held her hands above her eyes to shield them from the sun. Her charisma shimmered even then — Joanna's gaze kept returning to her. The other girl, smaller, had long dark hair and brooding eyes. "Vivienne," Joanna said. "And you."

"I've been looking at that photo all day. I still can't believe she's gone." She let a small breath escape. "It was taken in Toulouse where we went to school together."

"I thought you were from New Orleans." Those eyes. The Mother Superior still had that penetrating gaze.

"Oh, I am. My mother sent me to a Catholic girls' school in Toulouse, where she went. That's where I met Vivienne. We quickly became best friends, practically sisters. I used to go to her family's house for holidays." A smile passed over her lips. "I had quite a crush on her brother. After school, I came back to New Orleans, and she moved to Paris. We kept in touch for a while, but eventually — well, it happens."

"But you met again, here."

"Yes. It was God's plan. Had to have been. Vivienne is saving our convent." She reached a bony hand toward the armchair. Joanna placed hers near it, and Mother laid her hand over Joanna's. Her skin was cool and dry. "That's why I need to find out who killed her. I owe it to her. But not at your expense, daughter. I'm sorry."

Joanna had never seen the Mother looking so vulnerable. "I want to find who killed her, too. And Poppy."

"No, dear. You were shot at tonight. You could have died."

Joanna shook her head, then stopped as a ripple of dizziness came over her. "It was only a warning. I'm fine. Really."

"Joanna, I'm telling you it's time to stop. You owe me nothing." Some ferocity had returned to her voice. "You remember when you first came how I told your friend Apricot—"

"Apple."

"—I heard music and saw lights? It's getting louder. I don't feel good about this at all." She lay back and pulled up her blanket. She closed her eyes. "Now go to bed. And please turn off the light as you leave."

In the hall, she could already hear the snoring from Mary Alberta's room.

⁎

Joanna awoke to the sound of angels singing. Or was it children? No, definitely women's voices, and they melded in a benediction that sent chills down her arms.

She rolled over and squinted at the blush of sun bleeding into the horizon. Barely dawn. Mary Alberta's bed was empty. She swung her feet onto the floor and grabbed the bedpost until her head settled. The back of her head was even more tender than last night, and her elbow was beginning to bruise. She rose slowly—good, the floor stayed level—and reached for her robe. On the nearby dresser Mary Alberta had left a note, "Matins at 6, breakfast at 7." Was that coffee she smelled?

Downstairs, the sisters were lifting their heads from prayer. Mary

Alberta caught her eye. "How did you sleep?" she asked.

"Really well," Joanna said. Odd in a strange bed in a new place, but she'd slept like the dead.

"The concussion. One thing I can say about concussion patients is that they're no trouble once they get to sleep. And your appetite?"

"The coffee smells delicious."

"Good. Come in the kitchen and have some breakfast."

A long wooden table filled the east end of the kitchen. The Mother was already seated at the head of the table in her wheelchair. The fragrance of sweet, warm yeast filled the kitchen. One of the Marys, oven-mitted, hoisted a pan of cinnamon rolls to the table to join a large bowl of scrambled eggs and a dozen halved grapefruits. The nuns began passing the platters and scooping food onto heavy stoneware plates. Only Mary Frances waved the food by. A small bowl of dry cereal sat in front of her.

"Reducing plan," Mary Alberta whispered.

After breakfast, and after the sisters had refused her pleas to help with clean-up, Joanna and the Mother sat alone at the table. Joanna nursed a cup of coffee. The sun was up now, and yellow tulips, wet from the night, waved along the driveway.

"Considering I was shot at last night and have a funeral to go to this morning, I feel — peaceful," Joanna said.

The Mother adjusted her wheelchair so she faced Joanna. "Remember last night, how I told you I had feelings about Vivienne's death?"

"Yes. The music and lights."

"They came again last night, child." She grasped her crucifix with one hand. "I know you must go to your friend's funeral today. Grieving the dead is essential, and she meant a lot to you. But then it's time to let it go. You're too young to risk your life for someone's that is nearly already over."

Joanna searched the Mother's face. Her words were earnest, intent. At the same time, the Mother's mind was somewhere else. What was she up to?

Chapter 31

The funeral home's windows looked down the bluff to a swamp studded with rain-blackened oak trees. Inside, folding wooden chairs flanked an aisle as if for a wedding, but where the priest would stand to bless a couple, a white coffin with gold handles lay. A pillar candle on a tall brass stand burned next to it.

Joanna had left the convent with Mary Alberta's post-concussion care list — get plenty of rest, no sudden movements, no drinking, stay hydrated — and the invitation to stay another night if she wanted. What she wanted was a normal night at home. She'd quickly stopped at her house, popped a few ibuprofen, and changed for the funeral. Then she left Apple a message, saying there had been an "accident" at the store, and the window in the front door had broken, and she'd give her the details later.

Seats were filling fast. Joanna slipped into one near the rear next to a hunched man. It was Poppy's former hand, the one who had unwittingly tipped her off to Ben's diamond sales. "Travis?" she said.

The corners of his mouth lifted in recognition before he dropped his head to stare at his folded hands again. "Hi." Slumped in a dress shirt that was too big for him, Travis looked more like a boy than a man just starting out on his own.

What to say? "I'm sorry we have to meet again here."

"Yeah." He brushed something from his face and averted his eyes. "This music is dumb."

A man played a white upright piano near the door. Right now it was "Dust in the Wind." For crying out loud.

A woman with a skunk streak and a nose ring sat next to Travis. "You know my son. I'm Karen, Poppy's neighbor. We'll really miss her."

Joanna understood. Travis wasn't the only one with an aching heart. Toward the front of the room sat Poppy's ex-husband and other people who must be relatives. Otherwise Joanna didn't see many people she knew. But the room was crowded. Poppy was popular. Had been popular, she corrected herself. Why had she convinced Poppy to do the NAP art auction? A leaden lump settled in her throat.

"It's not fair," Travis said.

"No, it isn't," Joanna echoed. Murder, too. Oh, Poppy.

"Why would she kill herself? Shouldn't have happened."

Travis's mother patted his hand. "Sometimes unfair things happen, Travis." She glanced at the coffin. "Although this is especially hard to accept," she added under her breath.

The piano segued into "My Favorite Things." "This music is stupid," Travis said. He rested his head in his hands. Poppy's ex-husband said a few words to the pianist, and the tune morphed to "Margaritaville."

Nearly everyone was seated. From the corner of her eye, Joanna saw Detective Crisp take a chair near the edge of the room. He nodded at her and scanned the crowd.

The piano music ceased, and the elderly minister took her place just beyond Poppy's coffin. "Dearly beloved," she began, just like in the movies. "It is a deeply sad occasion that brings us here." She paused. Someone coughed. "But it's also a chance to rejoice in love and giving — qualities Poppy practiced abundantly in her too-short life." The minister spoke about "how you can't take it with you," and how Poppy's life was testament to that. Her role was to sell the things people had gathered through the years, but also, she said, she left her own legacy of kindness.

Yes. Normally Joanna would have ignored the sermon in favor of examining the audience's clothing or the room's wallpaper and moldings. But these words, words the minister had probably delivered scores of times, rang true, every one.

Travis doodled on his program. He'd drawn Poppy's head in a corner, surrounded by the tips of palm trees and a sun. His idea of heaven, perhaps. Or maybe Poppy's heaven, the Florida Keys.

The service over, most of the congregants drifted to a room next door for what the funeral home staff called "refreshments," as if coffee and a danish would satisfy the emotion dislodged by death. Joanna wandered to the wide windows and gazed into the distance.

Detective Crisp appeared beside her, his hands clasped behind his back. "How's your head?"

"My neck's a little stiff, but it's okay. Thanks."

"You going to the reception next door?"

"No. I'm not hungry." Wind ruffled through the trees outside. The sky was clear, but the earth was still wet. Joanna knew birds would be chattering warnings about the stormy weather blowing in.

"You're still feeling guilty about Poppy, aren't you?"

Joanna didn't reply. Sure, she felt guilty. But leaden grief overshadowed it. She touched a finger to the window's cold glass.

Crisp stared out the window. "Don't. I'm not sure Poppy's death could have been prevented. Whoever wanted her dead may have found an easy option at the auction, but it wasn't the only option."

Apple had said the same thing. Crisp was kind — almost

grandfatherly—in his attempt not to let her blame herself, but the fact remained: if Poppy hadn't been at the auction, she might still be alive.

"I don't go to a lot of funerals," he said. "Funny, maybe, in my business."

"But you're here," she said. Beyond the marsh with its straggly trees reared the tip of a Ferris wheel. Oaks Park. Beyond that lay the flat green river.

"I am." Crisp didn't add to his short reply, but he didn't move away, either.

"How's the investigation? Do you have any idea who did this to her? Or who shot at me?"

"We're following up on a few things."

In other words, he had nothing. Why else would he be at Poppy's funeral, if not to hope for some kind of new lead? "I can't figure out who would want to kill Poppy. She was so loved. Even her ex-husband has nothing but good things to say about her."

"She was popular," he repeated.

"She's dead. So's Vivienne." Joanna rubbed her arms despite the room's stifling heat. "What's the link? Could it be the diamonds?"

"No. That one's in the bag. Kay was the ringleader, and Ben helped him. Poppy had nothing to do with it. Neither did Vivienne."

"Then what?" Her tone might have been harsh, but it was easier to release her emotion in anger than tears.

They stared over the marsh. The tip of the Ferris wheel began to rotate in the distance. The Mother Superior had said Vivienne saw something alarming at Oaks Park. Even the words "Oaks Park" seemed to rattle Helena. She could tell Crisp, but tell him what? That Helena had been anxious about meeting Clary, and Vivienne noticed it? That maybe Gil knew, too? The police wouldn't care. The link to the murders was too tenuous. But it was all she had.

"Look, I want to find who did this as much as you do, and I wish I had more to tell you right now." The detective moved a step closer, the ends of his bolo tie dangling. "You need to be patient. Let us take care of this."

Gaze fastened on Oaks Park, she nodded.

Chapter 32

Joanna stepped out of her car and breathed river-moist air. Oaks Amusement Park. Past the entrance gate, a carrousel wheezed a march, and a man in a seven-foot chipmunk costume walked by. Moms pushed strollers, and kids—most looked preschool age—waited in line to ride a towel down a wavy pink slide. Coming through the gate behind her were a dozen children wearing neon orange tee shirts emblazoned "Montavilla Daycare."

The Mother Superior had said Vivienne and Helena had been here the morning Helena ran off. It would have been colder then, the trees bare. Joanna walked down the fairway, passing a ride featuring child-sized cars, rolling in an eternal circle. Each car had four steering wheels—one at each seat—and the gas pump in the middle of the ride touted gas for 25 cents a gallon. Those kids would be in for a shock when they grew up.

The roller skating rink dominated this end of the fairway. Joanna turned and headed back, the river on her right. She passed bumper cars and a shooting arcade. She wasn't sure what she expected to find. Helena said she met Clary here. Why would that scare her? Unless word got back to Gil. How any of that related to Vivienne or Poppy was beyond her.

A mom pried a corn dog stick from a crying toddler's hands and threw it in the trash. Not the kind of place Clary usually hung out. Then again, he was on the board of a couple of nonprofits in town, including one serving homeless families. He might have accompanied a group of kids, like the nuns did. One thing was sure: with his wire-rimmed glasses and ramrod posture, he would have stood out. Maybe someone saw what happened between him and Helena.

Joanna reached the south end of the park, beyond the Tilt-a-Whirl and roller coaster, both darkened until the park opened to older kids in the afternoon. Along the river stretched a few acres of lawn dotted with old oaks beginning to leaf out. She sat on one of the cold benches.

Who was she fooling? She didn't even know what she was looking for. Did she think one of the Mother Superior's "clues" was going to fall out of the trees? Mother had warned her away from looking for Poppy's killer, anyway. Then there was the caller. She caught her breath, remembering his warning. A chill wind blew off the river. She tucked her fingers into her sleeves for warmth. Crisp hadn't sounded very encouraged by the investigation, either. She shook her head and surveyed the heavy river for a moment longer before deciding to turn for home.

A rustling rose from behind her. A short man in a gray jumpsuit set down a garbage bag with his work-gloved hands. Not only Clary, but the nuns would have stood out in the park, with their blue habits. And the Mother in a wheelchair. It was worth one more try. She stood. "Do you work here most mornings?"

"Most, sure. Why?"

"I wonder if you remember a few nuns, in pale blue, visiting a month ago or so. One of them would have been in a wheelchair."

The workman's face broke into a wide smile. "Yes, the Marys." He unzipped the top of his jumpsuit and dangled a crucifix on a chain from the leather finger of his glove. "The mother gave me this. I helped her with the chair, you know, especially on the grass. It gets mushy. Hard to push."

What luck. "Do you remember, about a month ago when they were here, seeing a well-dressed man with glasses talking to a woman who came with the nuns?"

He shook his head. "No. Nothing like that. I remember the sisters' visit, though. They showed up with a beautiful old lady and a younger one. Her daughter, I think."

"Exactly. The younger one may have been meeting someone else, a well-dressed man."

The workman shrugged. "Don't remember anyone in particular. Why?"

"Well, the Mother Superior saw him" — hopefully telling lies about nuns wasn't a mortal sin — "and wanted me to track him down. Her friends — the ladies you saw — were interested. He may want to support their charity."

He laughed. "I guess you don't tell the Mother no."

She pretended to chuckle.

"I didn't see any man, but Mother's friend, the younger lady, saw someone she knew."

Bingo. This was turning out to be a cinch. Maybe Clary had played down the prosperous WASP look that day to blend in with the fleece-bedecked moms. "What did you see?"

He looked at Joanna for a moment and fingered the crucifix. "Meet me at the roller rink." He abruptly turned and swung the garbage bag after him. It bumped along the ground as he took off in the opposite direction.

She stared after him. Well, what did she have to lose? She retraced her steps up the midway, dodging moms with strollers and accidentally jostling a few Seabees on shore leave for Rose Festival's Fleet Week. One of them grabbed her hand and pulled her in for a photo. "Come on. Let's take a picture." Her mind on the grounds worker, she quickly smiled for the camera, then hurried toward the barn-sized roller rink.

The rink's neon "Skate Today!" sign was dark. Joanna cupped her hands around her eyes and pressed them against the glass front door. Although the roller rink was closed, some kind of activity went on inside. Was that organ music she heard?

"You're here. Good." The workman she'd seen minutes ago took a key from his belt and unlocked the front door. "After you."

Dingy carpet paved the way to a brightly lit central room. The scent of stale popcorn hung in the air. A massive platform, as big as a small house and heavy with organ pipes, hung over the wooden skating floor. The organ tooted "Row, row, row your boat" while — could it be? — people seemed to be working under the skating floor.

"What's going on?" Joanna asked.

"Rain in the forecast. A huge storm," the workman said. "We're checking the barrels under the skating floor to make sure they're tied on good. Sometimes the river floods, but with these empty barrels, the floor just floats right up."

Amazing. She took in the rink's lockers, the snack bar, the benches where people swapped shoes for worn roller skates. "But everything else floods?"

"Pretty much. We roll the organ onto the skating floor, and some of us take sleeping bags and spend the night. Make sure everything's okay. Last time this happened, a German restaurant boated us in some bratwurst."

The organ music shifted to "Old Man River."

"Over here," the workman said, leading Joanna to an entrance to the skating floor. "Luisa," he called out. "There's someone I want you to meet."

From under the floor a set of small feet kicked out, followed by legs, then the body of a boyish woman. Her hair was pulled back into a ponytail and dust smeared her face and hands. The workman stuck out a hand and pulled her up. She raised her eyebrows at Joanna.

"Luisa, I'd like you to meet—I'm sorry."

"Joanna," she said and extended her hand.

"I'm Jorge, and this is my sister, Luisa. Luisa, this lady is a friend of the Marys. Tell her what happened when the sisters came here last."

"What?" Luisa asked. When she turned toward her brother, a tattoo of a unicorn's head showed on the side of her neck.

"You know, the lady with them and Whitey. Remember?"

Whitey? Joanna looked at Jorge and Luisa in turn. This ought to be interesting. Who was Whitey? Not Clary.

Luisa took off her work gloves and smoothed a piece of hair behind her ear. "Why does she want to know?"

"Never mind, I'll tell you later. Hurry. Tell her. I'm supposed to be on garbage detail."

Luisa shrugged. "I was working on the Scrambler with Whitey" —she gestured absently toward the midway outside— "and he saw someone he knew. A lady. She was with the Marys. It was really weird. He waved his hands like this" —she waved both hands excitedly— "and the lady ran over to see him. She didn't look too happy about it."

"Could you hear what they said?" Joanna asked.

Both Jorge and Luisa started at the creak of the rink's front door. Joanna turned, too. A large man strode toward her. Luisa's feet disappeared under the skating floor, and Jorge darted toward the snack bar.

"Ma'am, can I help you?" the man said. An Oaks Park ID badge was clipped to his pocket.

"Uh, yes. I was looking for the restroom."

"The restroom here's closed. In fact, the whole rink's closed to the public. We're getting ready for the storm. You can use the bathroom out on the midway."

"Yes, thank you." She glanced back where Luisa had disappeared—what was it she had been about to say?—and reluctantly fell into step with the man. A security guard, she guessed. Maybe he could help. "I'm here on business. I'm looking for a man called Whitey. Do you know where I can find him?"

The security guard stopped suddenly. "Whitey? How do you know him?"

She was getting somewhere. "For legal reasons I can't tell you, but it's very important that I find him." Whoever Whitey is, she thought.

"Here's the restroom," the guard said, pointing toward a door wedged between a stand selling curly fries and another with soft-serve ice cream. He glanced at the leaden sky. "Going to rain this afternoon, but that's supposed to be nothing compared to the front rolling in tomorrow."

"Sure, Rose Festival and all," she said quickly. "But what about Whitey?"

"I can't help you about Whitey. He packed up and left almost a month ago."

"What?" Joanna said. She was so close to finding out what had spooked Helena, only to arrive at this dead end.

The security guard seemed to take pity. "Look, there's not a lot I can tell you. Some folks say Whitey came into some money and left, I don't know. He was good at his job." He shook his head. "We wouldn't take him back now, though. Not after running out like that."

"Where would someone with his skills go to find work?"

"You might try Thrillmeister. They're local. Always looking for mechanics. Won't do you any good if he came into money, though."

If Luisa was right, maybe Whitey saw Helena and Clary together and knew Helena was married to someone else. Her picture turned up often enough in the paper. He could have blackmailed her, threatened to tell Vivienne. With Vivienne dead, Whitey would have lost his leverage over Helena and might have had to look for work again. Or maybe Joanna's imagination was running wild.

Once the security guard moved on, she returned to the roller rink, slipping in the back way, through the parking lot. The door was locked, and no one let her in this time. Jorge was no where to be seen on the grounds. She put a hand on her hip.

She had to know who this "Whitey" was. First step, track down Thrillmeister.

*
**

Joanna's phone calls got her nowhere. Without Whitey's real name, Thrillmeister's central HR department couldn't tell her if he worked for them, and no one in the local office would confirm or deny they had anyone named Whitey on record. It would be easy enough for Whitey, clearly a nickname, to call himself something else in his new job. Even the Central Library's reference staff came up dry.

Fine. If the phone didn't work, she'd visit in person.

Thrillmeister's local headquarters were east of town on the grounds of an abandoned drive-in movie theater. Joanna eased Old Blue past the theater's marquee, now studded with holes, past an unmanned ticket booth, and into the gravel parking lot. Her windshield wipers swished against the rain.

From the warmth of the car, she surveyed the Thrillmeister lot. What had once been the viewing area for the drive-in was now jumbled with amusement park rides probably waiting to be fixed or sent to a fair. Two Cobras, their cars lowered, were closest to Joanna. Beyond them loomed a House of Mirrors and a rusted roller coaster. The drive-in's screen marked the edge of the property. Her windshield began to steam up. Figuring the drive-in's old snack building was where the office was located, she clutched her sweater and darted through the rain.

Joanna knocked hesitantly on the building's metal door. The rain beat on its aluminum roof as she waited for a response. Finally, she gripped the cold handle and yanked.

"For God's sake, close the door," a voice shouted from the other side of a cubicle wall.

Joanna stepped inside and wiped the rain off her sleeves. The office was warm — almost oppressively so. The snack shack had been gutted and fitted with fluorescent lights, surplus desks, and cubicle walls in motley colors from the 1970s. She heard a thump, then saw a child-sized woman with an adult's head come around the cubicle corner. Her head was half shaved and the remaining hair dyed magenta.

"You — " Joanna started.

"Little person. Not midget," the woman said.

"I'm Joanna Hayworth." She proffered a hand. "I was going to say you have a gorgeous bracelet. That's not a Schiaparelli, is it?" She either got very lucky at an estate sale or paid a pretty penny at a boutique.

She touched the faceted black stones surrounded by carved silver leaves at her wrist. "In fact it is." She appeared to take in Joanna's leopard print sweater, added after the funeral, and stack of Lucite bracelets before her gaze settled on Joanna's feet. "Nice boots."

"Oh, thanks. I hope I'm not tracking anything in."

"Nope, nothing but the cold. I got this place rigged up with heaters. Still can't keep it warm enough. I'm Marla, the operations person here. What can I do for you? You haven't come by to complain that it isn't a drive-in anymore, have you?"

Someone else, a man, had answered Joanna's earlier calls to Thrillmeister. Maybe Marla would be more helpful. "I'm looking for a mechanic named Whitey. He used to work at Oaks Park."

Marla's lifted an eyebrow. "I'm not saying we have anyone here named Whitey — in fact, I can tell you for sure we don't. Besides, we're busy now. Loading out rides to the waterfront for the Rose Festival's fun center. But why?"

She clearly knew something. "I'm afraid I can't tell you much. Legal reasons."

Marla's face shut down.

"Good legal reasons," Joanna added hastily. "In fact, Whitey might stand to come into some money." She nearly held her breath hoping her lie would pass.

"You don't look like a lawyer. At least, I've never seen a lawyer in leopard and driving a crap Toyota."

So, Marla had noticed her arrival. "I work for a nonprofit law organization. Protecting the underrepresented." She laughed. "Vintage is about all I can afford."

Marla seemed to relax. "Me, too. They know me by name at the bins. That's where I got the the Schiap. Can you believe it? Needed a new clasp, that's all." She toyed with the bracelet's safety latch. "So, you represent travelers, then?"

Joanna's smile froze. What were travelers? The term was vaguely familiar, but didn't click into place. "Yes, we do. All sorts."

"I told you we don't have anyone named Whitey here, and that's true. But there might be someone you want to talk to working on the Rock-O-Plane right now. Northwest corner of the lot. Shut the door behind you." With that dismissal, Marla returned to her cubicle.

Outside, Joanna again scanned the Thrillmeister lot. The northwest corner would be up to the right of the old movie screen. She made her way past an abandoned Scrambler, its arms severed from its cars, and past a metal foundation painted "The Zipper" in bright red, but with no Zipper attached. Grass sprouted between cracks in the asphalt. At least the rain was beginning to let up.

A semi with a long bed crunched up the driveway rimming the

drive-in's lot. It stopped with a loud hiss of its brakes. The driver leapt from the cab and was met by another man in overalls. The two men stopped their conversation and stared as she approached.

"Hi," she said, a little breathless. Neither man spoke. "Could you point me toward the Rock-O-Plane?" Still silent, the driver gestured to the opposite side of the yard. "Thanks." She took off in the direction he'd indicated.

"Hey," the driver yelled after her, "You got a spot on your sweater." Joanna looked down at her sleeve. The leopard print covered it with spots. The two men laughed.

Beyond the pitted facade of a funhouse was the Ferris wheel-shaped Rock-O-Plane. But instead of a Ferris wheel's open, swinging benches, the Rock-O-Plane held closed cages. Each cage rotated freely from the larger wheel. With a lurching stomach, Joanna remembered being a ten-year-old trapped in one with Apple at the county fair. Joanna had gripped the bar in front of her to try to keep the cage from spinning, and when their cage dipped to the ground, she and Apple yelled for the operator to stop the ride. He was too busy flirting with a busty teenager to pay attention. Apple threw up caramel popcorn when they were finally on solid ground. Even the thought of the ride in motion set her concussed head spinning.

"Hello?" Joanna yelled toward the Rock-O-Plane's base.

"Who are you?" The voice came from behind Joanna. She spun around. Now she knew why the woman in the office had seemed so sure Whitey worked there, even though she didn't know anyone by that name. The man standing arm's length from Joanna had white hair and pink-white skin. Despite the dim weather, he wore sunglasses. Other than his grease-smeared overalls and glasses, the man was completely white. Albino.

"I'm Joanna Hayworth." She extended a hand, and Whitey removed a leather work glove to shake it. Even the tiny hairs on the back of his fingers were white.

"Leo," he said, eyeing Joanna's coat and shoes.

She struck a confident tone. "I understand you used to work at Oaks Park."

"What about it?" His eyes were hard to read behind the dark lenses of his glasses. He rested on hand on a long wrench in his tool belt.

Mentioning Helena wouldn't help matters if he'd blackmailed her. He'd just think Joanna was gathering info to prosecute him — or maybe even serve him papers. She had to try a different angle. "I heard you left work at Oaks Park quickly — no, wait!" Leo had turned and started to walk away. "I think we have the same interests at heart here."

"You don't know what you're talking about," he said flatly.

"I do. I think you saw something — someone — who didn't want to be seen. And that person was going to make things hard on you. Maybe you even found a way to, um, benefit from the situation."

"What are you talking about?" He slipped off his sunglasses. His face could have been that of a Roman sculpture with its straight nose and almond eyes — all marble white, except his irises, which shone almost red. They wavered, as if he had trouble focusing.

Joanna tried not to stare. "Helena, of course."

"You're having an affair with Gil?"

Helena's husband? "No, Clary. You saw Clary, right? And Helena?"

Leo started to laugh. Joanna smiled at first, then her face grew somber when he didn't stop. A drop of rain slid down the back of her neck into her sweater.

Leo's laughter subsided. "I saw Helena, sure." He turned to walk away, then looked over his shoulder at Joanna. "Oh, and if you see her again, tell her we know where to find her."

Chapter 34

On the drive home, Joanna puzzled over what she'd learned in the few minutes she had with the mechanic. Leo, Whitey — whatever he called himself — had walked away laughing and refused to answer any more of her questions. Plus, he'd practically threatened Helena. Puzzling.

At the next stoplight, Joanna mopped the dampness from Old Blue's windshield. Traffic moved again. The only clue Joanna had was that he was a "traveler." Whatever that was.

At home, Joanna tossed her purse on the dining room table and reached for the phone.

"Second time today," Kimberly at the reference desk said. "The last question was about Thrillmeister employees. I can't wait to hear this one."

"Can you tell me anything about people called travelers?" Joanna asked.

"I'm on it." The clicks of a keyboard filled the background as Kimberly plumbed digital databases. She came up with a response within a minute. "Ready?"

"More than ready."

"In short, travelers are a form of American gypsy. It looks like a really rich culture — lots of history. Fascinating. Many were traditionally tinkers, mechanics. They're clannish." Kimberly spent another minute describing their origins. "I can pull you a reading list, if you're interested."

Now she remembered — Helena had called out the girl in the shop as a traveler and said she'd written a paper on them. Could she have been more involved than that? It made sense, then, that Leo was a mechanic, but it didn't clarify the day's events.

"Thanks, Kimberly. I'll get back to you on the reading list."

Joanna put down the phone examined the row of bottles on her buffet. She wanted a drink. Yes, a Bee's Knees. Maybe it would put her in the right frame of mind to have Vivienne's cocktail. Mary Alberta said she shouldn't drink with her concussion, but surely a small one wouldn't hurt.

Joanna opened the jar of Helena's honey, cursing as she accidentally spilled some down its side. The ants would love that. Oh well, she'd clean it up in a second. She scanned her collection of cocktail glasses, mostly crystal orphans from the 1920s and '30s, before settling on a small glass with lilies of the valley etched on its side. She wrapped the shaker in a dishcloth and shook until ice formed, then poured the frothy liquid into the glass.

The phone rang. Joanna wiped her hands on a dishcloth and hesitated. It shouldn't be the caller from the store. She'd told the caller she'd do what he wanted. She glanced at the front door. Locked. At last the phone clicked to the answering machine. "Joanna? It's Apple, I — "

She grabbed the receiver. "Apple?"

"How was the funeral this morning?"

"Oh, it was — I hated it." Hated being there, hated that it had to happen at all. "A real crowd showed up for Poppy. Detective Crisp was there, too, and I don't think he's any closer to finding who killed her." Too bad she'd left her cocktail in the kitchen. The princess phone in the living room, while satisfying to hold, was the old fashioned kind connected to the wall with a cord. She lowered herself to the couch and pulled the mohair throw over her legs.

"I have something that might cheer you up at least a little. Sister Mary Alberta came by with a proposal for the store's website. I'm closing shop now. How about if I drop it off on my way home? It won't be a minute," Apple said.

Pepper jumped into Joanna's lap as she slipped the phone into its cradle. She stroked his ears, her brain full of images: Oaks Park, the diamonds, Poppy's coffin, the second cocktail glass in the North's den, Leo's white hands clutching a wrench. How did it all fit together? The cat stretched and flipped to his back, giving her the rare chance to pet his silky belly fur. How did Helena's study of travelers relate? Judging from her treatment of the girl who visited Tallulah's Closet, Helena was not a fan.

Pepper launched from her lap at a rap on the door. Apple shook out her umbrella before stepping inside and hugging Joanna. "I know it's been a rough day. I brought you a present." Vanna White style, she presented a powder blue book.

"*How to Catch a Man, Keep Him, and Get Rid of Him*. Zsa Zsa Gabor." Joanna laughed. "Thank you. Although 'getting rid of' seems to be my specialty."

"Ha ha. Thought you'd like it. And here's the proposal. I took a peek — it's pretty good." Apple slid a portfolio from her bag and set it on the table. Through the clear front cover read, "Website development proposal for Tallulah's Closet prepared by the Sisters of Saint Mary Salome the Myrrh Bearer."

"They could work on their business name," Joanna said.

"Look." Apple flattened the portfolio open. "The site's home page is laid out like a real closet."

"She pulled the typeface from the sandwich board, too. Clever."

"You click on the closet's front door, and it opens. Like this." Apple flipped the page. "See? You can sort by era or garment." The next page showed the open closet grouped with dresses in one section, blouses and skirts in another, and suits in still a third section. "Click on the drawer below and you get shoes, scarves, and purses."

"And that jewelry box —"

"Exactly," Apple said. "Sectioned by type of jewelry — bracelets, earrings, whatever." She tapped the page. "You travel through the store's stock just by clicking a mouse."

Travel. Travelers. "Have you ever heard the term 'travelers' as a kind of people?"

Apple drew back. "No. Why?"

Joanna told Apple about her trip to Oaks Park and the Thrillmeister center. "So this guy, Leo, said to tell Helena that they knew where she was. Someone else at Thrillmeister mentioned travelers and hinted that he might be one."

Apple pushed the portfolio away and rested an arm on the table. "It just gets more and more complicated."

"Whitey — that is, Leo — must have seen Helena and Clary together and threatened to expose them. Blackmail. He obviously knew Helena from another life. Her sociology work, maybe."

"But what does that have to do with Vivienne?"

"Hmm. Maybe Clary hired Leo to kill her. He might have shown up at the house when they were out and snuck poison into Vivienne's drink." Mentioning the drink reminded her of the Bee's Knees warming on the kitchen counter. She rose to fetch it.

"And his was the second cocktail glass? You think Vivienne was having drinks with an unknown carnie? Not likely."

"It does sound a little out there." Joanna set the Bee's Knees on the table.

Apple snatched it up. "For me? Thank you."

"That was mine." She shot her a dirty look. "Never mind. I'll make another."

Apple raised her glass in a mock cheer. Joanna pulled an ice tray from the freezer. "He wouldn't have been a stranger. She saw him at Oaks Park, remember. And Tranh — Tranh knew about Vivienne's Bee's Knees even though it hadn't been in the news. He said Gil told him, but now I wonder."

"What kind of poison was it?"

"Don't know." Joanna cut a lemon in half and pulled the reamer from the sink. "They found traces in Vivienne's glass but not in the gin. Someone must have slipped something in her drink."

"Which leaves out Gil and Helena since they weren't home." Apple fanned herself with a hand. "It's warm in here."

"Right. But there's still Clary, Tranh, and Leo." Joanna reached for the honey, then pulled her hand back. "Helena told me the police had tested the gin used in Vivienne's cocktail, but I wonder if they thought about the honey."

"Good question."

"Stop." Joanna pulled Apple's glass toward her. "Helena gave me that honey. She said she and Gil bottled it. I used it in your drink."

"You think there might be poison in there?" She looked at the glass. "Come on. Why would the killer poison the honey instead of Vivienne's cocktail?"

"Think about it. It would be safer that way. He could slip the poison into the honey any time, knowing eventually Vivienne would drink it. He wouldn't have to be around when it happened." That completely changed the range of possibilities for the murderer. If the honey had been poisoned, it could have been anyone who visited the Norths between the time the honey was bottled and Vivienne's death.

They looked at the honey. It was in a small mason jar with no label. The blood drained from Joanna's face. The drip she hadn't wiped up earlier had attracted a stream of ants. But they didn't move, didn't march food back to the queen. The honey had trapped their black bodies like insects in amber. They were dead.

"You don't think—" Apple started. "They probably just got stuck there."

"You don't look so good. Your face is kind of white." Joanna bit her lip. How long did poison take to act? Apple had only had a few sips, but maybe that was enough.

"It's always white. Besides, I'm not used to drinking. Remember what happened last time I had one of these?"

"You fell asleep. You didn't get sick."

Apple moistened her lips. "I'm fine. I just need to sit down. Could you open a window?"

Joanna set a glass of water in front of her. "Drink that. It will dilute the alcohol."

Apple put her hands around the water glass, then pushed it away. Holding her stomach, she slumped in the chair. "Take me to the emergency room."

Chapter 35

Apple lay in the hospital bed. The television suspended from the ceiling nattered a basketball game. Beyond Apple's curtained-off room, the emergency room bustled with moving gurneys and people in scrubs.

"I'm never drinking again. I'm sticking to tea for good," she said with a weakened voice. "God, I feel awful."

The curtain parted. Paul. Joanna rose abruptly from her plastic chair, dumping her purse from her lap to the floor. Paul glanced at Apple, then folded Joanna into his arms. She inhaled his aroma, a combination of soap and wood dust, and closed her eyes.

"What happened? I came as fast as I could," he asked.

"Apple was poisoned. She drank from a cocktail that had poisoned honey in it." Apple's red hair spilled over the pillow. "She could have died."

"I wanted to die when they were pumping my stomach, believe me," Apple said.

"What about you? You didn't have any of it?"

"I'd made the drink for myself, but Apple came by, and she likes them so much — really, it should have been me." Reluctantly, she left Paul's embrace. "Thanks for coming down to pick me up. I rode here in the ambulance."

"I'm glad you called."

"I wasn't sure if it was a good idea—I mean, I wanted to, but you know." She stared at her feet.

"I insisted," Apple said.

The curtain yanked open. Gavin, Apple's husband, rushed to the bed. "Apple," he said, ignoring Joanna and Paul. He rang the buzzer for a nurse. "What happened? I was at the office late, didn't get your message until now."

"Poison," Joanna said. She told him about the Bee's Knees and Apple collapsing in the dining room.

Apple, although quiet and gray-skinned, seemed to be enjoying the attention. She'd insisted on extra pillows and now had them fluffed and arrayed behind her.

"Who did this? Did you talk to the police?" Gavin asked.

"They just left."

"Why don't you guys go get some dinner?" Apple said. "I'll be fine. Gavin's here to keep me company."

An orderly appeared, wheeling a trolley with instruments on it.

Paul took her hand and led her from Apple's room through the emergency room and to the street. The night air was crisp. While she'd been inside, the clouds had dissolved, leaving patches of starry sky. In the parking garage, Paul opened the passenger door for Joanna and held out a hand. She boosted herself to the seat and settled into the smell of diesel and old truck. Paul's coffee mug and a red paper rose sold to benefit the Veterans of Foreign Wars sat on the dashboard. This, at least, was the same.

Instead of starting the truck, Paul turned to her. The springs in the bench seat creaked. "What's going on, Jo? Why was the honey poisoned?" His voice was tender but insistent. What had he been doing the past few days without her?

With regret, she looked at the stubble on his face and the bit of chest showing above his tee shirt, under the plaid wool shirt. He wasn't going to like this, but she was through avoiding it. She wasn't going to lie to him again. She met his eyes. "I've been trying to figure out who killed Poppy." She ran through the last few day's visits yet again — her meeting with Tranh, the visit to Helena's, Oaks Park, and the Thrillmeister yard. "The poison that killed Vivienne must have been in the honey. What I can't figure out is who put it there — or why."

"I thought that after Poppy you'd leave things alone."

"Poppy was murdered. I can't leave it alone." She dared him to meet her gaze.

He looked away and drummed a finger on the dashboard. "You told all this to the police tonight?"

"Of course." An officer had questioned her as the emergency room doctor hooked Apple to bits of medical machinery. Between worried glances at Apple, she had told the whole story as best she could. "They weren't in any rush to follow up. The officer said she'd get in touch with the homicide detective in the morning but couldn't do anything until then, and — " She switched gears. "Wait. The honey. We've got to tell Helena so she doesn't eat any by mistake."

Paul pulled his cell phone from his pocket. "Do you have the number?"

She dug through her purse until she found the scrap of paper Clary had jotted it on. Someday she'd consolidate all these and get them into an address book. "Right here." She pressed the numbers into the phone. It rang four times before clicking into voicemail. "Hi Helena, it's Joanna. Listen. I think the honey you gave me had poison in it — that's how Vivienne died. Don't eat it. In fact, set it aside. The police will probably want to test it. Give me a call to let me know you got this message." She pushed the "off" button and returned the phone to Paul.

"Better?" he asked.

"No. What if she's lost her phone or something and eats the honey by accident? I'm worried about her husband, too, that he might —"

"Her husband?"

Joanna nodded. "And Clary."

"Look," Paul said. "We don't even know for sure the honey's poisoned. Is it at your house?" She nodded. "Let's get it and drop it by the police station. Maybe by then Helena will have called you back." He leaned forward to start the pickup.

Yes, that was a good idea. She could check messages at her house. The last thing she needed was two friends in the hospital.

As the truck crossed the Hawthorne Bridge, the Rose Festival's Fun Center came into view. Amusement park rides churned at the waterfront, their lights bright against the black river. The Rock-O-Plane, maybe even the one Whitey had worked on, began to rotate, and crowds thronged carnival and food booths. Anchored to the river's sea wall on the other side of the bridge were three Navy ships docked for Fleet Week.

A few minutes later Paul parked in front of Joanna's house. She unclasped her seatbelt.

"I'll come in with you," Paul said.

"It's all right. I'll go to the police on my own." She grabbed her purse and opened the door.

"No. I'm coming, too."

She stopped and turned, but he brushed past her on the way to the door. Wasn't this what he'd been so dead-set against?

"Joanna, I get it. Besides, I'm not letting you get in deeper on your own. Grab the honey, and let's go."

Joanna clutched the honey jar, now sealed in a ziplock bag. The elevator opened into the lobby where she'd waited for Detective Sedillo the week before. She placed the honey gently on the ledge in front of the receptionist's window. "Detective Foster Crisp, please. It's Joanna Hayworth."

"What's that?" The receptionist squinted at the jar. He wasn't the receptionist there last time. His bright blue eyes were thrown into relief by a smattering of acne. Once his skin cleared up, he'd be a looker.

"Evidence," Paul said over Joanna's shoulder.

"It's for Detective Crisp. We called, and he said he'd meet us here."

"What case?" the receptionist asked.

What did it matter to him what case? "I worked with Detective Sedillo on a diamonds theft case, the one with Daniel Kay."

"That case is closed. It's an FBI matter now. Anyway, what does that have to do with your jar?"

"This has to do with Vivienne North's murder," Joanna said, increasingly frustrated.

"You mean 'homicide.' Vivienne North's homicide."

The elevator behind Joanna and Paul dinged as it opened. Crisp? Joanna glanced back, but it was just a janitor wheeling a large recycling container. He passed his keycard over the reader and entered the back offices.

"Fine, homicide. But the bottom line is that I just talked to Crisp, and he said to bring the evidence here, and he'd meet me." She leaned forward. "You're the receptionist, right?"

"I'm getting my degree in forensics, but for now, yeah, I guess I'm an office assistant."

"Then, assist. Please. Ring Crisp and tell him I'm here."

"Can't." He folded his arms. "He went home."

"What?" She looked back at Paul, who was studying the most-wanted list of criminals. She thought of Apple in the hospital bed. She'd surely have something to say about the criminals' auras.

"He left a message, though," the receptionist said. "I'm surprised he didn't call and tell you himself. He said to leave the evidence here. He'll get in touch with you later."

Finally the receptionist had deigned to give her some info. But Joanna didn't have a cell phone. If Crisp called her home number, she and Paul had already been on their way to the police station.

"Fill this out." The receptionist slid a form across the counter.

Joanna lifted a pen, chained to the counter as if someone would really steal a pen at the police station. "How long will it take to get back the results from the lab?"

"Depends on what they're testing for and what else is in the pipeline, but probably a week, maybe two. Without a rush, that is."

A week. Too long. Too much could happen in a week. She turned to Paul. "We have to tell Helena. She doesn't live too far, just up off Vista. Could you —?"

"Definitely. Let's go."

She remembered the blue dress hanging on the door of Helena's closet. "The Norths are supposed to go to a Rose Festival gala tonight, but maybe they haven't left yet. Come on."

Chapter 36

After the bustle of downtown, the Norths' neighborhood was quiet and dark. Paul pulled his truck into a spot near the bluff at the end of the street. Patches of clouds shrouded the moon.

"Can you see?" he asked Joanna. "Not many streetlights out here."

"Sure. It's a little chilly."

"Take this." Paul pulled a rag wool cardigan from behind his seat.

She slid her arms into the too-big sleeves. The North's house was dark, and the porch light was on. "I think we missed them."

"Let's check anyway. We're here."

Joanna rang the doorbell. "Maybe they're at the back of the house, and we can't see them."

Paul stepped down the brick-lined stoop and edged between the azaleas in front of the den window. He nimbly pulled himself up by the windowsill and with his toes resting on the lip of the foundation, peered into the room. He dropped instantly to the ground.

"Come here. Hurry." He clasped his hands for her to use as a step and hoisted her to the window.

"Oh my God." Wooden blinds sliced a chiffonade of moonlight over the den's inside wall, down a bookcase, and over the splintered remains of *Pacific Five*. The painting lay on the den floor, its canvas torn and frame cracked as if it had been stomped in a rage. Who could have done this? Her thoughts flashed to Tranh — and Gil. She leapt down from Paul's hands and scrambled up the stoop again. "We've got to get in there, make sure Helena's all right." She pounded on the front door.

A light came on at the house across the street, and the curtains moved.

"Come on. Let's try the back door. This way." He took her hand and led her across the front lawn. A light burned over the driveway, but it was dark around the side. He stopped at a small plastic box affixed to the side of the house. Its door was open. "Someone clipped the phone line to the security system," he said. "We should call the police."

"Open the gate," Joanna said. "What if they're in there, hurt?"

Paul hesitated, then reached over the shoulder-high gate and unlatched it. Amber light glowed from deep within the house.

"Paul, look." A window pane in the French doors was shattered. Joanna tried the door. Unlocked.

"Don't go in there, Jo, someone might still be there — "

She shoved past Paul to the stairs, taking them two at a time to arrive, breathless, on the landing. The light she'd seen was the upstairs hall light.

She braced herself for another body and pushed open Helena's bedroom. It was dark. Her eyes adjusted and she scanned the room. Bed made with military precision, nightstands empty but for a frilled lamp and a treatise on herbal remedies. The dress on the door was gone, and a hint of lily of the valley hung in the air. No body on the floor, though. Her shoulders relaxed. Gil and Helena must have gone to the Rose Festival gala after all. She turned to find Paul in the hall behind her.

"I take it no one's here."

"No. Not in this room, anyway," she said.

"You shouldn't have charged in here. Someone could have been waiting with a gun." He looked around warily. "Correction. Could still be hiding. Stay here while I look around."

Uncanny, that mention of a gun. He didn't know that she'd been shot at. "But I —"

"Wait."

She hovered near the door while Paul disappeared briefly into Gil's room, then into Vivienne's suite of rooms at the opposite end of the hall. He seemed to take longer in there. The house felt tomb-still. She thought of the destroyed painting in the den and tensed. Nothing but pure hatred could have wrought such damage. An otherworldly yowl erupted from the street, and Joanna started. Just a cat. Probably in heat — it was that time of year.

Paul returned. "Empty. Let's look downstairs." His hand rested on her lower back as they descended. He left her in the entry hall. "Wait here while I check the basement."

They needed to take whatever honey was left and have it tested. That would save the Norths from accidentally eating it. And since they were already here, well —

Paul shut the basement door behind him. "No one downstairs, either."

She nodded at the hall clock. "It's nine-fifteen. If the Norths are at the gala, we should have until ten, at least."

Paul raised his eyebrows. "What do you mean? We checked the house. Sure, the painting's destroyed, but no one's hurt."

Such beautiful eyes. And that tiny gap between his front teeth. Adorable. Damn it. She drew a deep breath."We're not quite finished yet."

Paul locked eyes with her. "What are you telling me?"

"We're here. We might as well get the rest of the honey and have a quick look around."

"For what?"

"Anything that would point to who killed Poppy and Vivienne." He opened his mouth to say something, and Joanna quickly added, "I really need your help. Please. There are a few things I haven't told you about Helena's husband, but he worries me."

He paused. He was clearly struggling.

"Please, Paul. I can't do this alone," she said softly. "Will you help me?"

He let out a breath. "All right. I guess we're already in. But just for fifteen minutes. Then we're out of here."

"Thank you." She touched his hand.

"Let's split up and look down here, then go back up to the bedrooms. We don't have a lot of time. I'll take the front of the house, and you take the dining and living rooms. If I see anyone, I'll whistle, and you run out the back door. If you make it back to the truck before I do, there's a spare key in a magnetic box in the driver's side front wheel well."

Joanna nodded, knowing there was no way she'd leave Paul behind. He moved quickly but calmly to the den. Intensely aware of being an intruder, she turned to the dining room. It seemed unlikely anything would be hidden in here. Too public. A long, Queen Anne-style table dominated the center of the room. China filled the buffet at the far end. She opened the buffet's drawers and found tidy stacks of silverware. Probably sterling. Instead of the floral Tiffany design she'd expected, though, they were a spare, mid-century shape. Likely Vivienne's.

The living room looked stiff with disuse. A crisp white sectional anchored one side of the room, but it was the room's only modern touch. Chintz-covered side chairs flanked a marble fireplace, over which hung a large painting of a fox hunt. Joanna wrinkled her nose. How did Gil feel about that? A few coffee table books, probably rarely perused, sat on the table next to a brass sculpture of a horse. The room could have been a stage set for a well-to-do Boston merchant's house.

The clock on the mantel chimed. It was nine-thirty.

A photo album lay at a crisp forty-five degree angle on the coffee table. Curiosity overtook Joanna. She knelt beside the coffee table and opened the album's stiff pages. The first page showed Vivienne as a young woman with a curly-haired, blond man and a baby. Gil. Even in the black and white photo, Vivienne's large eyes commanded the viewer. Joanna flipped a few more pages. All of Gil as a child. About halfway through the album was a photo of Helena in what looked to be a dorm room. A few pages later were Gil and Helena's wedding photos. Nothing of Helena as a child. Had Gil insisted on taking the place of honor?

She heard a rustle, and spun to face the doorway. It was Paul. "My God. You scared me."

"Nothing in the den. I checked the kitchen—it seemed like a good place to hide things—but didn't find anything unusual. Even the pantry was meticulous. Not a grain of flour anywhere."

"No honey? Not even in the liquor cabinet?" Joanna whispered.

"Nothing but a bottle of Irish whisky and, curiously, a handgun."

A gun. The skin on the back of her neck prickled.

"Come on, let's get this over with," Paul said. They climbed the stairs, Joanna following. The window over the landing was curtain-less, showing the faint lights of the house across the street.

"Gil's room is there." Joanna pointed to the closest door, at the back of the house. "Helena's is at that end, and Vivienne's old room is at the opposite end of the hall, over the garage."

"Let's start in Helena's room." Her bedroom door was open. Paul closed the curtains on the street side of the room. "Can you see without a light?"

She nodded. "There's enough from the hall."

"You check the closet and nightstand, and I'll start with the dresser."

Joanna opened the drawer on the nightstand. Inside were tissues and nothing else. So strange to think that French regency style nightstands even existed, as if Mary Antoinette put down her novel and snapped off the light every night before bed. Under the drawer was a cupboard with a shelf. Nothing in there, either.

She turned to the closet but stopped when she saw Paul going through the dresser. He carefully lifted each bundle of clothing and felt around the edges of the drawer. He moved quickly but methodically, a vague smile on his lips, but an expression of total focus. Despite all his warnings to her, he loved this. She could tell. The puzzle of breaking into a house, the challenge of finding something—he was in his element. The muscle on his jaw tensed. He lifted his head and caught her staring at him. She quickly turned away and opened the closet.

The closet was the same tidy row of dresses and blouses Joanna had seen earlier in the day, less, of course, the peach dress. The floor of the closet was clean, polished wood. A rack of shoes, clogs and European brands sold for comfort, lined the floor, but nothing else. The shelf above the clothes rack was outfitted with wire shelves to make the most of the old home's small closet. They held mostly purses in felt bags. Her pulse leapt. A lockbox shaped like a small suitcase leaned next to a pair of gold evening pumps.

"Look, Paul." Joanna reached for the box and set it on the bed. She tried the handle. "Locked."

"Bobby pin, please." She pulled one from her hair and handed it over. Paul bent it and slid it into the lock. It opened instantly. Joanna looked at him. First noticing the cut phone line, now opening the lock box in seconds. Maybe he'd picked up more from his uncle than he'd let on.

He rifled through the box's contents. "Not much," he said. "Gil's birth certificate, passports, a marriage certificate, but that's all."

"You'd think she would have kept these things in a safe deposit box," Joanna said.

Paul locked the box and slid it back in its place. "There's nothing here. Where next? Is there a room up here they use as an office?"

Moonlight cast an eerie glow through the batiste curtains. The darkness emphasized that they shouldn't be here. Uneasiness crept over Joanna. Maybe they should forget about the search and get out now.

Joanna opened her mouth to suggest they leave, when the wide beams of headlights swung into the driveway.

Chapter 37

Cold reality replaced Joanna's relief from not having found a body. She and Paul had broken into the Norths' house. Sure, the door had been open, and they'd done it with the best of motives, but this one would be hard to explain. She imagined telling Helena they'd seen the destroyed painting and thought she was in danger. She might understand. Or not. And what about Gil?

"We've got to go downstairs, tell them we're here," she said.

"And what? Get shot? Remember that painting," Paul said. "They're going to think we did that."

Yes, the painting. And the gun.

He pulled her to a crouch, below the window, and quickly parted the curtains. The rush of blood in her ears obscured his whisper, but she could read Paul's lips well enough: "Follow me," they said. Breathing quickly, she darted behind him past the window in the stairwell and into Vivienne's room at the far end of the hall. He pulled the door closed behind them. They stood, backs against the wall.

Car doors thudded shut. Helena's voice was a quiet buzz from the garage below, but Gil's low voice came through more clearly. Over the thudding of her heart, Joanna heard part of a complaint about the food and something about being "tired of all that bitching." The voices grew more faint as they passed out of the garage under them.

Paul grabbed her hand and squeezed. She wasn't alone, and he wanted her to know that. She squeezed back, longer. She'd been crazy to involve him in all this. He shouldn't go to jail for her. "I'm sorry," she mouthed to him. Sorry for everything.

They stood still. She opened her mouth slightly to soften her breathing. Where were the Norths now?

Voices drifted from the upstairs hall. "I'm going to bed," Helena said. She sounded too near to be at the other end of the hall, but maybe it was a trick of the space.

Gil's voice boomed from downstairs. "Fine. I'm going to watch a little TV, take in the news. See you in the morning."

Their conversation was flat and uninflected with emotion. Helena's footsteps passed down the hall. The painting. Surely Gil would see the painting and raise the alarm. Then what?

Paul put his mouth close to Joanna's ears. "Stay up against the wall. The floor won't creak here."

An anguished shout rose from downstairs. He'd found the remains of *Pacific Five*. Helena's steps sounded light and quick down the stairs. Joanna had never heard Helena yell, but her anger sliced the air. "I'm calling the police!"

Blood rang in Joanna's ears. Now there was no way they could announce their presence. God knew what would happen if they did. If Gil called the police — and why wouldn't he? — they'd be arrested for sure.

"No," Gil's voice shot out. After a shocked moment, Helena's higher pitched voice continued, but more quietly. "No, and that's final," he responded. A cupboard door was thrown open and another door slammed. Joanna's eyes widened. Maybe they'd have to save Helena after all. She held her breath.

After a long pause, Helena's footsteps re-entered the upstairs hall.

"We can wait here until they go to sleep, then leave," Paul whispered.

How long would that be? Hours, maybe. The evening news was at what—ten o'clock? She carefully leaned against the wall.

Helena's door creaked open. "Honey, did you close my bedroom curtains?"

Damn. They'd forgotten to open them again. Helena was obsessive about her space. She'd probably notice if even a bobby pin were moved.

"No. You know I don't go in there." Gil sounded tense, but calmer. "They're closed. I didn't close them."

"Maybe you did and forgot. You've been a little distracted since mom's death."

A pause. "No, I'm telling you, I didn't close them."

Joanna froze, every fiber of her body tense.

"Gil," Helena said, "Come up here."

Joanna felt Paul shift. Their smallest movement set off whispers of noise that seemed to reverberate through the house. She caught Paul's hand and hurried him to the bedroom off of the sitting area. "There's a window to the backyard." The bedroom door was already ajar. Paul closed it silently. Joanna glanced behind them. Helena and Gil's voices murmured down the hall. Don't come in here. Please.

The casement windows opened out. Paul unlatched one side and looked down, then back at Joanna. She nodded. They'd have to jump. She tied up her skirt. Paul hoisted himself into the window frame, legs first, put his hands beside him and jumped. He landed on his feet with a thud and fell to a crouch. Next door, a dog began to bark.

Steps sounded in the hall. She glanced back to see a ribbon of light under the door. No time to lose. Hands trembling, she perched in the window frame as she'd seen Paul do and looked down. It was at least a fifteen-foot drop. She heard the door to Vivienne's sitting room open behind her. She closed her eyes and said a quick prayer. She kicked off the window sill. The fall seemed to last a lifetime. Paul's arms cushioned her landing. He pulled her to her feet and the ground wobbled beneath her. She put a hand to the tender side of her head. The concussion.

"Come on!" He whispered urgently.

They raced through the backyard on a narrow stone path, beyond the vegetable garden to the stands where the bee houses once stood. Chests heaving, they huddled against the fence. It only took a few seconds to make it to the back of the yard, but it would take less than that for Helena to reach Vivienne's bedroom and find the window open. She peeked around the side of the empty bee house stands. Light glared from Vivienne's windows.

"They know we're here," Joanna whispered. She flattened a hand to her forehead. If only her head would steady for a moment.

Paul grabbed her free hand. They fled along the back fence toward an old rhododendron. He pulled her under just as the backyard filled with light. There way no way they'd make it to the front gate without being spotted. The rest of the yard was fenced shoulder-high. They were trapped. The police would arrive any minute now.

"I'm so sorry. I never should have—"

Ignoring her, Paul pulled himself into the large shrub's branches and gestured for her to follow. Joanna's country childhood came back as she gripped the trunk and hoisted herself up. Small branches scratched her thighs and face. Surely Helena and Gil would see the movement. Would they run to the street and cut off their escape?

Paul dropped into the neighbor's yard and waited for her to do the same. The neighbor's house was quiet, the TV now mute. Joanna moved toward the house, but Paul pulled her back. "They'll think of that," he said, nodding at the North's house. "This way." A small cedar fence divided this yard from the one behind it. Moonlight barely outlined the silhouettes of patio furniture and a swing set.

Paul boosted her over the fence and followed, yanking her through the yard, under an illuminated second story window. Joanna tripped over a tricycle, but Paul pulled her onward. No fence hemmed in the front of the house, and within seconds they were on the street.

Joanna quickly untied her skirt. It fell around her legs. She reached down to rub her calf, bruised by the tricycle, but Paul slipped an arm around her waist and pulled her upright. "Keep walking."

The street behind Helena and Gil's house fronted a ravine. Darkness, broken only by pale yellow porch lights, cloaked the sidewalk. They reached the end of the block where the residential street met the larger road, but instead of turning right to go back to the car, Paul led her across Vista. They plunged into the neighborhood. "We're taking the long way back," he said.

"What about the truck?"

"I'll go back and get it later." He still held her hand. The wide palm, the slightly calloused fingers, soothed her. Joanna's body settled into jittery exhaustion. Paul seemed curiously calm, even euphoric.

"You like this, don't you?"

They walked together a few steps before he replied. "I hope we never have to do anything like that again."

"But you liked it," she repeated.

A slight smile played on his lips. "It was exciting. I wasn't sure we were going to make it out of the house. Then the yard."

"Your uncle. You were thinking about him, weren't you?"

"Yes."

They walked another block together. She waited for more. She knew he had more to say.

"I always idolized my uncle. You know — he was the guy who broke into rich people's homes and took things they didn't need anyway. No one ever got hurt."

"Kind of glamorous, almost." Down in the city, a siren cried. Somewhere, someone had slipped on wet tile, or sank into an armchair clutching his chest, or hot oil had splashed from a skillet, searing an arm. It seemed so far away.

"I've been really down on your following up on Poppy."

"Yes." The sidewalk passed step, step, step under their feet.

"Kind of demanding."

She didn't need to reply to this.

"I want to tell you something. I should have told you earlier, I just…"

She let the anonymity of the night do its work. Up the hill they walked, then turned in to a side street.

"I helped my uncle on a few of his heists."

She drew a quick breath. "You were young — " she started.

"I loved it."

Her step faltered, then she caught up with him again. "You did?"

"I did. You saw me. It's a huge charge, breaking into a house. We always made it out, had the goods."

"What — what did you do?"

"Not much, really. I was good at cracking security systems. Then

I'd let Uncle Gene take over, and I'd wait in the car."

"But you were never caught."

"No." A few seconds lapsed. "No, I wasn't around when he was finally nailed. But I saw what it did to him." Paul turned to her. "His wife left him. He went to jail. He lost everything. I should have told you sooner."

Paul's uncle must have covered up for him. On some level he'd felt responsible. "That's old history now. A long time ago," she said.

"I wasn't even out of high school yet. But you see why Poppy's jail time for stealing diamonds got to me. I've lived completely straight since then."

As far as she knew, he had. Maybe that's why he was so cautious that he didn't even drink.

They turned to the main thoroughfare and continued to walk like any couple out for an evening stroll. Maybe their "break" was over. She hoped so.

They climbed the hill and crossed the Vista Bridge, pausing for a few seconds in the brisk night to take in the view. Red lights of traffic headed downtown streamed away, while the white headlights of traffic through the canyon came toward them. "When I was a little girl," Joanna said, "I remember standing somewhere like this with my grandmother and sharing my grand revelation that if you had red lights you drove on one side of the road, and everyone with white lights drove on the other. Grandma set me straight, of course."

Paul laughed, but not Joanna. She wondered if he'd be able to sleep tonight reliving the break-in and escape in his mind. If she didn't sleep, it would be worry — worry about Apple and about being caught. They hadn't been very careful. They'd probably left fingerprints everywhere. Plus, the nosy neighbor across the street had definitely seen them.

"Thank you for telling me about your uncle," Joanna said. "It explains a lot."

He squeezed her hand.

They traversed the neighborhood, away from the direction of the truck, then crossed Vista again. They were making a wide circle around Helena's house. The occasional car passed. Streets wound more here, and houses perched up against the hills. In some places the sidewalks narrowed to just a few feet. Paul and Joanna's gait was steady on the pavement.

They continued by a wooded area. His smile faded. A police cruiser crawled past them on a side street. She forced herself to calm down. There's no way the police knew what she and Paul were up to. They couldn't. All at once Paul pushed her against a tree, his back to the street, and kissed her. The tree's bark grated into her back, but she barely noticed as she relaxed into Paul's arms.

The cruiser passed, and as suddenly as he had held her he released her and pulled her back to the sidewalk. "Come on, it's only a few more blocks."

Joanna gasped. "For God's sake, Paul. Don't do that unless you mean it." With her fingers she combed a leaf from her hair.

He didn't say anything, and she couldn't read his face in the dark. "We didn't find anything at the North's. No honey, either," Paul said.

"No." Another siren sounded in the city below, bringing back thoughts of Apple in the hospital. Maybe she was home by now.

"So besides Helena and Gil, you think the murderer could be the artist who painted the painting in the den, or the carnie from Oaks Park, right?"

"They seem most likely. Don't forget about Clary. Yesterday Helena told me he was interested in her, but Vivienne didn't approve. Helena said it's all over now. I just don't know. Plus, what if Gil found out?"

"Clary. Sure. I remember him."

"Uh huh."

"Clary and Helena? But Eve——" Paul didn't finish his thought.

"But what?" Joanna rankled at the sound of Eve's name from Paul's mouth. Eve bought that dress for some big date. She was so damned coy about it, too.

"Nothing." He looked puzzled.

They continued to walk. The truck wasn't far now. The events of the evening—the whole day, in fact—had left her in a state of edgy exhaustion. But at least Paul got it now. He understood why she couldn't just leave things alone as he'd wanted. And she understood why he'd been so protective. She glanced at him. His profile showed determination, but the lines around his mouth had softened.

"I'm glad you came with me tonight," she said.

He squeezed her hand again but said nothing.

"I'm glad you see how frightening things were getting, how I had to do something for Poppy." Their steps hit the sidewalk in tandem. "I haven't even told you about the store."

Paul fell out of stride. "What about the store?"

She told him about the caller and the gunshot. "The window's shattered, but thanks to the safety glass, the bullet didn't do as much damage."

Paul stopped cold. "He shot at you?"

"Yes, but only a warning shot. That's what the police figure."

"I'm—I'm speechless." He walked, but now strolled ahead of her.

She hurried to catch up with him. "I fell, that's all. Just a slight concussion. Crisp says if the shooter had wanted to get me, he would have."

"Foster Crisp came? From homicide?"

"Well, yes. There were gunshots." She hadn't even told him about the first threatening call.

"This is insane. I was right in the first place. Joanna, you cannot follow up with any more of this. This goes way beyond whatever happened to Uncle Gene."

"But…" She bit her lip. "But I thought you understood. I thought you even enjoyed it, to tell the truth. And what about Apple? I can't stop now. I can't."

Joanna pulled Paul's rag wool sweater tighter. Paper crinkled in its pocket. Without thinking she pulled it out. "What's this?" She flattened the paper in her palm. Under the streetlight's weak glow she made out a few words, "can't stop thinking about you" and "want to" in Paul's messy script.

"Give that to me." Paul yanked the paper from her, but she'd gripped it tightly. The paper tore in half.

She moved away from him, surprised at the urgency in his voice. "What? What are you hiding?"

"Give it to me," he repeated. He snatched the rest of the note from her fingers.

"What?" Joanna's voice rose in fury. Eve. Damn it. She had been right about them all along. "A rough draft? And what did she say when she got the note?" Her face burned and hands shook.

"Jo, I just spent the evening breaking into a house for you. We narrowly escaped. We could have both been tossed in jail — and for good reason. But you don't trust me."

"Why should I when — when you're writing mash notes to Eve?"

His pleading turned to anger. "What makes you think it was to Eve? Besides, you should talk. I can't trust you to keep a promise.

You told me you'd butt out of all this diamond and murder business. Then I find out about the sting operation. And now someone is trying to kill you. What if you'd died?"

"Not kill me. Just warn me."

He shook his head. "I can't trust you. I can't trust you to keep a promise. I can't trust you to take care of yourself, even. You even came over to the shop when I wasn't there."

That's right — she'd forgotten. Her face burned. She should have told him. "How do you know?"

"Gemma puked up a blueberry muffin." He clenched his fists and released them. "I was wrong to think I could do this." His voice softened. "All we went through tonight, and still you don't trust me." He wouldn't look at her. "I can't do this. There's no way we can make it."

Joanna slowed, but Paul walked ahead. "Paul — " She started, uncertainly.

"I'll take you to the bus. I'm walking home."

Chapter 38

Joanna pushed open the door of the Night Light tavern. The bus had deposited her down the block, and she had been walking past to get home when she remembered Eve mentioning the Night Light as a place she visited sometimes. Maybe she'd be there now, and Joanna could give her a piece of her mind. Yes, she'd march up to that woman and let her know exactly where she could get off. Besides, on a practical note, the Night Light would be warm. She'd left Paul's sweater wadded up on the bus seat, and she shivered in the spring night air. And, oh, how she wanted a drink.

The familiar mix of 1980s music, dim light, and muffled conversation greeted her. This month's art show focused on wizards. Wizards riding horses, waving magic wands, and drinking foaming potions. But no Eve. She slumped into a corner booth under a water color of a wizard zapping a bulky demon with a lightning bolt.

The waitress set a cocktail napkin on her table. "Long time no see." She put a hand on her hip. "You don't look so good."

"It's been a hellish day. You wouldn't even believe it."

"Oh Joanna. I'm sorry." Her kohl-rimmed eyes drew together in sympathy. "The usual?"

"Nice and dry, please, with a twist." The day's events played and replayed through her brain. Poppy's funeral. Leo. Apple in the hospital. Breaking into Helena's. And, of course, ruining things for good with Paul.

She was going to get good and drunk.

The Martini arrived a minute later. "On the house," the waitress said.

Joanna slid the cocktail close and tipped the icy gin into her mouth. Except for the elderly woman at the bar—the one who used to play the drums for a Nirvana opening band, and she was no spring chicken back then—the bar was full of couples. One couple, both in stocking caps and too-short jeans, played backgammon. Another couple drained pint glasses, their lip piercings bulging against the glass. A middle-aged couple took a table in the middle of the room and studied the menu. Probably in for a nightcap after dinner at the French restaurant down the block. The man seemed particularly interested in the wizard painting nearest him, featuring sleeping unicorns.

Martini number two arrived. As Joanna poured the last few drops of her first cocktail into the second, the tavern's door opened and damp night air ruffled the stack of weeklies on a nearby bench.

That halo of golden hair. It could only be Eve. Oh good. She had some choice words for that home wrecker. She put her hands beside her to boost herself up, then dropped to the seat again. Behind Eve was a man. Joanna swallowed hard as the man turned to face the room.

Clary? What the hell was he doing here?

Clary put a hand on the small of Eve's back and guided her to a booth across the room. Eve delicately scooted down the bench and Clary settled close to her. Very close. It was unlikely they'd be able to see Joanna in the darkened corner, but she was perfectly placed to see Clary and the side of Eve's head. Eve lifted her jacket from her shoulders, revealing a spill of pale green silk. The Hermès scarf.

Clary had bought the scarf for Eve, not Helena.

Clary plus Eve. Joanna had been so wrong. Eve wasn't after Paul at all.

She'd totally blown it.

Joanna tapped her glass, signaling she wanted another drink. Someone once said, "Martinis are like a woman's breasts—one is too few, and three is too many." Tonight she preferred James Thurber's take on the old saying, "One Martini is all right; two is too many; and three is not enough."

Her stupid, stupid jealousy had ruined everything. The bartender strained the cocktail into a glass and dropped in a twist before signaling the waitress. Light reflected off the tiny ice particles floating on its surface. Joanna sighed. Drinking wasn't going to help anything. She'd just wake up in the morning with a sour stomach and an awful taste in her mouth. She'd pay her bill and leave. At home waited a stack of torch songs and a few boxes of tissue. If only she could get out without Eve and Clary seeing her.

The waitress deposited the cocktail on Joanna's table.

Joanna touched her arm and said in a low voice, "Is there an exit in the annex?" She nodded at the doorway to the bar's side room. It was only open for private events or when the bar was particularly busy. It would be a lot easier to sneak out through there than dart by Clary and Eve for the front door.

"Sure, but it lets out at the dumpsters behind the tattoo parlor. What's wrong with the front door?"

"Some people I know just came in, and I don't want to talk about" —she paused to find a good word— "everything that's happened today. It's all too much."

The waitress nodded, her shoulder-dusting earrings swishing.

"I'll turn off the alarm for a couple of minutes so you can make your getaway."

Joanna withdrew some bills from her purse and tossed them next to the untouched Martini. She slid from her booth and glanced toward Eve and Clary. Their heads were close, Eve talking while Clary, enraptured, looked on. The coast was clear.

She stood, slightly swaying. Sister Mary Alberta was right. Booze did not mix well with a concussion. She should have drunk more water with those Martinis. Had she even eaten lunch? She backed toward the wall and stood until the room leveled out. Man. This was ridiculous. On a normal day, she could handle two cocktails just fine. Hand against the wall, she moved toward the entrance to the back room, but her feet tangled with a bar stool, sending it careening to the floor with a crash.

All eyes turned to Joanna. The murmur of voices halted, and Herb Alpert's trumpet filled the void with a couple of bars of Spanish-inflected brass before people resumed talking. Joanna's face flamed with embarrassment. The bartender picked up the stool, and Joanna felt a hand at her elbow. Clary.

"Are you all right?" With his other hand, he pushed in his glasses.

Eve joined them. "Joanna. You've been drinking, haven't you?" She looked at the two empty cocktail glasses on Joanna's table.

"It's a bar. I might have had something to drink."

"Why don't you come sit with us for a minute? I'll order some coffee. You're not driving, are you?" Eve asked. Her voice was soft. She seemed genuinely concerned.

"No, no, I'm walking. It's just a few blocks. I need to get home."

"Are you sure?" Clary said. "It's no trouble to take you home."

"If you'd like, I can call Paul," Eve said.

That would be the final humiliation. Joanna willed a confident smile. "No. Please don't. Really, I'm fine. Clumsy, that's all. See you soon."

She strolled toward the back room. "Emergency Exit Only," the door to the alley read. She pushed it open and emerged into the alley, scaring a rat from under the dumpster. The bar's alarm bells clanged through the night.

Chapter 33

Had she really fallen asleep? The gray daylight seeping through the curtains signaled morning, so she must have, despite tossing and turning all night.

She dragged herself to the closet and pulled out an old house-dress in drab gray and dark blue to wear. Rain splattered from the gutters, matching her mood. She dialed Apple's house. With any luck they had released her from the hospital last night and she'd be home by now.

Gavin answered. "Oh, she's fine. A little worn out, but all right. I think she's enjoying the attention. I'm just glad she's okay." Apple's voice sounded in the background. "She wants to talk to you."

"Joanna," Apple said. "You've got to be careful. Someone is really dangerous—unhinged."

"I know, believe me."

"No, I mean it. I'd never felt so out of it last night, but I kept having dreams. Horrible dreams. It's cold and wet and I smell engine grease. I hear screaming. Warn the sisters, too."

"I know. I mean—obviously."

"Call the police again. I'm worried. See if they know anything new."

Detective Crisp. He'd be happy to hear from her. Right. Joanna hesitated, and Apple added, "Promise me."

Joanna sighed. Maybe he'd have news about the honey, at least. "Okay, I promise."

"Good. I need to go now. Gavin's bringing me breakfast in bed." She must have moved the phone away from her mouth. "Gavey? Don't let that steep too long." Then, into the phone's receiver, "Be careful, and call the detective."

Joanna hung up, then picked up the phone again and dialed.

"Foster Crisp."

"This is Joanna Hayworth. I —"

"Ms. Hayworth. I was just going to call you. We need to talk. In person."

In person? Alarmed, she said, "I was just going to the store."

"Fine. Can you meet me there right away?"

Despite being in such a rush to meet her at Tallulah's Closet, Detective Crisp was nowhere to be seen when Joanna arrived. Why was he so eager, anyway? He couldn't possibly know about last night at the Norths, could he? Her throat tightened.

The store's lights barely illuminated the gloom cast by the rain outside. The radio had broadcast a "severe weather alert" warning about floods. Not a very welcoming environment for customers. Replacing the window in the door would cost at least three cocktail dresses — or a part of one of Vivienne's suits. Hopefully she'd get some business today.

She flipped through her record albums to find something suitable for the morning. Maybe the Carpenters. That song about rainy days and Mondays would hit the spot. Record in hand, she started at the sharp knock on the plywood nailed over the door. The detective.

"May I?" Crisp shook out his umbrella and set it next to the door. He sat on the bench in the center of the store, the scent of wet wool rising from his pants. He motioned for Joanna to join him. "I'm sorry about your friend. Why don't you tell me what's been going on?"

Joanna picked up a gold lamé mule near her feet and set it on the bench. Another loose end, just like everything else in her life right now. She'd find its mate later.

"Apple was poisoned by honey that Helena Schuyler North gave me. I'm sure of it. I bet the honey was what killed Vivienne North, too. We need to figure out who poisoned it. I brought it to the station last night."

Crisp's cowboy boots scuffed the floor as he repositioned himself. "You have ideas?"

She couldn't tell if he was serious or just humoring her. "A few, actually."

"Let's hear them." He couldn't have seemed less interested.

"You don't care, do you?"

"It's not that, Joanna. It's just—"

The emotion of the past weeks teetered like a snowball on the top of a cliff. If she let go now, the detective was in for a real treat. "Poppy was my friend. She was in the wrong place at the wrong time and ended up dead. First you guys wrongly arrested her for selling stolen diamonds, so she spent time in jail. Some of her last days. In jail." She leaned forward. "That last night Vivienne was alive, she called Poppy. Did you know that?"

"Yes. We know."

"Poppy said she sounded delirious. It had to be the poison. Every night Vivienne drank a cocktail called a Bee's Knees. It's made with gin and honey. I know you tested the gin, but you must have for-gotten the honey. That's all I can think."

Crisp's expression remain unchanged. "I know. We got preliminary results this morning."

"And?"

"No poison."

Joanna's jaw dropped. "Nothing?"

He shook his head.

"You said 'preliminary' results. You just haven't found the right poison yet. Apple—"

"She must have eaten something else. Maybe at lunch."

For a moment, Joanna couldn't find words. "But I…" It had to be the honey. Had to.

He fastened his gaze on Joanna. "Speaking of telephone calls, the Norths reported a break-in last night. We discovered they'd received a call from a cellphone that evening. Your boyfriend's phone."

Joanna's anger melted into fear. She fidgeted and looked at her lap. "Really? A break-in?"

"You didn't ask if anything was stolen."

She drew a breath and looked him in the eyes. Less suspicious that way. "Was there?"

He paused, still watching, and said finally, "No. Nothing they could find. One of Gil North's paintings was damaged, though."

Fearing her lower lip would quiver, she put a hand over her mouth. She wanted to scream and blurt out that it was already destroyed when they arrived. But she couldn't. "That's awful. He must be really upset."

"Strangely, he isn't. That doesn't mean we won't find out who broke in. People try to hide things from us all the time, and we find them out." He stood. "I suppose you'll want to be opening the store now." He headed toward the door, then turned around. "One more thing. Where were you last night? We tried to call."

"Me? I went to the hospital, of course. Then I — " Flustered, Joanna paused. "I guess I was in shock and went to sleep. The concussion, you know. The last thing I was thinking about was talking on the phone." Now she was lying to the police. Again.

"I see. Oh, I almost forgot. One of the Norths' neighbors reported seeing a pickup truck in front of their house last night. Not a truck she recognized, either, although she said she's sure she would know it again if we showed her a photo."

Paul's truck. Damn. His phone, and now his truck. There's no way she was letting him take the blame for her terrible plan. No way. She drew a shaky breath.

"Maybe I didn't tell the whole truth. I didn't want to tell you where I was last night because — because it was embarrassing. I needed to ask Helena something... personal, so I used Paul's phone to call her — you know I don't have a cell phone — then borrowed his truck to go see her." Should she have called a lawyer before talking to Crisp? He wasn't taking notes. Too late now. "She wasn't home, so I left."

Completely unconvincing. Even as the words left her mouth she knew how bogus they sounded. Despite the blood hammering at her ears, she felt faint. He would surely reach for the handcuffs now and take her away.

Instead, Detective Crisp picked up his umbrella. "I see." He stood and stretched. He pointed behind her. "By the way, that other gold shoe? It's under the chair."

She turned her head. The lamé mule's toe peeked from under the chair's ruffle.

Crisp looked at her for a moment longer than necessary, then left the store.

*
**

Rain pounded on the aluminum awning and gushed down the gutters. No one had been in the store for hours. Joanna had already spaced the dresses evenly along the racks and tidied the hat and jewelry displays. She moved a lamp to illuminate the shadow caused by the plywood nailed over the door. Now she was scrubbing the seams of a pair of patent leather stilettos. They were already clean, but she'd do anything to keep from thinking of the mess she was in. Maybe Detective Crisp was talking to Helena right now, and maybe Helena was telling him she saw Joanna running through the backyard when her house was broken into. She pushed the stilettos to the side.

Just as Joanna had decided to sort through a jar full of buttons, the bell jangled. It was one half of the nearly indistinguishable couple who usually shopped together. Natalie — or Nicole.

Natalie or Nicole shed her coat by the door. "Is it okay if I leave this here? I'm drenched. What happened to the door?"

"Accident. I'm hoping to get the glass replaced some time this week." Change the subject. "Where's — uh — "

"Nicole? Cleaning the gutters. They're predicting floods. The mayor's even talking about stacking sandbags along the river." Natalie smoothed her wet hair and set down two to-go cups with tea bags dangling from them. "I just dropped in to see Apple."

"She's — she's not feeling great today." Big understatement. "Can I help you?"

"I brought her some tea, that's all. There's a Zandra Rhodes caftan

I wanted to show her a picture of, too."

Joanna expected Natalie to pull out her phone with the photo, but she wasn't paying attention. She stared at Vivienne's peach dress behind the counter. Joanna hadn't had time to price it and put it out.

"Did Eve sell you that dress?" Natalie asked.

Eve? "No, I picked it up a few days ago from the owner's daughter-in-law. Why?"

"I could swear I saw it at Eve's. Is it an Adele Simpson?" She pulled the dress from the rack. "It is."

Joanna grabbed the dress's right sleeve and fingered the seam near the wrist. Yes, there it was, the tiny, telltale hole left by a price gun. She dropped the sleeve as if it were molten metal. The truth took a moment to sink in.

Helena had lied to her. Why?

Natalie slipped on her raincoat. "Well, tell Apple I stopped by, and I hope she's feeling better soon. I'll leave the other tea with you. If you don't mind my saying so, you look like you could use it."

"Thanks, and stay dry," Joanna said absently.

Helena had used the dress to lure Joanna to her house. She wanted to tell Joanna about Clary, cast blame on him. And give her the honey.

No. Couldn't be. Crisp said the honey wasn't poisoned. Plus, the killer had tried to implicate Helena by making Joanna tell the police she'd seen her leaving Poppy's body.

Joanna circled the store, straightening hangers and spacing dresses evenly along their rods, even though they didn't need it. If the killer were Helena — ridiculous, but consider it a moment — she would have known the police would clear her immediately. By calling Joanna and forcing her to lie to the police, she made Joanna look bad, not her. After all, Joanna herself had seen Helena at her table before she went to the green room in search of Poppy. But earlier, Helena had been away from the table. She could have killed Poppy then.

And Helena let Ben find her in Poppy's office. The bit about a call from Gil could have easily been an excuse. She didn't want Poppy cleared. No, she wanted her in jail not just for selling diamonds, but for poisoning Vivienne.

Joanna shivered. Why? Why would Helena do it? Poppy's voice came back to her. "Voyeurs," Poppy thought Vivienne had told her. What if it wasn't "voyeurs" at all, but "voyageurs"—or, in English, travelers? Leo was a traveler and knew Helena. Could she be one, too? She pictured Helena's patrician features and New England-touched accent. But what if her features were bleached white? Albino? Helena and Leo might be twins.

She returned to the tiki bar and took a deep breath. The killer wasn't Clary or Gil or Tranh at all. It was Helena. Helena murdered Vivienne and Poppy. Joanna had to talk to Crisp. Immediately.

Her hand nudged a package next to the phone. Natalie must have set it down and forgotten it. Through the plastic bag showed the lurid, 1950s-style cover of a battered paperback. *My Gun is Quick* by Mickey Spillane. The book on the Mother's nightstand.

The breath went out of her like she'd been hit. The Mother. She must call the convent to warn them. First the convent, then Crisp. The dial took forever to spin then click each number. Come on, come on, pick up.

Mary Alberta's voice sounded distracted. "Hello, Sisters of the—"

"Mary Alberta? Joanna. Listen, you—"

"Thank the Lord you called. It's the Mother. She's missing."

Chapter 40

"Hold tight. I'll be right there." Joanna fumbled for her keys and locked up the store. She ran to dodge the rain, and the inside of the car began to steam up as soon as she started the engine. She mopped at the windshield with a rag. Old Blue's windshield wipers batted weakly at the downpour.

Apple had warned her to tell the nuns. Of course, Helena would make sure the Mother wouldn't repeat to anyone the story about Oaks Park.

Joanna swerved and pushed the horn when a car tried to move into her lane. How could the Mother have disappeared? She couldn't even walk. Helena was solid and the Mother was frail. Still, it was hard to imagine Helena sneaking into the convent and hauling the Mother out over her shoulder.

Ten minutes later Joanna pulled up by the convent's kitchen entrance. Mary Alberta stood at the door, her usually placid expression twisted with worry.

"Come in, come in." She gestured toward the kitchen.

Joanna dashed in, holding her coat over her head. "What happened?" Water streamed from her coat to the linoleum.

"About an hour ago Vivienne's daughter-in-law, Helena, came by. We weren't expecting her. Mary Frances and I were finishing up lunch. Helena said she was in the neighborhood and wanted to stop in for Vivienne's sake. She wanted to see Mother."

Helena must have left the house right after the detective's visit, Joanna thought.

Mary Alberta paced. "Mother didn't seem surprised she was here at all. I led Helena upstairs, then came down to clean up the lunch dishes." The dishes in the drainer shone in the kitchen's yellow light.

"Yes?"

"She didn't stay long—Helena, that is. Maybe ten or fifteen minutes. After she left, I made the Mother a plate of leftovers from last night's supper and brought it up to her. She wasn't there."

"Are you sure she's really gone?" It seemed impossible she could have left on her own. "Maybe she just went down the hall. Maybe she's still here."

"She's not, I'm telling you. I searched the whole house."

"You're certain Helena left alone, right? How long was it from when she left and you discovered Mother was gone?"

"I was in the kitchen, but I heard the front door close, and right after that I heard a car on the street in front. It had to have been her. I admit I wasn't paying a lot of attention. Mostly I was thanking the good Lord that even in this rain the exhaust fan in the kitchen doesn't leak anymore."

The good Lord and Paul, Joanna thought.

"We've looked everywhere—downstairs, the garden, even the basement," Mary Alberta said.

If Helena took the Mother away, they might never find her. She was undoubtedly desperate enough. Joanna should have warned the nuns. Instead of wasting time at Tallulah's Closet, she should have been at the convent. "Mary Alberta, there's something I have to tell you."

Mary Alberta gestured, indicating Joanna should get on with it.

"I think Helena killed Vivienne and my friend, Poppy."

"What?" Mary Alberta and Mary Frances said in concert.

"It takes too long to explain, but Mother shouldn't have been left alone with her." Joanna's voice choked in frustration. "Listen, is there any chance the Mother could have left on her own?"

The Marys shot glances at each other across the hall. "Well—" Mary Frances started.

"She didn't like to advertise it, but she could get around a little better than she made out," Mary Alberta finished.

So there was at least a small chance that Helena didn't take her. "Could she get downstairs?"

"I don't know about that," Mary Alberta said.

"I have noticed a little pie missing some mornings," another Mary said.

"But that would have been Mary Catherine, don't you think?"

"And found a plate and fork in the Mother's room," Mary Carmen added.

"If she went anywhere, she had to have taken her cane." She trotted up the stairs to the second floor where Mother's bedroom was. "It's not here. She took it. Mother took her cane and went somewhere," she shouted from the landing.

If the Mother left the house on her own, in this rain, she had to have a good reason. Something sparked by Helena's visit. "Is there a cab company you guys use?"

"Mother likes Radio Cab. A lot of veterans drive for them. She likes to talk to the older drivers about the war," Mary Alberta said, downstairs again. "Their number's in there."

In the kitchen, Mary Alberta handed her a small notepad with Radio Cab's number and logo printed across the bottom.

"May I use your phone?" Joanna asked.

"Right here." Mary Alberta pointed to a mustard yellow phone affixed to the kitchen wall.

Joanna dialed the cab company's number. "Hi, yes. I'm calling about a customer you picked up at the Sisters of Saint Mary Salome the Myrrh Bearer convent."

The Marys looked at each other. Another Mary joined them in the kitchen, and Joanna heard the front door close. Business at the rectory must be over.

"Yes." Relief washed over Joanna. Mother had taken a cab. "I know you don't normally give out this kind of information, but we need to know where the customer went. You see, she's the Mother Superior." She grasped the phone more tightly. "Me? I'm, uh, the Mother Superior's secretary, and we urgently need to get in touch with her. She doesn't carry a cell phone." The dispatcher paused. "It's very important. God's business. Thank you. I'll be right here. Yes, that's the number."

Joanna hung up the phone. "We were right. They picked up Mother a little while ago. They're going to call the driver of the cab that took her." She wanted to get in touch with Detective Crisp, but didn't want to tie up the line until the cab company called back.

"What happened?" a short, plump nun Joanna vaguely remember as having the unlikely name of Mary Marsha, asked as she shook rain off her habit.

Mary Alberta hesitated. A few more Marys joined the group in the kitchen. "I guess you'll find out sooner or later. Mother has disappeared." A clamor of voices rose.

As if on cue, the phone rang. Joanna grabbed it and took a breath to relax her voice. "Sisters of Saint Mary Salome the Myrrh Bearer here. May I help you?"

"We never answer the phone like that," a voice murmured at the back of the kitchen.

Joanna nodded. "Yes, thank you. Oh, and God bless." She hung up and reached for her coat.

"Where is she?" Mary Alberta asked.

Joanna ignored her question. "I'll come back with her, don't worry." The sisters were too mixed up in this as it was. She slapped Crisp's card on the counter. "Call this number right away and tell the detective everything I told you about Helena. Tell him to meet me at the Rose Festival's Fun Center." She slid on her coat and opened the kitchen door to a thunder of rain. A half-inch sheet of water flooded the driveway, the lawn unable to absorb it.

Through the water streaked windshield, Joanna saw a passel of Marys in the kitchen doorway, and another few with their faces plastered to the side window.

The cab driver had said the Mother asked him to go out Powell Boulevard to the Thrillmeister yard. They'd stopped a few minutes while she talked to someone in the office, then continued to the Fun Center.

Joanna could be there in ten minutes—soon enough?

Joanna found parking only a few blocks from Waterfront Park, where the Fun Center was set up. On a normal spring day, the park would teem with people eating elephant ears, playing the arcade games, and lining up for rides. The torrential rains changed all that. As she hurried toward the park, she only saw a few security guards and a policeman, fully tented in rain gear.

Portable chain link fences encircled much of the fun center, and amusement park rides ran down the two-block length of the Fun Center.

As Joanna reached the fenced-off area, a security guard stopped her. "We're shutting down. The rain." He gestured toward the ground where his feet had left indentations in the muddy grass. "It's flooding." He was holding large pieces of foam core with "Closed Until Further Notice" printed on them.

"I don't want to go on any rides," Joanna said. "Have you seen a nun? In the past fifteen minutes or so?"

The guard looked at her as if she were unhinged. "No nuns, ma'am."

"I need to look around. It's important. It's—"

"Uh huh. Right." He grunted as he wired the sign to the fence. "Fine. But you gotta be out of there in ten minutes. We'll have the whole area fenced off by then. Good luck with your, uh, nun."

Joanna's feet sank an inch when she stepped off the cement path. Her foot made a sucking sound when she lifted it again. Her suede pumps would be completely destroyed, and the 1940s wool suit so perfect for a day at Tallulah's Closet already smelled like a wet dog. She squinted against the rain and scanned the park, looking for the Mother. Cursing her lack of an umbrella, she felt her way down the park, trying to stick to higher ground.

Undoubtedly, the Mother Superior was also looking for someone—Helena's brother, Leo. She must have figured out he was in danger and wanted to warn him. If he hadn't gone home, he'd most likely be working on one of the rides. But which one?

Most of the rides were covered in tarps. A woman draped in a rain poncho checked the padlock securing one booth and headed for the exit. Rain dripped down Joanna's neck and saturated her blouse. Walking in the mud was slow going, but Joanna moved as quickly as she could.

She spotted motion at the red and black frame of the Rock-O-Plane straight ahead. She walked toward it, pausing behind the inert arms of the Scrambler to get a better view. She pulled a rain-drenched lock of hair from her eyes.

Yes, there was Mother and Leo standing partly in the Rock-O-Plane's shelter. The Mother leaned on her cane. She was intent on explaining something to him. Leo's bleached complexion and hair nearly glowed against the muddy fairway. Tools spread at his feet. Bits of their voices drifted to Joanna, but the splattering of the rain on the tarp wrapping the base of the Scrambler obscured most of the words. Well, Joanna was going to take Mother home right now. Crisp could deal with the rest.

Just as Joanna stepped from the Scrambler's shelter, Helena, eyes trained on the Mother and Leo, strode to them. She seemed impervious to the rain that plastered her hair to her skull. Fury had contorted her features. Her voice cut clearly through rain.

"You." Helena spat out the word. "You selfish son of a bitch. You can't ruin me."

Helena was focused completely on her brother. Mother might not have been there. Joanna lurched forward to intercede, but she slid and hit the ground, her elbows and knees first. With the noise of the rain, no one seemed to hear her.

Closer, Leo's voice was more clear. "Well, if it isn't my big sister. Mom always said you'd do good if your temper didn't get in the way. Ellen."

Ellen? Joanna pulled herself up at the rear of the Rock-O-Plane and stopped cold. A gun. Helena had a gun. She'd drawn a small gray handgun from her purse and held it on Leo.

Heart hammering, Joanna looked up and down the fairway, but saw no one. Where was the security guard? Should she rush Helena? Try to wrest the gun from her hand? No. She could barely stand in this mud, let alone tackle someone. Helena stepped closer to Leo.

"Elly, what are you doing? I said I wouldn't tell. No one knows you're here."

"It's too late for that, isn't it? I gave you the money to move on, and you didn't. Now you have to face the consequences."

"I couldn't sell that bracelet. With all the diamond thefts lately, it was too risky."

Helena's fingers tightened on the trigger.

"No," Joanna yelled and rushed out from behind the ride. Before she reached Helena, a thwack split the air — the sound of Mother's cane striking Helena. Instantly, Mother's body hit the muddy ground. She must have fallen from the effort.

"You." Helena kicked the Mother in the side, and her whole body went limp. Leo stood, mouth agape, seemingly frozen with fear.

"Stop it," Joanna cried. Her own head was jerked back by the hair. Helena.

"And you, too." Helena said, rain pouring over her. Now jabbing the gun in Joanna's ribs, Helena led her to one of the cages on the Rock-O-Plane and pushed her inside. "I'm sorry, but it has to be this way."

Joanna tried to kick Helena but lost her balance. Helena slammed the Rock-O-Plane's caged door and thrust a screwdriver into its latch. Joanna was trapped. She screamed and banged at the cage.

"Shut up," she yelled at Joanna. "I'll deal with you later."

Leo pushed Helena and turned to run, but Helena grabbed the back of his shirt and pulled him into the mud. She pressed her gun against his throat. Joanna screamed again. Muzzle still trained on Leo, Helena reached up and flipped a switch on the Rock-O-Plane's control panel.

"No. Not in this rain. It's not grounded right now. I'm not finished — " Leo shouted above the storm.

The ride's giant engine began to groan, setting off the bells and organ notes of carnival music. Locked in the cage, Joanna was heaved up and around. On one side loomed the dreary shapes of downtown Portland. On the other, the Willamette River, swollen muddy brown, flowed slowly. The landscape wobbled faster than the ride, and Joanna took a deep breath to keep from vomiting. Her skull throbbed.

She pushed her fingers at the cage's mesh covering. She had to loosen the screwdriver, had to get out of there. The mesh was too small. She dug her fingertips into it and rattled with her full body's weight. The screwdriver refused to budge.

Below, Helena pulled the lever further. The Rock-O-Plane's speed increased and Joanna's cage began to spin. She shivered uncontrollably. Her head whirled. When the ride's giant wheel rotated Joanna toward the ground, Helena and Leo's yelling reached her ears, but she couldn't make out their words over the grotesque carnival music. She pounded on the cage again. The gray metal of Helena's gun shone dull. Her car passed them and rose again.

Grab the central bar, Joanna thought. Stop this car from rotating, at least. She clutched the rain-slicked bar in the cage, her grip firm but still hands still trembling. Breathe slowly. She remembered the bent bobby pin Paul had used to get them out of a locked bathroom on a boat. She pulled one from her hair and vowed always to wear bobby pins. Her fingers trembled as she maneuvered it. Yes. Now if she could just get it to dislodge the screwdriver.

A gunshot exploded, and Joanna loosened her grip on the bar. The cage began to rock. "No," she cried out. She grasped the bar again and held tight, the bobby pin still in her hand. As the car lowered, she saw Leo's pale form limp in the mud. Blood flowed from his throat.

Helena wasn't looking at him, though. She had fixed her wild-eyed gaze on Joanna. She raised the gun to Joanna's cage. Joanna shoved the bobby pin through the mesh and nudged the screwdriver. Just a few inches would do it. The screwdriver edged up a fraction of an inch. She let the bar slip, and the cage spun with the rising wheel of the Rock-O-Plane. Please let someone see me.

A bullet tore through Joanna's cage, ringing in the metal. Joanna gulped air. She rattled the cage's door, trying to shake loose the screwdriver. At last, it dropped to ground. From her height, she saw a dozen white-uniformed sailors running up the waterfront toward them from their ship anchored below. The cage circled lower. Helena smiled and lifted the gun at her again. Joanna breathed in gasps.

Behind Helena, the Mother struggled to her feet, the front of her habit black with mud. With deliberation, she lifted her metal cane and knocked the gun from Helena's hand. Scowling, Helena turned to grab her by the neck. The Mother pointed the cane toward the control panel.

"Don't," Joanna yelled and pushed open the ride's door. The sailors were too late. Mother would be electrocuted. Joanna closed her eyes and leapt from the Rock-O-Plane, higher than she'd wanted. Her whole body slammed the slick mud just feet from the Mother, but she wasn't close enough. Mother's cane plunged into the control panel.

The Rock-O-Plane's motor spewed orange sparks and blue smoke into the wet afternoon. Joanna's sobs were absorbed by the sound of the giant machine grinding to a halt.

Like a raft of butterflies, the blue and white habits of a dozen nuns fluttered from a van, the sailors close behind. Sirens wailed in the distance.

Chapter 41

Leaning against several pillows on starched white linens in the hospital bed, the Mother Superior looked much as she had back at the convent. An orchid even occupied the table next to her. Its nodding petals mimicked her wimple. Only the bandage wrapping her right arm bore evidence of the struggle and electrocution. Mary Alberta, tapping on her laptop's keyboard, sat by the far side of the bed.

"Thank you for coming to see me," Mother said.

"Thank you for saving my life," Joanna replied. She set a paper-wrapped packet of macarons on the table. "Framboise and menthe. Mary Edwina said they're your favorites. And this." She pulled Mickey Spillane's *Vengeance is Mine!* from her purse and laid it next to the pastries. "I hope you haven't read it already."

"So thoughtful, dear. Sit." She patted the edge of the bed.

A tattooed man, bicycle helmet on his head, appeared in the doorway with an armload of yellow lilies. "Flower delivery."

"Right here." Mother lifted the card from the bouquet while Mary Alberta searched under the sink for a vase. "They're from your friends in the Navy, Mary Alberta. Such nice gentlemen, and so kind of them to help out at the Fun Center."

The Seabees had secured the area before the police arrived and given the Mother and Leo first aid. Unfortunately, they weren't able to save Leo, but CPR kept the Mother Superior breathing until an ambulance arrived.

"You're looking good," Joanna said. "Considering."

"I should be out of here soon, although they're telling me I'm going to have to do physical therapy now. Some ridiculous young man seems to think I can walk if I do a few exercises each morning."

"But you can walk," Mary Alberta said without lifting her head from the screen.

"Nonsense. That was just a little shuffling around." Her fingers grasped the buzzer for a nurse. "We need some tea."

Leave it to the Mother to turn the hospital into a five-star resort. She probably had a team of candy stripers on alert in the lounge. A harried-looking woman popped her head through the door. "Tea again, I suppose?"

"Yes," the Mother said. "A little milk, too. No honey," she emphasized.

"Detective Crisp said the honey wasn't poisoned." Although she'd given a complete statement to the police after she was rescued from the Rock-O-Plane, Joanna hadn't talked to the detective yet. In the two days since, she flinched every time the store's bell rang and took a fortifying breath before answering each phone call. Surely he'd show up any time to arrest her for breaking into Helena's house.

"It was poisoned all right," Mother said. "He told me the results of the comprehensive screening came in, the follow-up they did to the basic screening. The honey was made with rhododendron pollen. Deadly."

A thick ring of old rhododendrons sheltered the North's house. Helena's bees ate from them, and Helena must have known it — planned it, even. Thank God Apple hadn't drunk enough of the cocktail for it to kill her. She was already well enough to work at the store tomorrow.

Good thing, too. Since the website Mary Alberta built for Tallulah's Closet had gone live with items from Vivienne's wardrobe, she'd had a steady stream of shoppers.

"I'd better get back to the store." Joanna rose. "I'm glad to see you looking so well."

"Thank you, daughter. That machine gave my ticker a real shock, but I'm not so frail as I look, thank the Lord."

Down the hall, a uniformed policeman slumped in a folding chair outside the door to one of the private rooms. Helena's room. The newspaper said she was badly burned— much more so than the Mother Superior— but was expected to live. Joanna mended her pace.

"Ms. Hayworth." The voice came from behind her. Detective Crisp.

Her heart dropped. She turned, slowly. This was it. By now he probably had a statement from the neighbor that she'd been seen at the Norths, plus fingerprints.

"I need to talk to you. Come to the lounge." They settled on a small couch covered in nubby fabric. Hospital staff came and went at the nurse's station, but they were far enough to be out of earshot. "Are you all right?"

Wary, Joanna looked up. Surely he'd be reading her her rights about now. "Yes. I'm fine. A few nightmares, but I got off easy." Much easier than Poppy and Vivienne. And Leo.

"Helena is conscious, and we questioned her. I thought you might want to know her story."

Joanna nodded and tried to control her breathing. Was this a lead-in to being charged?

"She grew up as a traveler, a sort of American gypsy. Her family did odd jobs, mostly mechanical things, and moved throughout the south."

Joanna nodded again. This would explain how Leo picked up his skills working on amusement park rides. "I figured that much out."

"She was deeply sensitive to being an outsider — there's still a lot of stigma surrounding gypsies — and ashamed of her brother being albino. She left home at sixteen and adopted a new identity. Apparently, she took her family's stash of savings with her, which didn't make her too popular."

"No kidding." Although she knew Helena was a murderer, it was still hard to reconcile the pedigreed academic with her past.

"We found a police record for her in Pennsylvania and Connecticut. Mostly minor things — shoplifting, check kiting. She's no dummy, though. She made it into Yale, where she met Gil North. When they married, she must have thought she had it made. New name, new family, new home far away from where she grew up. Of course, she refused to have kids. She was terrified they'd turn out with white hair and red eyes."

"Then she saw her brother at Oaks Park," Joanna said.

"Right. Her family still wanted to get hold of the money she stole. Vivienne North saw him, too, and may have asked too many questions. She could have blown Helena's world apart."

Helena killed her mother-in-law to protect her new life. "And Poppy. She knew about the phone call from Vivienne including her mistaking voyageurs for voyeurs. She was afraid Poppy would figure it out." Joanna dropped her head to her hands. She was the one who alerted Helena to Vivienne's call to Poppy.

"It would have come out soon enough. Don't blame yourself. She feared you might figure it out, too — thus the phone calls and warning shot." He gave Joanna a moment to compose herself. "But there is one thing I want to clear up with you."

The break-in. Here it came.

"The night the North residence was broken into—"

"I admit it," Joanna said. "I did it. I wanted to warn Helena about the honey being poisoned. I didn't know she was the murderer. When I looked in her front window and saw the destroyed painting, I panicked. Her back door was open, so I went in."

"We spoke to your boyfriend, and—"

Ex-boyfriend, he meant. "He had nothing to do with it." Her voice was firm. "It was all me. I told you. I borrowed his truck and used his phone. Don't drag him into this, because—"

"Shut up," Crisp said. Stunned, Joanna clamped her lips closed. "That's what I told him you'd say, even though I know better." He fastened his gaze on Joanna and let the full force of his disapproval sink in. His children must have grown up terrified of crossing him. "Anyway, it doesn't matter, because Gil North refuses to press charges. He claims he busted the painting himself, on accident. That the broken window in back was another accident. He clearly knows something we don't." Another pointed look at Joanna. "A lot of people are having trouble telling the truth these days, it seems."

At some point Gil would have to own up to claiming Tranh's painting as his own, but apparently he wasn't ready to confess yet. At least, not to Detective Crisp. As to whether Gil destroyed the painting himself, or Tranh did it before she and Paul arrived, she'd likely never know.

"So," she said, then hesitated. "So, that's it?"

"For now." He rose and shifted his raincoat to his opposite arm. He saluted goodbye. His steps rang down the hall.

Joanna nearly went limp with relief. She wouldn't be going to jail. And she wouldn't be dragging Paul with her. This, at least, she could do for him.

***

The door bell jangled at Tallulah's Closet. Joanna glanced up from arranging a jewelry display. It was Paul. She lowered a pearl-encrusted brooch to the glass counter and clasped her hands to keep them still.

He broke the silence. "How are you?"

"Fine," she said. Dumb. For all the time she'd spent thinking of what she'd say if she ran into Paul again, she could have come up with something more clever.

"Mary Alberta filled me in on what's been happening. Crisp came to see me, too."

"Yes." Another brilliant statement. She was sorry for dragging him into the Norths, sorry telling him one thing then doing another. If she had to do it again, she still would have continued to try to find Poppy's killer. But she would have told Paul about it. And lost him fairly, at least.

"Do you mind if I sit?"

She moved the dustpan from the red velvet bench. "Please."

He took a breath. "I'm sorry."

"No, I'm the one who's sorry. I should have been honest with you. I — "

"Please, listen to me. I had no right to tell you what to do. I was afraid for you, and I felt so out of control. The only way I knew how to make it stop was to make you stop. But that wasn't right." He patted the bench next to him. She sat. "I was throwing on you all the guilt I had over taking part in my uncle's jewel heists, and it wasn't fair to you."

"But we talked about that. After we went to the Norths. What changed your mind?"

Another moment passed. "My mind didn't really change, it's more that I figured out what was most important to me."

"I don't understand."

"Well, I was repairing some siding at the convent, and Mary Alberta found me. She pulled me off the ladder and said, 'You love Joanna for who she is, don't you?' That's all. I had all afternoon and all night to think about it. And about you."

As if occupying her hands would quiet her mind, she grabbed a scarf from a nearby display and wrapped it through her fingers.

"Part of what I love about you is your decency, the way you stick up for your friends," Paul said. "I don't want that ever to change." He paused. "Joanna?"

She looked up, still silent. He'd said "love." Present tense.

"I've been such an idiot. You had to help Poppy. I know now. Will you forgive me?"

She glanced at his work-roughened hands, the lock of sandy hair that never seemed to stay in place. "There's nothing for me to forgive. I was terrified you'd leave me if I told you what I was up to." She caught his gaze, hoping he'd understand. "So I stuck my head in the sand about it. It was wrong. I was wrong. I'm so, so sorry."

As she apologized, a queer mixture of laughter and tears swelled in her throat. Paul came back. He understood. She should have known he'd get it. She should have trusted him.

He reached into the pocket of his Pendleton shirt, the one with the frayed cuffs she'd always tried to replace but that he insisted on keeping. He handed her a small package wrapped in newspaper.

She glanced at him, surprised, and peeled back the paper. It was the box he'd made for her, the one she'd seen when she went to his shop alone. Her fingers slid over its surface, over the inlaid "J" on the top.

"Open it," he said.

She did. Inside was a folded sheet of paper. She opened that, too.

"Green light," it said.

Acknowledgments

Travelers in the United States have a complex and often misunderstood history. *Dior or Die* doesn't even begin to skim its rich lore.

I want to thank the Xtabay Vintage Clothing boutique for inspiring Tallulah's Closet. If you ever find yourself in Portland, you must stop by to marvel at the amazing clothing Liz Gross has assembled. Be sure to visit Dot's Café next door for a tuna melt afterwards, and if you have time, don't miss a roller skating session at Oaks Park, especially on Thursdays and Sundays when an organist is at the Mighty Wurlitzer.

Thank you, also, to the patient and persistent members of my writing group: Christine Finlayson, Doug Levin, Dave Lewis, Ann Littlewood, and Marilyn McFarlane. The superb editing of Mary Rosenblum and Christine Finlayson, as well as Robin Remmick's and Jared Pierce's comments, elevated the story several notches.